AF267345

Something to Be Saved

A NOVEL

MELANIE RIGNEY

Arlington, Virginia

Library of Congress Control Number Data
Name: Rigney, Melanie, 1956-author
Title: Something to Be Saved / Melanie Rigney
Description: Arlington, Virginia: Rejoice! Be Glad!
Identifiers: Library of Congress Control Number: 2025927983
ISBN 978-0-9909376-1-6 (paperback)
ISBN 978-0-9909376-2-3 (ebook)
Subjects: LCFFT: Christian fiction / Novels
LC record available at https://lccn.loc.gov/2025927983

This book is a work of fiction. Names, characters, places, and incidents are the product of the author's imagination or are used fictitiously. Any resemblance to actual events, locales, or persons, living or dead, is coincidental.

Interior Design: Linda M. Au
Cover Design: Barry Hansen
Cover Image: Jon Bilous via iStock

1

Six o'clock. He was going to be late.

Rachel Gregory added a few zucchini and tomatoes to her rattan basket, straightened up to her full five-feet-two, then ran her fingers through her cropped red hair. Their adult daughter called it "Mother's peace place," the forty-by-forty garden that took up most of the little tri-level's backyard. Jill certainly was right about that.

Rachel and Peter had a deal: supper at six-thirty unless he was on the night shift. But he was finishing up a round on days. There was no sign of the truck, and he liked to shower and change before eating.

She prayed the prayer she'd been praying for years, the prayer that had become rote, the prayer she wasn't even sure she meant anymore: *Jesus, there's good buried in that man somewhere. Bring him back to You. Make him a husband again. Deliver us from the Land of Settling.*

She passed through the carport and into the kitchen, where evidence of her gardening and canning prowess was displayed in homemade frames: six straight years of 4-H blue ribbons from back in the day, and a certificate from a couple years ago proclaiming her a Northern Shenandoah Valley Master Gardener Association member.

Six thirty. Steamed cod, two small green salads, and sliced home-made bread were on the wooden table. Still no Peter. Rachel checked her phone. No voice mails. No need to check for a text because that was a skill her husband had no interest in mastering.

⁂

Peter Gregory couldn't believe it. He was being dumped. That hadn't happened to him since, well, ever.

"Why?" he croaked for the third time.

Kara sighed for the third time. She walked to the window that looked out onto the low mountains. He couldn't help but admire the way the late August afternoon sunlight played off her long red hair, and how trim her rear looked in those khaki shorts.

They'd been seeing each other for a year, and he couldn't remember ever fighting about anything: music, politics, books, anything. It'd been easy for them both, or so he thought.

He joined her at the window, pressing his chest into her back and resting his chin on the top of her head. She smelled good like she always did, like wash on the line from when he was a kid, like Rachel used to smell when she bothered with perfume. He inhaled deep and wrapped his arms around her.

"I know you haven't found anyone else, because there ain't anybody better around here," he said, only half-joking.

Kara leaned back into him and grabbed his hands. "No, I haven't found anyone else. It's because you did, a long time ago. I saw you last Saturday afternoon with your wife and daughter."

Peter thought back. The truck had needed new tires, and Rachel had come along to the warehouse club to get stuff for a 'do at her church. Jill had been over for lunch and joined them. Afterward, they'd stopped at Schumacher's Hardware.

"I went to the bakery to buy some of those cookies you like," Kara said, tightening her grip on his hands. "You were outside the hardware store next door, talking to an old guy by the bags of dirt. Rachel and Jill were looking at bulbs. Jill started singing something. You hoisted a bag over your shoulder and turned and looked at Rachel. Not at Jill, but at Rachel. You smiled at her the way you do at me when you don't think I'm watching. She could feel it. She turned and smiled at you too."

Peter snorted. "You're dumping me because I looked at my wife? Here's a news flash—I live with her. I look at her all the time."

"No. I'm dumping you because she loves you, and I think you love her too. Your faces showed it."

Peter swallowed hard. "Woman, if you don't want to be with me, don't be with me. But me and Rachel, we're roommates on a good day, and that's the way she wants it. As for me, I can't even tell you where my wedding ring is."

Kara disentangled herself, moved to the front door, and opened it. "You told me from the first that you weren't going to leave her because it'd take too much effort. And I appreciate that you never trashed her to me. But you told me the love was long gone, and you're wrong about that. One of you needs to humble themselves enough to make the first move. Maybe it should be you. Godspeed, Peter."

He stared at her, eyes pleading for her to reconsider. She stared back, not saying a word. Then he walked outside, hoping he was moving fast enough that she didn't see the beginning of tears. He fired up the truck and roared out of the driveway, scattering gravel as he headed for Marshall Road. He was going to be late.

The cod was getting cold when the truck turned into the carport at six forty-five. Rachel took the plates to the counter, moved the cod pieces to a third plate, covered it with wax paper, and started the microwave.

"You're late," she said, not turning around, as the door into the kitchen opened.

He gave a big sigh. "Yes. Yes, I am. I apologize. Gotta wash my hands. I'll skip my shower." The clump-clump-clump of boots sounded on the wooden stairs as he went down to his bedroom, just off the laundry area.

She heard his boots on the stairs and brought the plates back to the table.

"You're late. Third time in two months. That's not like you. Do we need to talk?"

Peter rested his face on his hand and stared at her. Rachel began to fidget with her napkin. She still felt a little tingly when he looked at her. She just couldn't help it.

"No," he said finally. "No, we don't. And it won't happen again."

After Rachel said a quick prayer, she passed him the butter for the bread.

"Say, that's nice." He gave her what looked to be a smirk. "It's been a while since you did that."

"Passed you the butter?"

"No." He picked up the bottle that was next to his plate. "You bought some of that blue cheese dressing I really like."

"It was—" Rachel stopped herself before she spit out "not for you." What was up with him? "It was nothing, really. I wanted to have some to take to work for dipping vegetables, and the bottles were two for one. It's reduced fat."

"Whatever. But I thank you. I do love that dressing."

Rachel felt herself fidgeting again. "Jill came by the library today. She wondered if we might keep the dog next week. She's wanting to meet Eric in Vegas for the Labor Day weekend before he leaves Twentynine Palms to deploy."

"That came up all of a sudden."

"She found a great last-minute airfare. Still, a silly thing after two years of marriage, if you ask me. She'll spend almost as much time getting there as they'll have together."

"Beautiful thing after two years of marriage, if you ask me. Once he's deployed, who knows when they'll see each other again? I suspect we would have wanted to do the same in the day."

"They'll grow out of it. Time and trouble have a way of making people keep their hands to themselves."

"It doesn't have to be that way."

Rachel got up to clear the table, then felt more than heard him behind her. Then she smelled him. Sweat and perfume. The same perfume she used to wear.

"That was a fine meal," he said. "The salad dressing made it special. I thank you. I wondered—"

"Wondered what?" she asked without turning around.

"I wondered if you might want to take a walk down the road. It's considerable cool for late August, and the light's already starting to go in the evening."

A walk? When he still smelled of *her*?

"I have to get work schedules done before I go to bed. Need to do some wash too. I'll fetch your basket in a bit."

"I'll leave it by the washer. G'night."

After an hour at the computer in her bedroom in the tri-level's top floor, Rachel realized she had forgotten to start the wash. Well, it was going to get later before it got earlier. She took her pink plastic basket from the closet, then went down to the laundry area. His door was closed, and she could hear some sports thing through it.

She sorted her clothes into lingerie, towels, and cottons piles. She'd do the cottons tonight anyway, as she wanted to wear that lavender blouse in the morning. She held it up to check for spots. Size four petite, just like she'd worn since high school, other than when she was pregnant.

She put in her cottons, and moved to Peter's rough wood basket next to the washer to fill out the load. The chambray shirt he'd been wearing was on top. It still smelled of *her*.

Rachel held it to her nose. Jesus, there's good buried in that man somewhere. Bring him back to You. Deliver us from the Land of Settling.

She started the washer.

2

Some day off.

Peter fed more magazine pages into the shredder. He had spent the past fifteen minutes destroying articles he'd stashed among the truck manuals in his closet. They carried titles like "Ten Ways to Look Ten Pounds Thinner," "Secrets Your Lover Won't Tell You," and "How to Simplify Your Beauty Regimen."

Peter didn't need to look ten pounds thinner, had just lost his lover, and had never had a "beauty regimen," whatever that was. Why had he kept the stupid things?

Still, he couldn't keep himself from running his right thumb over "By Kara Lane" that appeared on each before he shredded it. He'd always been proud when she pointed out her articles in the big-name magazines you'd see at the supermarket checkout.

What was it about the woman that had got so deep under his skin? he wondered as he stacked up birthday, Valentine's, Sweetest Day, and "just because" cards, all of them goofy, all signed only with her big green lazy K.

Then he got to one that was different. Homemade, with a child's handprint on the front.

How had that got into this pile?

Slowly, Peter opened the card, though he knew what was inside:

a kindergartener's drawing of a short, red-haired woman standing very close to a little girl with curly black hair and a red scrawl intended to be a dog. On the opposite page was a tall man with shaggy black hair kissing a woman with long yellow hair.

"DAD," Jill had written in crooked block letters. "Happy Birthday," Rachel had written in crisp, perfect letters above Jill's.

It had been the June after the second miscarriage. They were fighting over everything from whether to paint the living room gray or blue to whether Jill could have a gerbil. Rachel's cancer had probably started, but they didn't know yet. The neighbor had been doing yard work when he blew out of the house after an argument. She came over to talk with him and, well, the kissing just happened. He knew he should have pushed away or told Rachel, but it had felt good that something female wanted to be near him. In the following weeks, they'd had a few tongue dances, nothing more, but it shamed Peter then and even now, truth be told, that Jill had seen enough of them together to draw that picture.

While Rachel put Jill to bed, he headed out to the front porch swing, hoping to get in a smoke before World War III began.

But Rachel was quiet as she came outside and sat on the rocker opposite the swing. After a few moments, in a very soft but firm voice, she said, "I told her yesterday that if I ever see the two of you within fifty feet of each other again, I will kill her."

Peter blew smoke and air out in a slow whistle. "All right."

"You and I have a big problem."

"We have a lot of problems." He was about to begin listing them when she shook her head.

"That's a true fact. But we have one big problem, and that's the way Jill sees us."

Peter wanted to grab her in his arms and beg pardon and kiss her like he hadn't in weeks. Instead, he took another drag. "If you can't forgive one mistake, well, that's up to you. If you want a divorce, go ahead. But you won't take Jill with you without a fight."

Rachel gave a low laugh. "I don't want a divorce. We said 'till death do us part,' and that's that. But we neither of us had the most normal of family situations growing up. I believe we both want that for Jill, and that means a mom and a dad who love her enough to put her first. No more fighting in front of her. I want you home for every supper you're not working. I want us to eat together like a family."

"That's reasonable. Now, about what you think happened with me and her—"

She raised a hand, stood up, and went to the screen door. "And Peter?"

"Yes?"

"Don't ever, ever cat around again with someone I know." Then she went into the house.

He stood the little card on his nightstand. By and large, he'd stuck by their bargain. He hadn't missed many meals. There'd been a lot less catting around than she probably thought. Most importantly, Jill had grown up to a wonderful young woman.

Peter had thought about leaving exactly once: seven years ago, when Jill went off to the University of Virginia, and Rachel kicked him out of their bed. She said it was his snoring, but he still wondered if there was more to it, not that he was going to ask. A man has his pride. But then she came in a few days later after planting some bulbs, dirt on her gloves and on her glowing face, just like when they first moved into the tri-level. His heart started beating so loud he was sure she could hear it, and he decided he wasn't quitting this.

They were the only two women who had ever closed doors on him, Rachel and Kara. Rachel had done it again the night before. It had cost him to ask her for that walk, and it still hurt to be rejected by her.

He took the bag of confetti to the garbage, then went to the refrigerator for a slice of salami before a nap.

"Peter," a folded-up piece of paper held by a refrigerator magnet read. Who else did she think was going to read it? He opened it. "I put together a snack that's better for you than salami. Rachel."

Inside the fridge was a see-through container with fresh vegetables from the garden next to that bottle of dressing. He put them both on the counter, poured too much dressing on the vegetables, then sat at the table.

Cherry tomatoes, yellow squash, radishes. They were good, as always. Rachel could coax anything out of that Virginia clay. It was funny that they'd been buying stuff for the garden when Kara saw them. They probably had looked happy together; maybe they even had been happy. They both liked being outdoors and physical. How they ended up as a librarian and a factory mechanic, inside all day, he couldn't exactly say.

Peter ran the empty container under the faucet, put it in the dishwasher, and headed to bed. But sleep wouldn't come. What did he and Rachel look like when they were together and happy?

He went back up to the living room and looked through the photo albums. It was in their photos with Jill when she was born, when she was confirmed, when she won this or that award, when she graduated high school and college, when she and Eric got married: big smiles that proclaimed to the world they knew their daughter had hung the moon.

But he couldn't find anything of just the two of them, other than a photo from their wedding day. It showed a tall, handsome man with bushy black hair and icy blue eyes towering over his pretty red-haired bride, who was twisting toward him in hopes of making her pregnant belly a little less visible.

"We were scared half out of our wits, both of us, that day," Peter said to Callie the calico cat, who was more interested in grooming than in his ruminations. "But I know we were happy then, and later on too, when Jill was little. Maybe Rachel's got some other pictures somewhere. Maybe if I ask her…or see Kara, just to get her to explain what she saw…"

He closed the album and put it back on the shelf.

3

H e's done with this one, I guess," Rachel said to Lizzie, plucking the soggy tomato from her sandwich at the Busy Bee. "He always gets like this afterward."

Lizzie dumped four sugar packets into her coffee. Rachel shook her head. Lizzie Davis didn't seem to mind that in the years since their high school graduation, she'd gone from a size six to a size twelve.

"He always gets like what?" Lizzie stirred her coffee, her armload of silver bracelets jangling against the white china cup.

"Oh, you know. Last night, he gave me a shirt to wash that reeked of perfume instead of stashing it away and washing it himself. He's a careful man. He wouldn't have done that if it was still on. He's probably shredding pictures and cards from her right now from one of his hiding places that he doesn't know I know about."

Lizzie poured raspberry vinaigrette dressing on her cranberry gorgonzola salad and nodded.

"Last night at supper, it was almost like he was trying to woo me. He thanked me for buying some salad dressing he likes. He asked me to take a walk. Of course, I didn't go."

Lizzie sighed. "Let's go sit in the park for a while. With ice cream. My treat."

Rachel didn't allow herself dessert very often, but a little self-indulgence sounded good. She loved that Lizzie knew she needed it, and that Lizzie almost always knew the right thing to do or say. It was a gift Rachel knew she did not possess.

Dishes of chocolate ice cream with sprinkles in hand, they walked two blocks to the park across the street from the library and Lizzie's antique shop. Rachel led the way, walking briskly in her no-nonsense flats, Lizzie clopping along behind in three-inch mules.

"I'm not sure where you were going back there at the Bee," Rachel said as they sat down on a bench.

"I just wonder what was so horrible about your husband asking you to take a walk with him. There was a time the two of you hiked for hours, Jill strapped on one of your backs. My recollection is you enjoyed it. And remember all those campouts we had with the kids when they were little, even after you and he…"

Rachel gave a harrumph. "You've been my best friend for thirty-odd years. You're the one who encouraged me to go out with Peter in the first place—"

"Which you were dying to do."

"Which I was dying to do, yes. But you know what our marriage has been like. Why are you going soft on him now? Whose side are you on?"

"Oh, honey, you know I'm always on and at your side." Lizzie put her free arm around Rachel. "We always cluck about Peter strutting around when he's done with one of his women. We cackle about that he never has figured out that you know all the places he hides cards and pictures and such."

Rachel laughed. "Remember the time he used the bread machine because he thinks I knead by hand?"

"Yes, that man is nowhere near as smart as he thinks he is—or as good looking as he once was, for that matter, though you and he seem to be the only folk who don't realize that. But him being mopey at the end is different, right? Maybe the Lord is going to give you that changed man we've been praying for for years."

Rachel could feel her face flushing and her throat swelling up. What if Lizzie was right? But she couldn't be. She just couldn't be.

"I wasn't looking for a sermon, Lizzie, just for someone to laugh with me like usual." Rachel put down her ice cream cup and crossed her hands across her chest.

"All I know is, I wish John were here right now to ask me for a walk. A walk's a simple thing. Would it have cost you so much?"

Rachel gulped, but the big knot in her throat still wouldn't go away. "Yes," she choked out.

"Now, just stop that," Lizzie said, pushing back the ash blond hair that fell below her shoulders and, frequently, into her eyes. "It sounds like this time might be different, and I think you think so too. You usually joke about pitying the one to come. You've told me time and again I was lucky that he broke up with me at his senior prom before I had a grown-up heart, because he couldn't break it the way he has yours. But now you're condemning him for asking for a simple walk. Is this about fear? Or maybe pride?"

Rachel narrowed her green eyes. "Pride was stomped out of me long ago. In twenty-two years, John never cheated on you. You never had to see women at the grocery store give you pitying glances and then whisper to their friends. You never—"

Lizzie put up her right palm. "Stop. John and I had our own problems, but we took every one of them to the Lord. I've missed him every day the past two years, but my soul is at peace with him having gone Home. Could you say the same if the Lord took Peter tomorrow?"

"That won't happen," Rachel snapped. "He's healthy as a horse. But I get your point. That said, I think we need to let this dog lie, and get back to work. I'm short-staffed this afternoon."

"Sure enough," Lizzie said as they started across the street. "I'll be in West Virginia for estate sales the rest of the week. Pick you up

Sunday for services like usual, or are you going to hate me forever for speaking my soul?"

Rachel laughed and shook her head. "You know me too well, Miss Liz. Yes, I'm upset, but I'll get over it. As for Sunday, I'm driving with Jill. I'm taking her to Dulles right after church. She's going to Vegas to be with Eric before he deploys, and leaving the dog and her car at our place. Save us space?"

"Right side, third row from the front like always. But if you don't want to talk with me serious about what's standing between you and Peter, maybe it'd be good to visit with Pastor Doug."

Rachel didn't need to talk with Pastor Doug to find out what stood between her and Peter. But as she reviewed her presentation for the library board, she couldn't get the conversation out of her head.

Yes, Rachel could always tell when he put a woman to the curb because he destroyed his little trophies. And every time, she had said a little prayer that maybe this was the time—and been disappointed. But the night before was the closest he'd come to reaching out to her since her hysterectomy when Jill was ten. She'd pushed him away then, a lot harder than she had last night. Told him he was an animal, and she wasn't interested in his lustful ways.

Maybe Lizzie was right. Rachel called the church office, number 8 on her cell phone's speed dial. She wasn't surprised that the secretary promised to find Pastor Doug right away. Still, it took a few minutes.

"Hello, Rachel. Doug Brown here. Sorry for the delay. I was with the building inspector. How can I help?"

"I wanted—" Somehow, the words "to set up an appointment to talk about my cross of a husband, whose name you don't know and whom you've never met" wouldn't come out. "I wanted to let you know there are some books left over from last week's Friends of the Library sale that you might want for the church library. I'll drop them off sometime soon."

"Wonderful! Thanks so much for everything you do for our community."

She turned off the cell phone and returned to her spreadsheets. But she couldn't stop thinking about what Lizzie had said at lunch. Why was she making such a big deal out of a simple request for a walk? Why was it taking up so much space in her brain?

"Because we're a couple of old dogs," she said aloud as she hit Print. "And you know what they say about old dogs."

4

C'mon, Fifth! Step lively, now!"

Peter chuckled as he positioned the sprinkler in Rachel's garden, then started walking to the front of the yard and his daughter's voice.

"Dad! I didn't think you'd be up and about. Didn't you just start on the graveyard shift?"

"And let you go away without saying goodbye? What kind of father do you think I am?"

Jill tossed back her long black hair. "Is Mother ready? She said to come early."

"I heard the shower when I came outside to fiddle with the sprinkler. Let's go find out."

Inside, Rachel had coffee brewing and french toast on the griddle. Strawberries were nestled in three little white stoneware bowls on the kitchen table.

"Good morning," Rachel said with a smile. "Thought we'd all have breakfast together before church, then Jill and I can go directly to the airport."

Peter watched the women as they bowed their heads. Meal prayers were about the only time he saw Rachel quiet and still, not working on some project or another or fussing about something.

Her face was lovely as the day he'd met her back in school. He wondered why it was he always bragged on her brains but not her looks.

Twenty minutes later, the gals were ready to go. Peter walked them to Rachel's hybrid, Fifth shuffling behind.

"Now, don't lose too much money," Peter said as he hugged his daughter. "My son-in-law's not a brigadier general yet."

"Oh, Dad!" Jill giggled. "You know we don't gamble. Besides, we'll be too busy working on getting you guys a grandbaby to do much of anything else."

"Speaking for myself, at forty-four I'm in no rush to be a grandmother," Rachel said, opening the driver's door.

"That may be, but we've waited long enough to be parents. If Doctor Kidder hadn't said there's nothing to be worried about, we'd both be concerned."

Rachel pushed the ignition button and put down the front windows, then leaned across the front seat.

"Peter, would you like to come to church with us? Then you could ride along to the airport. You'd have more time with Jill."

Peter couldn't remember the last time he'd been to services or been asked for that matter. "Um, thanks, but I'm tired. Remember, I worked last night and ain't been to bed yet. Me and Fifth are looking forward to a good nap. Jill, safe travels. Love you."

"Love you, Dad! Don't cry, Fifth, Gramps will take care of you," she said as she and Rachel pulled away.

Peter headed back into the house, Fifth trailing behind. He went to the counter and took a dog biscuit out of the bag of stuff Jill had brought. "Step lively, now," he said and headed down the stairs. Peter helped the dog up onto the double bed and gave him the treat. Rachel wouldn't be happy if she knew Fifth was on the furniture, but what Rachel didn't know wouldn't hurt her.

He drew the room-darkening shades tight and took off his jeans and shirt. Then Peter lit his going-to-bed cigarette and joined the whimpering Fifth.

Peter inhaled and with his free hand stroked the dog's head. "Don't cry, Rusty."

⁓∾⁓

Jill had been three when Peter found a setter by the side of the road. He was surprised when the animal let him load him into the back of the truck without a battle, especially once he realized one of the moaning dog's rear legs was broken.

Peter dashed home for the checkbook before heading for the vet. When he got back outside, Jill was standing by the truck bed. She raised her arms up and, against his better judgment, Peter hoisted her high enough to see the setter. He waited for her to start crying herself. But instead, the child said in a sing-song way, "Don't cwy, Wusty. I take care of you." The dog's crying slowed and then stopped.

Nothing would do but that Jill would come along to the vet and watch as the dog's leg was set, and from then on, the two were inseparable. Over the years, four other abandoned setters had come into the Gregorys' lives. They stopped calling them Rusty and started calling them by number with the third one.

Peter took another drag. Of course, the part Jill didn't remember was that, at the time of Rusty the First, Rachel's nickname also had been Rusty. "My dad says it's the color of a rusty nail," Rachel had told him when he touched that beautiful hair on their first and only date, a few weeks after she graduated high school. It was long then, in a tight braid. Until he took off the rubber band and let it tumble free.

She was wearing a tight braid again the next time he saw her, three months later. As she walked toward him, Peter wondered for the millionth time why she hadn't been returning his calls until the night before.

"I'm pregnant."

Peter's heart leaped with fear and excitement. "Are you sure?"

She stared at him, breathing rapidly. Yes, he decided. She was sure. And she was ashamed.

"Now just listen," he said. "I love you. I want to marry you. Everything will work out. I promise."

"How can you promise me anything? You're an uneducated construction worker who lives in a trailer." She reached up and began beating her fists against his chest.

Peter grabbed the fists and raised them to his mouth, kissing each knuckle. As he kissed the last one, she sobbed, "I'm so scared!"

He drew her to him, stroking her back and kissing the top of her head. "Don't cry, Rusty," he murmured. "I'll take care of you." And then, she hugged him back.

"Don't cry, Rusty. I'll take care of you." How many times he had said that in those days, and believed it. No wonder it was among the first things Jill said.

Peter stubbed out the cigarette. Some job he'd done taking care of Rachel. She had cobbled together a bachelor's degree with community college classes and went to work at the county library when Jill started high school. Rachel had earned a master's online, and even before her latest promotion six months ago, she was making more money than he ever had. They owned the little two-bedroom trilevel free and clear because they both always had known how to squeeze a dollar. But they had nothing like the life she'd dreamed of back in high school, working for the Library of Congress over in the District. The few times they'd taken overnight vacations, it'd been camping with John, Lizzie, and the kids. No jaunting off to New York or Europe or Disneyworld for the Gregorys. And then there were the women.

It was a lot to think about, especially at naptime. Peter put out the cigarette, rolled on his side and drifted off as Fifth was licking his face.

§

The first half of the drive to Dulles was quiet, other than Rachel's dulcimer music in the DVD player. But as they left the four-lane and entered the toll road, Jill turned off the music.

"Mother, I need to talk about what you said back at the house. It hurts me when you say you're not ready to be a grandmother, even if you're joking, and you've said it so many times I'm not sure you are joking. A loving grandma is important to a child. I know, since Grandma Gregory died before I was born, and your mother…" Jill let the unfinished sentence hang for a few seconds. "Anyway, you've been the best mother I could ask for. I just don't believe you won't be the best grandmother ever too."

Rachel swallowed hard. There wasn't much she wanted more than to be a grandmother. She'd love her grandchildren the way Grossmutter Grossman had loved her, give them everything she and Peter hadn't been able to give Jill. But the problem with being a grandmother was that that would make Jill a mother, and that meant danger.

"Well, first off, with Eric in the Marines, he'll be moving every few years for a while. Do you really want to bring up a family that way? Why not wait until you're a bit more settled? You're only twenty-five."

"And you were eighteen when you had me."

"And it was a struggle with not much money and your dad having no folks, and my folks, well, you know. If it hadn't been for Lizzie and John, I don't know what we would have done sometimes."

"Marines look out for each other, Mother. That goes for Marine families too."

"All right then." Rachel felt herself starting to tear up and doing her best to fight it. "Truth be told, I'm worried after you. Remember, your Grandma Gregory died with her second, and I had two miscarriages before they took everything out. If something happened to you, well, I can't imagine a greater blow."

Jill sighed. "We have had this conversation, many times. Doctor

Kidder knows my family history. She doesn't believe anything should keep me from conceiving or carrying a child to term. And I've never wanted anything as much in my life as to be a mother. So please, put your fears away and pray for a beautiful little baby to come, all right?"

A few quiet minutes passed. Then Rachel asked, "Did your dad seem a little off this morning?"

Jill turned her eyes away from Rachel and looked at her phone and started scrolling. "How did we get from me wanting to be pregnant to Dad? And what do you mean, off?"

"Seems like he's been underfoot more than usual, and more quietlike. I guess that's why I asked him about services today. Just wondered if you'd noticed anything."

"I don't know, Mother. What goes on between a husband and wife is no one else's business. Just be careful." Jill reached over and turned the player back on. Rachel's favorite track, "Just as I Am," started up.

A half hour later, they were at the airport. "Love you, Mother," Jill said as she brushed her lips on Rachel's cheek, then got out of the hybrid and took her suitcase from the back seat. "Remember what I said, just be careful." She waved, and disappeared inside the airport.

As Rachel drove home, she couldn't get stop thinking about Jill's comment. As if Rachel hadn't been careful all her life, except for getting pregnant and falling in love with Peter.

Even in high school, he had been different from the others. He carried himself like a man, though he was just a year older than her, maybe on account of his dad dying in the hunting accident a year earlier and him living with Shoe, the hardware store owner. There'd been a lot of talk about what Peter and Shoe said happened on that West Virginia mountain and what might have really happened, but Rachel didn't find much interest in gossip. It was a true fact that Peter's drinking and smoking had started after that. Rachel had found that edginess attractive despite her best efforts, especially once she learned they'd be chemistry lab partners, what with Grossman coming right after Gregory alphabetically. She was surprised he'd even take chemistry. He didn't need it to graduate, and he planned to go straight off to full-time work. Rachel thought that showed there was more to him than dark good looks, a slow smile, and eyes that seemed to stare into your soul.

But it wasn't just his looks. It was the way that, starting with that class, he came to know all the bad things about her—her temper, her impatience, her fears. She started to fall in love with him a little at that lab table, even though he and Lizzie were dating. Rachel didn't seem to be able to do anything that upset him. She was safe with him.

She was still safe with him, regardless of the women. She knew what to expect from him—home maintenance projects, other than that bathroom tile project he'd been putting off for months. Keeping his truck and her hybrid running. Helping with the yard when she needed it. Keeping his dalliances out of her space. Sticking to the budget they both agreed to. And he knew what to expect from her—a clean house, good meals, and minimal interaction. Maybe it wasn't love anymore, but it was predictable.

In some ways, Rachel thought as she exited the toll road, she longed for him to take on the next woman so they could both get back to that predictability.

5

"What do you have on today?" Peter asked, smacking his lips over a last bit of wheat toast smeared with Rachel's home-made strawberry jam.

"I've got someone from Charlottesville coming over to give a workshop. How about you?"

"Take a nap. Give the furnace a going-over for the winter. Walk Fifth. Maybe go down to Shoe's and price out sabre saws."

Rachel nodded. "Sure would be nice if you could get my bath-room retiled one of these decades." She stood up and adjusted that green checkered scarf she liked to wear with her black suit. "Figur-ing on grilling a pork loin for supper if that suits."

"Sounds good. Go on to work. I can clear."

Peter shifted in his seat while the yellow kitchen wall clock shaped like an apple ticked off the seconds loudly. Fifth, curled up in front of the refrigerator, his legs twitching, provided the room's only other sound, letting out the occasional "mmuff! mmuff!" Callie the calico had taken up residence on the bay window sill and was asleep as well.

"Probably help you to get to work a couple minutes early, set things up before that suit comes," he said, standing and placing his plate on top of hers. "I have been known to load a dishwasher or two in my time."

Rachel gave him an odd little smile. "Not very often in the morning when you're on graveyard. You're usually in a hurry for that nap."

"I—" I what? Peter wondered. I want to ask if you know I helped Jill pick out that scarf for you for last Christmas? I want to tell you that I'll be taking my nap here instead of leaving for Kara's house fifteen minutes after you're gone? He settled for, "I can clear the table. You go on."

Rachel nodded. "I'll just go brush my teeth, then."

Not so much as a thank-you, Peter thought as he put their plates and her coffee cup into the dishwasher. He wrapped the remaining bread and put it in its place on the counter, then returned the butter and jam to the refrigerator.

He was washing the skillet when he felt Rachel's arm graze his back, a couple of inches above his belt. It took everything inside him to hold back a shiver for the split second the touch lasted. He wondered if it'd been intentional. Slowly, he turned around.

"Thank you for helping," Rachel said, almost shylike.

"No problem. Drive safe."

He walked to the front window and watched her back out of the carport. As she drove out of sight, he wondered if she'd noticed his wave.

And now, what to do? Peter had determined the easiest way to deal with the graveyard shift was to sleep for four hours when he got home, and then nap again for a couple hours after supper. When he was on the shift the past several times, he had spent his mornings at Kara's, sleeping while she wrote. In the afternoons, sometimes he'd amuse or more likely frustrate himself by tinkering around with that fool green Mustang of hers.

The car had a short; sometimes it just wouldn't start. If you found the right wire, you could jiggle it to get the thing going. Maybe a month would go by without a problem. Then she'd get stuck somewhere.

"You got the bucks," he'd told Kara time and again. "Take it to an expert. I'm good, but I ain't that good. Nobody is. It's a problem with this model."

But Kara said her parents had bought it for her when she graduated college up in Connecticut, and it was the biggest piece of them she had with her in Virginia. Peter tried telling her she could keep a piece of them by transferring that KLN 699 vanity plate to a more reliable car, but she wouldn't budge.

"You'll figure it out eventually," she'd say with a laugh. "I have faith in you."

Well, now someone else would need to solve the mystery of the short, Peter thought as he whistled Fifth awake and headed to bed.

A half hour later, Peter still wasn't asleep. He picked up his trusty flip phone from the nightstand. No voice mails, other than one he'd heard a few hours earlier from Jill, saying she'd made it safely to Vegas, and Eric was even handsomer than she remembered. No missed calls from any of Kara's numbers.

Well, he sure wasn't going to call her.

Envying Fifth his ability to fall sleep anywhere, anytime, Peter padded to the kitchen in his stocking feet. He'd read the newspaper, then look at the furnace. If he still couldn't sleep, maybe he'd go to Shoe's and get the sabre saw ordered. Rachel had been complaining about her bathroom floor's chips and cracks for a while, but he'd been putting it off, worried about the subfloor's condition. If it was bad, the project would end up being a lot bigger than he was inclined to take on just now.

Peter poured himself a big cup of coffee, black and caffeinated, and took it to the table. The newspaper was the same old, same old. Folk complaining about neighbors who didn't sort their recycling properly. The county attorney whining about kids drag racing through downtown. The area's minor league star pitcher being called up to the majors for the playoffs. Peter wondered why they bothered to publish the fool thing, and why Rachel bothered subscribing to it since they could get all that news online.

He folded the paper back up, and went to put it in the box. They recycled properly, thanks to Rachel. But what was up with the big notice on the front page of the church bulletin that sat on top of the pile? Peter removed the bulletin and settled back in at the table.

"Won't You Help?" read the headline right below the church photo on the front page.

Too early for Commitment Sunday. Rachel always upped her giving sometime around their anniversary on October 20.

"We thank Jim Schumacher for donating the insulation we need," the pastor had written. "However, illness in his family will prevent Shoe from installing the insulation himself. Shoe estimates the project would take a good handyman just a few weeks. If you can donate your talent and time, please contact me at the church office."

Shoe? Illness in the family? Peter shook himself the way Fifth did. Why hadn't he heard about this?

He punched 7 on his trusty flip phone and got Shoe's voice mail. "It's me. I'm on my way over. Put on the coffee pot." He went to the truck, bulletin in hand.

Weaving in and out of traffic, Peter tried to focus on something other than what might be wrong with Shoe's family, but couldn't. The problem probably wasn't major, or Shoe'd have called. But then again, Shoe was part of Redeemer's backbone, so for him not to do this job himself, it had to be something.

Peter scanned the bulletin again while he was stopped at a light. Insulation was a messy, itchy job, but not that hard. Almost anyone could do it with a little instruction. He considered lighting up a cigarette, then decided against it. He wouldn't finish the thing before he hit the hardware store, and Shoe had never liked his smoking.

The light changed, and he hit the gas.

6

Introductions done and name tags on, Rachel exchanged glances with the thirtysomething man with the gold stud in his right earlobe. She watched as he surveyed the seventy or so people seated in the central library's big conference room, then nodded.

"Okay. Let's count off into groups of five for the first exercise," he boomed. "I call it 'Magical Moments.'"

Rachel, seated in the first row on the left-hand side as befitted the county's head librarian, obediently said, "One." She'd seen Robert Carlson present at a state conference, and thought he might help her bridge the gaps that seemed to be widening within the county's three library facilities.

First, there was Brian, who still was upset that Rachel and not he was selected to run the whole show when the former head librarian retired. He was ten years older than Rachel and managed to "mention" at every staff meeting that he was just twenty-five when he was awarded his master's in library science from Carnegie Mellon. Rachel, on the other hand, had received her master's just two years earlier from Drexel University Online. But the programs were accredited by the same association, and the county board members decided they preferred Rachel's businesslike approach over Brian's more academic style. To that end, the board had encouraged Rachel to do what she could to nudge the library's finance person into retirement. Nancy couldn't make head nor tails out of computers, which meant Rachel reentered all Nancy's work or did the work herself to begin with. Yes, it was time for Nancy to retire, past time, really, especially given how tight the next budget was going to be.

Then there were Felicity and Sandy, the Gilroy County natives and University of Maryland graduates who were Rachel's first hires after becoming head librarian. In six months, they had gone from best friends forever to not speaking to each other. Felicity spent as much of the workday as she could planning her wedding, set for the following summer. Sandy spent as much of the workday as she could looking sad because Felicity had filled the bridal party with family members. Add in the other personalities, and there were days Rachel wondered why she'd applied for the job.

And, wouldn't you know it, it turned out that Brian, Nancy, Felicity, and Sandy were the others in Rachel's group. God's certainly got a sense of humor, Rachel thought as everyone resettled.

"I'm going to give you ten minutes to write down magical moments in your life," Robert said. "Make one a school or work accomplishment, one when you helped someone, and one when someone helped you. Don't think a lot; just write down the first things that come into your head."

Rachel frowned. The first two came easily, but as for the third, well, she wasn't one to sit around and wait for others to do for her. She leaned over the paper, pencil between her teeth.

She heard the ding of an alarm, then footsteps. She looked up to find Robert standing by her, and everyone else in the room looking at her.

"Rachel, almost finished?" he asked.

How could she be behind all the others? Still missing that third moment, Rachel folded her paper in half and nodded.

"Now, I'd like you to go around your table and share what you've written. Select a scribe, please, so someone can report out to the larger group. You can always say pass. Let's go."

"Nancy, perhaps you could be the scribe," Rachel said. She probably didn't have much to share anyway.

"That's fine, but can I go first?" Nancy said with more excitement than Rachel had seen in years. "I have a moment to share that'll surprise most of y'all."

"A surprise? How lovely, dear Nancy. Do tell," Brian purred, turning to give Rachel a butter-wouldn't-melt-in-his-mouth smile. She gave him one back.

"Well, I haven't told any of y'all, not even Rachel, but I'm retiring at the end of the year," Nancy said with a big smile. Rachel managed to hold back a sigh of relief.

"Why the secret, darling?" Brian asked. "We'll have so much to do to prepare the festivities. Schedule the flowers, gather up the donations…"

"That's why I haven't said anything. I don't want a party for me. I want a party for you," she said, pointing at Brian. "Because I'm going to tell about the magical moment you did for me."

Rachel studied Brian's face as it went from white to red to white again.

"Brian did something for me that none of y'all know about. Back in the day, they hired me as a receptionist. But they didn't know I couldn't read or write very well."

"What? How could that be?" the other women chorused.

"My sister filled out the application for me and I signed it and brought it in and got hired. I was good with people, and I thought that'd be enough. But I mixed up numbers and letters in phone messages. Brian got a wrong message the first week and figured it out. Every day at lunchtime, he'd work with me. After a few months, I wasn't messing up anymore. I kept my job, and took a couple finance classes at vo-tech to get the one I been doing lately. Now I have my retirement. But it would have never happened without Brian."

Rachel sat, stunned. Who would have guessed it? Maybe a little tutoring and Rachel wouldn't have been slaving away at home on spreadsheets Nancy should have been doing. And who would have thought Mr. Superior would deign to help someone?

"Me next! Me next!" Sandy and Felicity both said after a few minutes, their hands in the air, looking to Rachel for permission.

"Felicity, you first," she said, nodding at the statuesque blonde.

"Well, you might not think it's as big a deal as Nancy's story, but it was important to me and it was someone who was really nice to me and I'll never forget it as long as I live," Felicity said in a rush, brushing the bangs out of her eyes.

"Yes?" Rachel asked.

"It was high school prom night and I had on this killer midnight blue dress that so totally matched my eyes and my nail polish, and then my boyfriend Joey dumped me because I wouldn't do some stuff he wanted and there I was, all by myself at dawn at the truck stop with a bunch of guys leering at me."

"You never told me!" Sandy said, moving around the table to take the vacant chair next to Felicity. "I thought you dumped Joey!"

Felicity shook her head. "And my folks were out of town and I was miles from home and my phone wasn't working and I didn't know what to do. So, I started walking out of the parking lot, and an old geezer with green teeth got out of his car and grabbed my arm. But right then Mr. Gregory drove up in his truck and told the guy to get lost. I guess Mr. Gregory had just gotten off work."

Why don't I know this story? Rachel wondered.

"We went inside and he bought me coffee and told me I was a rare jewel"—Felicity smiled—"and not to give Joey a second thought. He told me I was right to save myself for my husband and to stand by that. When he dropped me off at my house, he shook my hand and waited to leave until I got inside and turned on the lights."

Felicity turned toward Rachel. Then Sandy did. Then Nancy did. Then Brian did.

"That is a magical moment, Felicity," Rachel said finally. "Thank you for sharing it."

"How about you, Mrs. Gregory, I mean Rachel?" Felicity said. "How about one of your moments?"

"Yes, Rachel," Brian said with more sincerity than Rachel had heard out of him since the battle for the top job had begun. "Please do."

Rachel unfolded her paper and read it to herself. "Magical moment of a work or school accomplishment: The day I testified before a Virginia Assembly committee against sharing patron information with criminal investigators. Magical moment when I helped someone: Helping Jill get dressed on her wedding day."

She refolded the paper.

"I had a magical moment of someone helping me just this morning," she said. "It was my husband. He was dog-tired after being on his feet at the factory for eight hours straight on the graveyard shift."

"Did he bring you breakfast in bed?" Felicity asked.

"Was there a rose on the tray?" Sandy chimed in.

"No," Rachel said. "He cleared the table. He loaded the dishwasher. He stayed awake long enough to watch me get out of the carport. And he waved."

Felicity, Sandy, Nancy, and Brian all looked at each other.

"That was magical?" Nancy asked.

"Yes," Rachel said, not caring who heard her tone of wonderment. "That was magical."

7

If you didn't know the brick hardware store was there, you'd miss it. The bakery and the pet store both were practically on the frontage road. Schumacher's, to the west, was set back close to a half block to allow plenty of room in the front for topsoil, peat moss, sand, and such.

Peter drove around to the back, where the older man was lugging some large contractor's bags to the trash. "Lord, what a glorious way to start this beautiful day," Shoe hollered as Peter got out. "Got your voice mail. What's on your mind?"

"Need to talk with you about this thing in the church bulletin. Did you put the coffee on?"

"'Course. It's done brewed."

The smell of paints, thinners, and wood hit Peter as they walked in. It always took him back to the spring day Peter and his daddy came to get him a trike for his fifth birthday, the year after Mama died. His daddy called the odor "sweet perfume," and Peter had learned to love it when he started helping at the hardware store when he was thirteen or so. He learned to love Shoe too, Daddy's best friend. The men were so close that, when Daddy died, there was no question but that Peter would move in with Shoe's family above the store. That part, the accident, Peter didn't like to think about much—or that Shoe had spent most of the next few years doing his mourning in a bottle, not objecting when Peter joined him from time to time.

Inside the musty office, Shoe poured the coffee, his into a chipped blue mug that read "World's Best Grandpa" and Peter's into a "Virginia Is for Lovers" one.

"What's on your mind?" Shoe asked as they sat down on the beat-up green couch.

"This," Peter said, pushing the bulletin toward his friend. "Who's so sick that you can't do a job for church, and why don't I know about it?" Peter managed to avoid the places where springs were threatening to break through the upholstery. He knew them because he'd spent more than a few nights there in the past seven years since Rachel kicked him out of their bed.

"David's ma."

Peter frowned. He liked Shoe's son-in-law and had met David's mother once when she came to visit.

"Ain't she out in one of them cold states?"

Shoe nodded. "Minnesota. She had a bad fall, broke her hip. She'll be fine, but tweren't anyone there that could help. Him and Dot left last Monday, and won't be back for a few weeks. Kevin's staying with me."

Peter nodded. Shoe's grandson Kevin, a good kid, was in high school. But Dot was his right-hand woman at the store, handling all the bookwork. It'd be hard for Shoe to stay on top of that stuff and still give customers the service he prided himself on.

"I can help."

Shoe laughed. "You're worse with numbers than I am."

"So, run the numbers, Einstein, and I can help out front. Just started three months on graveyard, and I'm looking for something to fill my days when I'm not sleeping."

"How's that?"

Peter drained his coffee. He shifted the mug to his left hand,

and traced the slogan with his right. Then he set the mug on the floor.

"Let's just say Virginia ain't for lovers anymore."

He stared at his hands. He could feel Shoe's eyes on him.

"I got dumped. Can you believe it? Mr. Love 'Em and Leave 'Em, dumped." He gave a hard laugh. "Anyway, it's done and there won't be any going back."

Shoe said nothing.

"You wouldn't have to pay me or anything. It'd be my pleasure. You'd be helping me more than I'd be helping you."

He turned to look at Shoe, whose face was scrunched tight.

"Here's how you can help me. Do the insulation job at Redeemer."

"Say what?"

"I know how you are on graveyard. Sometimes you fall asleep mid-conversation. With Dot and David gone, someone's gotta be here and awake to help the customers. This here insulation job is custom-made for you. You could come and go as you like."

Peter stood up and put his hands on his hips. "Church is Rachel's place, not mine. She likes things separatelike." He remembered Rachel had asked him to go to church with her and Jill that Sunday but decided not to tell Shoe that.

Shoe rose and took the same pose. "What if you could do it without her knowing? She's at the library all day long."

Peter laughed. "Right, I go to this pastor and say, 'I can't tell you who I am or my background, but I'm here to do your insulation'? And he's going to trust me to crawl around in his building?"

Shoe pulled his phone out of his jeans pocket and pushed some buttons. "Becky? It's Shoe. How's by you and your family?" Pause. "Glad to hear it. Yep, David's ma is doing better, thanks for asking. I need to talk with Pastor, please. Thanks."

Peter felt his heart starting to pound. "Wait," he whispered. "Don't do this."

Shoe nodded like the person he was talking with on the phone was in the room. "Yep, she's doing good. Yep, they're good too. Say, I got a volunteer for the insulation. Good friend. I can vouch for his work, and he could start pretty much right away. Only thing is, he wants to be anonymous."

This time, the pause went on longer. Peter ran his finger across his throat to signal Shoe to end the conversation. Shoe ignored him.

"I know, I know. But he has his reasons." Shoe nodded again.

"I don't know as he wants you to know his first name even. Why don't I just put him on right now and you can find out?" Shoe handed the phone to Peter.

"It's your call, son. Hang up or talk."

Peter inhaled and shut his eyes.

"My name's Peter," he said, holding the phone to his ear. "When can I start?"

❧

When he arrived at the Church of the Redeemer late the following morning, Peter took stock. On the outside, not much had changed in the three years since Jill and Eric's wedding: a red brick structure that looked to date back to the 1950s, with a bell tower that could use some tuckpointing. Window casings that needed painting. A parking lot that begged for resurfacing. About the only thing to recommend the place was the garden just outside the office door. Salvia, some autumn clematis, mums, asters. That burst of color almost was enough to make you overlook the rest of it. Rachel had to have had a hand with that.

He tallied up the odd jobs. Wouldn't take more than a thousand dollars and some elbow grease.

"Hello! May I help you?"

Peter turned around to face a balding man who looked to be at the most thirty-five, maybe younger—not a wrinkle on his pasty white baby face. What hair the guy had was the color of straw. He was short, maybe five-foot-six, and he was wearing khaki pants and a green polo shirt and carrying a set of golf clubs.

"Oh, I'm good," Peter said. "I'm early for a meeting and didn't want to waste the weather."

Pasty-Face smiled. "Well, I don't think you're here for the Moms Club or the Arts and Crafts Guild, and I know everyone on the development committee."

Peter laughed and shook his head. "Couldn't balance a checkbook, much less ask folk for money. I'm here to talk with Pastor Brown. Well, not exactly talk with him, as there's nothing wrong, but to—"

"I'm Pastor Brown," Pasty-Face interrupted, extending his hand. "Most call me Pastor Doug, though. You must be the man who's interested in helping with the insulation. I'm sorry; I don't remember your name."

"Peter."

"Peter, I'm pleased to meet you. I have a few things to do before our meeting, but let's go on in." With that, Pastor Doug walked toward the office door and, after jiggling the key in the knob a few times, opened it.

The inside didn't look much better than the outside. Orange industrial carpeting that probably hadn't been replaced since Peter's own wedding day. Duct tape covered the bigger rips. The walls were a dingy yellow; not dirty, just worn out. Peter wondered where all the money Rachel donated was going. Not to the building, that was for sure.

"Pastor Doug! You almost beat me back!" A young woman in a wheelchair was rolling herself behind a low reception counter.

"Hi, Becky. How'd it go at the doctor?" the pastor asked as he checked the pile of messages waiting on the counter under a large rock that had "PD" painted in white on it.

"He upped my allergy meds, so I should be good till there's a frost. Oh, and the Johnsons are in your office. They came in the back with me."

"Thanks much, Becky. This is Peter, and he wants to help us with the insulation." Peter and the woman traded nods. "Peter, the library is to your left. I'm going to park you there for fifteen minutes or so. If you need anything, just holler for Becky."

The library was in the same place as it'd been when Peter and Rachel had their hasty wedding service with Rachel's parents, Shoe, and Pastor Miller. But unlike the rest of the office, this room had been painted recently—eggshell, he thought Rachel would call it. The blue-and-green checked linoleum was cheery and new. The dark oak bookshelves looked like they'd been around a couple million years, but they were sturdy. Someone had made signs for each color-coded section: DVDs. Bibles. Biographies. Praise Books. Holy Land Travelogues. Now this room felt homey and welcoming. He wondered if Rachel was responsible for it as well.

On one wall under a sign that read "Volunteer of the Year" hung plaque after plaque and picture after picture of people accepting awards and shaking hands with Pastor Miller or Pastor Doug. He moved along the wall, starting with the oldest. He recognized a few faces, starting with Rachel's parents. He hadn't seen Mavis and Maarten in years and wondered why Rachel had started bothering with them again, even if it was just for their birthdays and anniversary. Strange to think they'd been valued members of the church community for establishing Lyman's first food pantry that same year they'd made Rachel feel so small about being pregnant.

When Peter got to the more recent plaques, there was Rachel from the year Jill left for college. In the photo, Rachel was wearing a navy pantsuit, looking serious and shaking hands with Pastor Miller. The plaque read: "Volunteer of the Year/Rachel Gregory/Landscaping."

Ah, yes, of course. And it was just like her to keep the landscaping up once she'd done it. Peter smiled with pride and moved on down the line of photos, not expecting to recognize anyone else.

Except he did. The plaque from the previous spring: "Volunteers of the Year/Eric and Jill Stanton/Library."

The photo showed Pastor Doug, glistening with sweat, shaking hands with Jill, wearing a short-sleeved ruffly pink dress, her black hair piled up on top of her head, and Eric, standing ramrod straight and smiling big as could be in dark pants, white dress shirt, and a tie the same pink as Jill's dress.

They had to have told me about these awards, Peter thought. *Maybe I had to work. Or maybe I didn't understand how important this was.*

"I'm sorry," Pastor Doug said as he entered the room. "That took longer than I expected. Now, let me show you around and tell you about the project."

The two men took a quick tour, with Pastor Doug pointing out his own office, stacked with books and papers; the space for Sunday school class; and a couple of meeting rooms, one of which contained bundle after bundle of pink rolled insulation.

"Shoe figured that would take care of the attic above the areas we've seen plus this room," Pastor Doug said when they returned to the library and sat at the table.

"That looks about right," Peter said. "He's lending tools too, right?"

"Yes. Now, Shoe said you've done this type of work before."

"Yep. He taught me when I"—he caught himself; he'd have to be careful not to give anything away—"a long time ago. I've done my own and helped friends. Learned a lot from my own mistakes."

"Haven't we all. Now that you know what would be entailed, are you still willing to help?"

Peter nodded. "Shouldn't think it'd take more than three or four weeks in my spare time. Be done by late October, beat the frost."

"Peter…" the pastor paused. "Peter, something about you seems familiar. Are you a member of the church?"

The best defense is a good offense. Peter had always believed that. He met Pastor Doug's eyes and tried to stare him down, but Peter had to look away first.

"We have a congregation of about five hundred families," Pastor Doug said. "I take pride in knowing everyone. You're not a member, are you?"

"Not exactly. I don't come very often. I went to Shoe because I was worried after I saw the item in the bulletin my wife brought home."

"And she is?"

"I mean no disrespect, Pastor," Peter said, trying to keep his voice at an even level but feeling an edge come into it, "but who I am shouldn't matter a hill of beans to you. You got a project, I got the time and skill."

Peter stood up to his full six-foot-two and walked to the library door and faced the pastor, who was watching him much as Peter watched the birds that make it to the backyard feeder, determining each of their species.

"Why are you doing this, Peter?" It was as if the pastor had asked Peter whether he wanted cream or sugar with his coffee, the tone was just that calm.

Peter tried the stare-down again, and it didn't work this time either.

"I just started three months on the graveyard shift. I'd like to keep busy in the afternoons for reasons I'd rather not talk about."

Pastor Doug was still watching him, right elbow on the table, chin resting on his hand.

"I'd like to keep my mind and my hands occupied. Didn't God say something about idle hands being the devil's playground? Well, I can tell you the devil's got more than a playground for idle hands. There's a whole theme park."

Pastor Doug got up and walked toward Peter, right hand extended.

"Fair enough. Now, how soon can you start?"

8

Rachel put the hybrid in park, took off her sunglasses, and sighed. As always, the Grossman farm looked perfect. Even in late September, the lawn appeared freshly mown, without a single leaf cluttering it. Had the shutters been painted a deeper shade of green? It was hard to remember. Even though Duffy was just a twenty-minute drive from Lyman, she came here only three times a year—her parents' birthdays and today, their wedding anniversary.

She prayed the same prayer she prayed every time she entered that driveway: Lord, let me find favor with my parents. Then she took the gift from the passenger seat and put it in her oversized purse.

Her mother was watching through the screen door as Rachel approached.

"You're late," Mavis said, arms crossed across her ample chest over a spotless white apron.

Rachel looked at her watch. 12:05 p.m.

"I apologize," she said. "Pastor Doug's sermon today was on the woman at the well, and…" Her mother turned and walked further into the house.

Rachel entered the kitchen. Enough fried chicken to feed the county was draining on paper towels by the ceramic sink, even though it'd be just the three of them. Mashed potatoes, still steaming, sat in a Meissen bowl on the counter next to a smaller bowl of creamed corn. It was the same menu for every important meal that had ever occurred in the house, including Peter's only visit there, two days after she told him she was pregnant.

More than twenty years ago. So much and yet so little had changed.

Since she was old enough to balance a serving dish, one of Rachel's duties had been to bring the food from the kitchen to the dining room table. She washed her hands, then moved the chicken to a waiting platter.

Her parents, dressed in their Sunday black as always, were at opposite ends of the large cherry table that seated twelve, eyes closed and hands in the praying position. Their lined faces and stooped shoulders gave them the appearance of people twenty years older than their actual ages. Rachel coughed.

"Here's the chicken. I'll be right back with the corn and potatoes." Neither of them looked up.

After bringing in the remaining dishes, Rachel slid into her usual place and unfolded an orange cloth napkin. The color matched the tiny oriental garden pattern on the plates. She'd always wondered how they'd come to choose that pattern. It was cheerily at odds with the furniture and the somber dark green wallpaper. But Maarten and Mavis—she had been unable to think of them in any other terms since her wedding day, and when she spoke to them, called them "folks"—weren't people you questioned.

"Lord, we thank You for this food in front of us and the hands that made it," Maarten intoned in his deep bass. "We beg Your forgiveness for all our wrongs and pray that You will keep us from the fires of hell. In Jesus's name, amen."

"Amen," Mavis and Rachel said at the same time.

Typical prayer from Maarten, Rachel thought. The God her parents had shown her was a vengeful one, the kind who threatened to wipe out villages on a whim and who left women barren. Only Maarten's mother, her beloved German-born Grossmutter, talked about Jesus and how much He loved the sparrows and the lilies of the field and, yes, even Rachel. Rachel accepted Him as her personal Lord and Savior during her senior year in high school just before the Grossmutter died. She still doubted sometimes that He'd accepted her.

"Well, happy forty-seventh anniversary," Rachel said as she passed the chicken to her father. The wide man studied the plate and proceeded to take a breast, a thigh, and a drumstick.

"Don't know what's happy about it," Mavis said. "My knees and hips aren't what they were. Takes me longer to get out of bed every morning."

"Poultry prices are down so bad, the Lord only knows if we'll still be on the farm this time next year," Maarten grumbled. "We may be in the poorhouse by then."

Rachel nodded, then did her best to tune them out by thinking about Pastor Doug's sermon. He had talked about the way that Jesus asks His followers to worship the Father in both spirit and truth if they wanted to drink of the living water, and how His followers today continue to reap the benefits of the resurrection.

"It's a shame you stopped going to Redeemer all those years ago," Rachel said, interrupting Mavis's diatribe about something to do with the apple orchard. "Pastor Doug, the one who married Jill and Eric, he preaches a thoughtful message. Remember how when I was in high school, we'd discuss Pastor Miller's sermon all the way home in the car?"

Maarten harrumphed. "We're fed at Calvary. You know why we left Redeemer. No need to go into that again."

"So," Rachel said, "Eric is leaving his Marine Combat Center training in California soon to go overseas. Jill met him in Las Vegas for a long weekend at Labor Day."

Maarten and Mavis looked at each other. "Can't see why anyone would want to go to California," Maarten said, turning his head toward Mavis.

He went there because that's where his training is, Rachel wanted to say, and he and Jill met in Las Vegas, which is in Nevada. But instead, she gave a fake smile and forged on. "Peter's on the grave-yard shift again. I'm hoping he'll take advantage of the time to get my bathroom floor retiled. And I'm loving the head librarian job so far. It's been six months."

Rachel could feel her mother's eyes on her—or rather, on her plate. "You ate like a bird. Are you on a diet again? You picked off the skin. That's the best part. And why didn't you have any gravy? You should have taken more potatoes."

Rachel stood. "I'll clear the table. Are we having coffee and cake for dessert?" Of course we are. Decaf, because they won't sleep all night otherwise. Chocolate cake with seven-minute frosting, and Mavis will complain that it didn't peak the way she wanted.

She had tried to stay in contact with her parents when Jill was little, the two of them going to dinner at the Grossmans' every so often—without Peter, who was adamant he and Rachel were owed a big apology. The last visit of that sort occurred when Jill was seven or eight and asked Mavis and Maarten why they didn't love the Gregorys. Her parents had looked at each other uneasily, and then Maarten started talking about how the Bible said if an eye offend-ed you, you should pluck it out. That ended that. The Grossmans weren't even invited to Jill's high school graduation.

But after Jill went to college, Rachel humbled herself and called on their anniversary that year. Over the past seven years, she had learned to tolerate them for a couple hours three times a year. It wasn't much, she knew, but it was something.

Cake finished, Rachel opened her purse and brought out her gift, an oblong box wrapped in silver and white paper with a big silver bow. "Happy anniversary!"

She held her breath as Mavis opened it with Maarten looking

on. The eight-page "Marriage Memories" book Rachel had made included a photo of the two of them on their wedding day, Mavis in a calf-length, long-sleeved white dress, Maarten in a tux. An explanation of the meaning of their names: Mavis, "song thrush"; Maarten, "do not deceive." A brochure from the Smoky Mountains, where they had honeymooned, from 1968 that Rachel bought online. Photos from the movies *The Horse in the Gray Flannel Suit* and *The Shakiest Gun in the West.* She had purposely not included images of political figures, violence, and rock musicians; no need to upset them. The exercise had reminded Rachel of the troublesome time in which her parents came of age and made her think that perhaps that helped to explain their sour view of the world.

"I hope you like it," Rachel said.

Mavis nodded. "We're not much for tchotchkes."

Or gratitude, Rachel thought. She said her goodbyes, no hugs or kisses, of course, and was five miles down the road before she realized she didn't have her purse. Back she went.

"Left my purse," she said when Mavis answered the door.

Mavis sighed. "Careless. I'll get it for you."

As Rachel waited for her mother to fetch the purse, she saw the anniversary present, perched on top of the garbage can just inside the door.

9

"Hello, Peter! Did you have a good nap?" Becky sang out as he entered the church office for week three of the insulation project.

"Yes, I did, thanks. What's new in the kingdom, Becks?"

"Oh, the usual. Choir's trying to decide whether introducing a couple new songs on Sunday will upset people or inspire them. The printer printed the inside of this week's bulletin upside down, and there's no time to redo it."

Peter laughed. "Trouble do have a way of coming all at once, don't it? Everyone in the county must be here for meetings. I had to park across the way at the coffee shop. Say, any chance the pastor'd have a couple minutes for me before I head upstairs?"

"Can't imagine that he wouldn't." Becky picked up the phone and pressed a few buttons. "Peter's here. He'd like a word." A short pause, followed by, "Thanks."

"You can go on back," she said with a smile. "But remind him Seniors on Call is going to want to see him in a bit."

"You got it, Becks. Wouldn't do to keep Seniors on Call waiting—whatever that is."

Pastor Doug was seated at the little round table near his office door when Peter walked in. You couldn't have a meeting with Pastor Doug at his desk, because he wouldn't be able to see you through the stacks of papers.

"Someday, someone's going to call the fire marshal on you, you know," Peter said.

"Some days, I think that'd be a good thing. Seems like every time I get through a pile, Becky brings in new stuff for me to review, or somebody sends me a book or article they think I'd like, and I can never say no. How are you today?"

"I'm good," Peter said, taking a seat next to the table in a ratty overstuffed chair that looked ready to burst a spring at any minute. "I'm near done with the insulation."

"That was fast."

"That was fast and good. You'll save a bundle on heating this winter. What was left up in those rafters was about as bad as nothing."

"It's been good having you around. Becky and I are both going to miss your face."

"That's what I'm fixin' to talk about," Peter said, pulling a folded piece of paper from his jeans front pocket. "I got another two months on graveyard. The whole office, other than the library, could use a coat or two of paint. The entryway carpeting anyway should be replaced. And that leak in the sanctuary roof ain't bad now, but it will be if you don't take care of it."

Pastor Doug sighed. "You're right on all counts. We tend to look at the way we minister to those in financial or spiritual need a lot more often than we do at the building. But those things aren't in the budget, and all our volunteers are tapped out with projects right now."

It was the response Peter had expected.

"Pastor, I can do the labor—" Pastor Doug started to speak, but Peter raised his hand to quiet him. "And I've priced out the materials. I'll cover it."

The response Peter expected was effusive thanks to God and to him, and probably a strong hand clasp and maybe even a slightly uncomfortable man-hug. Instead, the pastor pushed his chair back a bit and leaned back.

"Peter, what's this all about?"

"What do you mean?" Peter was a little irked. He was offering to donate a good chunk of change on carpeting, primer, paint, and other materials, not to mention his time.

"I don't know who you are other than Shoe's friend, a good craftsman, a man with whom I enjoy discussing local history and books, and someone who makes my receptionist smile. What's this all about?"

Peter looked at the wall clock. "Listen, you got to meet with Seniors on Call. Maybe we'll talk about it another day."

Pastor Doug shook his head. Then he took off his glasses, polished them with a tissue, and walked over to the desk and picked up the phone.

"Becky, is Seniors on Call here yet?" Pause. "All right. Please tell Connor something's come up and to start the meeting without me." Another pause. "I'll try, but I'll catch up with him later if they finish before I can get there."

The pastor moved back to the table. "I appreciate the gifts—your time, your donation, getting to know you. But why?"

"I don't see as that matters."

"It matters because something is sitting on your soul. Otherwise, there wouldn't be so many secrets."

Peter stood up, stretched, and walked to the windows near Pastor Doug's desk. The Blue Ridge Mountains were just a couple weeks from full splendor, the sumacs, dogwoods, and maples nearly ready to explode into gold, green and orange. On days like this, most days really, Peter wondered how anyone would want to live anywhere other than the Shenandoah Valley. Why look for something different when you already had perfection?

"Me and the wife, we live together and that's about it," he said, keeping his gaze out the window. "A certain other lady I thought had my heart, but she told me it's still with my wife. I'm working on figuring out whether she was right about that, and being here at your church keeps me safe. Much more than that, I can't say."

He heard Pastor Doug get up, and turned around. This time, the pastor's head was nodding, not shaking.

"I'm happy you feel safe here. When you want to talk further, I'll listen. And now, just when do you expect to start on turning Redeemer into the Palace Beautiful?"

Peter laughed. "I'll finish the insulation today. Probably start work tomorrow on that leak, and then the painting when I'm through with that."

"Won't you need some time to buy supplies for all these projects?"

Peter turned toward the door and pulled his dust mask out of his front jeans pocket. Then he grinned.

"Bought 'em before I came over today." He put on the mask and headed for the attic.

You could divide the world into two kinds of people, Rachel thought, drawing a neat box on her notepad: those who knew how to conduct a meeting and those who did not.

Connor Newman, a man in his mid-sixties with a bad comb-over, was one of the second kind.

Inside the church library, ten minutes passed in silence, then fifteen. Rachel tried not to think about the things she had left undone at work. She was rightly proud of Seniors on Call, which she'd set up five years earlier to link up local nonprofits with retired church members who had so much to offer in finance, marketing, and other areas. But becoming the county's head librarian had increased her workload substantially, so she had asked Pastor Doug to find a new chairman. She appreciated he'd done it so quickly, but it made her ego smart a little bit that he had turned to Connor. One of Connor's first actions was to move meetings from evenings to afternoons so he and the other members, all except her retired, wouldn't have to drive after dark. Oh well, another meeting or two and the transition would be finished.

"I wonder, Connor, if we couldn't move along on the agenda," Rachel said. "I understand you'd like Pastor Doug to see the logo. But perhaps we could discuss dividing up the business contact list in the meantime."

Connor shook his head. "We have to settle on the logo before we can do anything else."

"Stephen? Carol? Karen? What do you think?" Rachel asked.

Stephen kept checking his phone. Carol shot Rachel a pleading look. Karen, it appeared, had fallen asleep.

All right then.

Rachel had drawn sixteen smaller, perfectly matched boxes in four rows of four by cutting the larger box into quarters, and had inked in the upper right and lower left corners of each by the time Pastor Doug walked in.

"Well, this is a surprise!" he said with a pastoral smile. "I didn't expect that you'd all stay."

In short order, Pastor Doug provided some gentle but effective guidance on the logo, thanking Connor for creating it but suggesting he consider some other color schemes besides purple and green. Everyone agreed to divide up the business contacts list. Everyone told Carol the homemade brownies she'd brought were the tastiest ever—everyone except Rachel, who said they looked delicious but she didn't dare.

Finally, Connor said they were ready to wrap up, and the committee members bowed their heads. "Who shall we pray for?" Pastor Doug asked.

"For my granddaughter, whose volleyball team has a big game tonight," Carol said. "Lord, please show these young women Your joy and grace in victory and Your wisdom and love in defeat."

"For my brother, who can't seem to stop coughing," Connor said.

"For the Seniors on Call volunteers, that their experience and expertise multiply a thousandfold at the charities that use their services," Karen said.

"For people suffering with mental illness, that they find comfort in God and help in our community," Stephen said.

Rachel hated this part of church meetings. Twenty years on, and she still was uncomfortable sharing anything personal, and Karen had taken what she had planned to say. She coughed.

"For my daughter and for her husband, who will be deploying overseas. Lord, please hold them safe in Your hands," Rachel said. While she sincerely prayed for Eric's safety, it was Jill who concerned Rachel more these days. The child had seemed so preoccupied ever since that drive to the airport.

"For a new friend You have brought to this church, Lord," Pastor Doug said. "Help him to understand that Your forgiveness and mercy are infinite and to open himself up and come into Your light. In Christ's name we ask for Your help on these and on all the petitions we hold close to our hearts, amen."

"Amen," the committee members chorused. As the others exited, Rachel walked over to Pastor Doug.

"Remember those books on religion and philosophy left over from the Friends of the Library sale? I have four boxes in my car. Do you have a minute to help me get them inside?"

"Absolutely! Let me get a cart."

Rachel checked her watch. Getting rid of the boxes wouldn't take long, but still, it'd be close to five thirty before she got home. She'd planned to bake a quiche for supper, but that wouldn't work now. Maybe some poached fish with a tossed salad. Peter had said he was going to the hardware store in the afternoon. She hoped he'd been able to get everything he needed to get the yard ready for winter. And was that sabre saw ever going to come in? Her bathroom tile was looking worse by the day.

Pastor Doug came out, wheeling a small hand truck, and they walked to the hybrid. "Let me load it up, Rachel," he said, as she began lifting one of the boxes out of the trunk. "Any more on when Eric deploys?"

"Just after the new year. He'll be here for Christmas."

"Fantastic! We can always use his voice in the choir, especially at Christmas. All set. Let's go inside."

Rachel walked ahead to hold the door for Pastor Doug. She couldn't see Becky, but she heard her laugh and the clomping of work boots.

"You are really something," Becky said. "See you tomorrow."

"G'bye, Becks," a strong, masculine voice called out. Before Rachel could process the identity, Peter strode into view, jeans and chambray shirt covered in fibers, goggles resting on top of his head and a dust mask pushed down over his Adam's apple. She let go of the door so fast that it hit Pastor Doug and the hand truck.

Rachel stared.

Peter stared.

Rachel tried to summon up some Scripture: 1 Thessalonians 5:4? "But you, brothers and sisters, are not in darkness, for that day to surprise you like a thief." 1 Peter 4:12? "Beloved, do not be surprised at the fiery ordeal that is taking place among you to test you, as though something strange were happening to you." Nope and nope. After a few seconds, Rachel couldn't help but shout: "What are you doing at my church?"

10

A million things to say zipped around Peter's brain: "Your church? Last time I checked, it was God's." "Helping people. How about you?" "What are you doing here? Shouldn't you be at work?"

"Peter Jackson Gregory! I asked you a question!"

At this second outburst, Peter heard Becky's wheelchair roll closer to the entryway. The outside door opened and Pastor Doug, panting, took a step inside.

The best defense is a good offense. Peter had always believed that. But as he turned to look at each of the others, he felt his own heart rate and breathing slow. Rachel, red-faced, shaking. Becky, eyes wide open and body leaning forward in her wheelchair, like she was watching a TV show. Pastor Doug, looking like he was the quarterback and the coach had sent in a play that he didn't understand.

"Good afternoon, wife. Let's do this at home. Goodbye, Becky. Goodbye, Pastor." And, with as much dignity as he could muster, he walked out the door and to his truck.

Peter was tempted to take the truck out on the four-lane for twenty or so miles to clear his head and figure out what he was going to say, but instead he found himself going directly home. He had nothing to hide. Well, nothing but that he'd spent a few hundred bucks and some of his free time on that church of hers.

He parked the truck in the carport, started some coffee, and changed. He put his work clothes in the washer, and was walking back into the kitchen when Rachel came in.

"What was that all about?" she said in a cold, even tone.

"Let's sit." Peter pulled out Rachel's chair at the table. She shrugged her shoulders and plopped down.

The coffeemaker gave its distinctive gasp. "Coffee's ready. Decaf. Want some?"

Rachel nodded.

Peter went to the cupboard and started to grab the usual bright blue stoneware mugs, then reconsidered. Instead, he took down from the top shelf—the one Rachel couldn't reach without a step stool—two of the Queen Margaret bone china cups and saucers that had belonged to his great-grandmother. Maybe pretty cups would make the conversation a little less ugly. He rinsed them under the faucet, then poured the coffee, added sweetener to his own—he knew better than to ask Rachel if she wanted any—and brought them to the table.

Rachel gave him a curt nod and took a sip. She spent what seemed like forever examining the saucer's pink rose pattern, then put the cup back on it.

"I don't want you at my church."

"It wasn't so very long ago you asked me to go to services with you, the day Jill was leaving for Vegas."

"That was different. I knew you wouldn't go."

"If you knew I wouldn't go, why did you ask?"

"I asked because…well, yes, I did hope you'd go that day, but it was because I was trying to be a good Christian and give you more time with Jill before she went away. Anyway, this isn't about that. What were you doing there?"

"I saw the item in your bulletin about Shoe not being able to do the insulation work. Thought I'd make myself useful during the day beyond talking to Callie. She's a good cat, but her conversation leaves something to be desired."

"You ran out of projects around here? How about the bathroom tile, for starters, or the furnace?"

Peter reached in his shirt pocket for his pack of cigarettes, but stopped. He'd been cutting back because it didn't seem right to smoke at church. If he could make it through this conversation without lighting up, he could make it through anything.

"I'm fixing to do the tile as soon as the sabre saw comes in. Told you that. I was worried about the furnace, but new filters solved the problem. Told you that, too."

She gave him a look he couldn't quite read, her lips twisting and her hands clasping and unclasping. "For years, I've held my head high when people told me they'd seen you with this woman or that. But at church, all most people know is that my husband doesn't worship. Now, there you were, flirting with a receptionist who's Jill's age. And I can assure you she's already texted all her friends about what she saw today."

Peter remembered what he had learned back in high school. The easiest way to deal with Rachel when she was like this was to say three magic words, "As you wish." But he liked Pastor Doug. He got a kick out of Becky, and he was being friendly, not flirty. He was proud of the work he'd done, and was looking forward to doing more. He was grateful that whole hours now passed without thinking of Kara, and that his new route to the factory avoiding her house was second nature now. Still, he surely hadn't intended to embarrass or hurt Rachel; that's why he had tried to keep his work a secret.

"As you—" Peter started, but that final word wouldn't come. He started again. "About embarrassing you in public, that's a whole 'nother discussion that maybe we'll have and maybe we won't. But right now, we're talking about me doing work for Redeemer. Today

I bought a few hundred dollars in paint, carpeting, and materials for other jobs there. It's all in the truck."

Rachel put her hands over her face. "Where did you get that money? When were you going to tell me about it?"

"You know how we agree on the budget and then you give me cash spending money for the week on Sunday nights? I always have some left over. I keep it in my sock drawer. I used that."

When Rachel put her hands down, he could still see the imprints of her fingers. "Please let me have my church. Please."

This time, there was only one thing to say.

"As you wish. And as for supper, well, I'm not hungry." Peter picked up Callie and headed for his room, softly shutting the door.

∽∾

Peter was at the Church of the Redeemer at 9:30 the next morning, after coming home from work to a silent breakfast with Rachel. Becky didn't stop him as he walked toward Pastor Doug's office.

"I've come to drop off the paint and such," Peter said.

"Good morning, Peter," Pastor Doug said, moving from behind his desk.

"Can't say as it is a good morning. I just need to leave the materials, then I'll be on my way."

The pastor gestured toward the table. "Do you have a minute?"

"Not really," Peter said, remaining standing. "If I'd had any idea Rachel would find out, I never would have gotten us all into this mess. She feels this is her territory, and she's mighty perturbed I've infringed on it. Thinking about it from her view, I don't blame her. Now, none of the work's urgent other than that leak. If you get a volunteer, I can tell them by phone what to do."

"Is that it?"

"That has to be it, Pastor."

"You told me something once about trying to get back with

your wife. Rachel and I have gotten to know each other pretty well, and I could try—"

"If you want to try, I won't stop you. But I wouldn't hold out much hope. Goodbye, now." He turned and left.

11

Is this about yesterday, Becky? I'm not sure five this afternoon will work for me," Rachel said. She and Lizzie were scheduled for their monthly pedicures at four.

"Pastor Doug didn't say what it was about, just that it was important."

"All right. I'll be there."

It had to be about yesterday. Why else would Pastor Doug want her to come in on such short notice? She knew she had been wrong. She'd beaten herself up about it most of the night.

How do you get so angry at someone who's doing a good deed for God? she had asked herself repeatedly. The only reasons she could come up with weren't pretty: Because he's a charmer and I'm not. Because I'm afraid Pastor Doug and the rest will like him better than me.

She didn't even want to guess how much money Peter had saved the congregation by installing the insulation. She believed he had saved some of his Sunday-night money in his sock drawer. They both had learned to be careful with their dollars in the early days when there were so few of them. That was why they owned their house and vehicles free and clear. And he had never protested that tithing was built into their budget.

She'd ask for forgiveness from Pastor Doug, Becky too. Then she'd go home and apologize to Peter. Or maybe the first apology belonged there.

She texted Lizzie, asking her to go ahead to the salon herself and let them know Rachel wouldn't be joining this time. Then she tried calling the house, but there was no answer. Next, she tried his cell phone. The generic voice said, "No one can come to the phone right now. Please leave a message at the tone."

She hung up, angry all over again. Peter would know she'd called because of the missed calls list, and she didn't care. He'd gone back to that announcement a few years earlier after a man had called a phone number he'd found in his wife's purse and heard the message that began, "This is Peter Gregory…." There being only one Peter Gregory listed in Lyman, the man got their address and drove to the house to tell Rachel that, if she'd keep her husband satisfied, he wouldn't be sniffing around other women's skirts.

That night, Rachel read Peter the riot act. "As you wish" was all he said. The next time she called his cell, the generic message was on.

Finally, it was four thirty. Rachel was heading for the door when her cell phone rang with Jill's ringtone.

"Hi, Mother, it's me," Jill said in the same flat tone she'd been using lately. "I'm wondering if there'd be room for me at supper tonight."

It figured. Here they'd been waiting for Jill to open up about what was troubling her, and she chose tonight.

"Jilly-Bean, I'd love to have you, and I'm sure Dad would. But I'm just leaving for a meeting that could run late. How about to-morrow night?"

The silence on the phone struck Rachel right in the heart.

"Jill?"

"Um, I'm not sure. Hope the meeting goes well. Bye."

Rachel was so lost in thought about Jill that she drove through a four-way stop intersection and didn't hear the angry honking that followed. But she came back to the moment when she arrived at Redeemer. Peter's truck was parked in front of the office.

Three adults were a tight fit around Pastor Doug's little table. Rachel wondered why they weren't meeting in the library, which was so much more comfortable. *Maybe he's concerned that it's too close to the receptionist's desk,* she thought. *Maybe he's concerned I'll blow up again and Becky will hear.*

She knew Becky and some of the volunteers called her Mrs. Perfect. "She's got the perfect daughter, the perfect job, the perfect clothes, and she knows it," Rachel once heard Becky telling the Sunday school leader. "And she's got the pastor wrapped around her finger."

Rachel was quite sure Becky had now informed many people that the good-looking older guy who had put in the insulation was Mrs. Perfect's non-churchgoing husband and that Mrs. Perfect had yelled at him, right in the office. This time when the tongues wagged, the fault would be hers, not Peter's.

"Thanks to both of you for coming," Pastor Doug said. "I thought perhaps we could talk about yesterday."

It felt like the one time in Rachel's school days that she had been sent to the principal's office, for passing a note to Lizzie in study hall. She had cried that day. She wouldn't cry today, no matter what.

"Not sure there's a lot more to say, Pastor." Peter folded his hands on the table. "Wife, I dropped off those materials this morning and told Pastor Doug he'd need to find someone else for the labor."

Would it really cost so much to say, "I think you should go ahead with it if you like"? Yes, she decided.

"This isn't about the work," Pastor Doug said. "I can find someone to paint, carpet, and fix a leak eventually. This is about the two of you. Peter, I've enjoyed our conversations and getting to know you over the past few weeks. Rachel, you've been like a mo—" He stopped as Rachel shot him a glare. "—Like a big sister to me the past few years."

What had the two of them talked about? Rachel wondered. Back in the day, she and Peter talked about everything—the stars in the sky when they camped, their dreams for the future, the books they were reading. But she couldn't remember the last time they'd talked about anything much beyond Jill, their budget, the weather, and the house.

"You're both engaging, intelligent people. Until yesterday afternoon, it wouldn't have surprised me to learn you're married to each other. What did surprise me was the intensity of negative emotion. Is there anything you'd like to say to each other in the safety of this room?"

Rachel looked at Peter's face, and he returned her gaze. The eyes were as beautiful and ice blue as they were back in high school. But the face was softer, less angular now, the years and the lines working together to make him even more handsome. Not a spot of gray on that jet-black head. He was past due for a haircut; a bit of a wave played just below his ears. She wondered if, below the navy crewneck cable sweater, his arms and chest still had the muscles she remembered, then felt both embarrassed for thinking about it and ashamed for not knowing.

She wondered what he saw when he looked at her.

"Pastor, Peter and I have been married twenty-five years—"

"Twenty-six next Tuesday," Peter interrupted.

"Twenty-six next Tuesday," Rachel continued, a little surprised he'd remembered and she hadn't. "I apologize for the inappropriate way in which I reacted yesterday."

"That's it?" Peter asked, slapping his right hand on the table, hard.

"Was there something you wanted to say, Peter?" Pastor Doug asked.

"Pastor, the law may say we've been married almost twenty-six years, but it ain't been a real marriage for a long time. I been out of her bed for seven years, and I don't even remember why. We ain't truly been together for a lot more than that, because she got this crazy idea we couldn't be physical because she had those miscarriages and—"

"Crazy idea!" Rachel stood, hands on her hips. "Why are you telling him all this? One baby, then two miscarriages, all in five years. They told me not to get pregnant again—"

"And I got a vasectomy so we wouldn't have to worry about that—"

"Which you didn't tell me about until after it was done!"

"—and you still pushed me away, even after your hysterectomy." Peter stood up as well and folded his arms across his chest.

"Please!" Pastor Doug moved between the Gregorys and put a hand on each of their shoulders.

Rachel bit her lips and watched the old clock tick off the seconds. Five. Then ten. Then thirty. She was embarrassed for them both, but mostly for herself. It seemed like every time she thought she'd gained some control over her emotions, the devil found a way to undo her efforts.

Pastor Doug went to his desk, rummaged through some of the stacks of paper, and pulled a piece out. Then he wrote something on a sticky note and returned to the table.

"I apologize to you both," he said. "Rachel, you're right. I don't know what it's like to be married to someone for twenty-six years. But I don't think it has to be this way. I've written down the name of a Christian marriage counselor who was one of my instructors at seminary."

"I don't know, Pastor," Rachel said, shaking her head. "Good or bad, the two of us have settled into a life. I'm truly sorry for what happened yesterday and for my strong words today, but that doesn't happen with us much. We coexist pretty well."

"I'll take that, Pastor," Peter said, reaching for the sticky.

What's this about? Rachel wondered. "Why?"

"Because maybe there is something here to be saved, wife. I'm not even sure what coexist means. I do know that once there was a lot of love and passion and trust. We both know we can't get back there on our own."

Seconds ticked off the clock again. Finally, Rachel said, "I've got some work to be done yet this evening. Pastor Doug, I'll see you Sunday. Peter, see you at home."

Peter came in just as she was setting the table. They both were quiet until Rachel brought out a slice of homemade apple pie with ice cream for his dessert.

"Jill called me at work," she said after a few minutes. "She wanted to come to supper tonight but I said no because I didn't know what was going to happen with Pastor Doug. In fact, I was surprised to find you there. I asked her to come over tomorrow night but she didn't say yes or no. I think she's maybe ready to talk about what's bothering her."

"Good," he said with a decided nod. "Now, tonight, should we talk about what's bothering you?"

What was bothering her? Rachel felt like her insides were all tied up in knots. Maybe there'd be a time to try to talk about it, but not yet. So, she just shook her head.

"You're forty-four. I'm forty-five." Peter leaned forward. "We got a lot of years ahead of us. If we mean to spend them together—and I ain't heard either of us say otherwise—we need help. I'm going to see about talking with that counselor. I hope you'll join me. But I'm aiming to go either way."

"Suit yourself," Rachel said, getting up to clear the table. Peter went downstairs to his room. It wasn't long before she heard his snoring, catching a nap before work.

It was funny, Rachel thought as she went up to her room to work on her computer. It was the snoring, not the women, that had led to them sleeping in separate rooms.

They hadn't been physically intimate for a long time, but there still had been something good and right about waking up in the same bed. They'd talk about the day to come, what was on their minds about the house or work or Jill. Or, if the time was right, they'd watch the sun rise through the east-facing window, not talking much at all. I was still honest with him then, Rachel thought as she ran the scheduling program one more time, finally finding a way to accommodate everyone's time-off requests. I could tell him about how angry I still was with Maarten and Mavis, or little things like how much Lizzie's antics made me laugh. And he always listened.

Then Jill had left for the University of Virginia, and the house didn't feel the same. After several mostly sleepless nights, Rachel had fussed at Peter about his snoring. He raised an eyebrow, said, "As you wish," in that way that made her blood boil, and took his pillow to Jill's room.

Rachel waited a few minutes, then went downstairs, ready to beg pardon and explain that she missed Jill's light step and giggles. But he'd closed the door.

Early one Saturday morning a few weeks later, Rachel found Jill in the kitchen drinking coffee and reading a magazine. She'd caught a ride over from Charlottesville. "I thought I'd surprise the two of you, but I got the surprise instead," she said. "Dad's sleeping in my bed."

Rachel started to explain, but Jill waved her off. "Really, it's none of my business. I'll take the couch when I'm here."

"No," Peter said as he came up the steps. "When you're home, you can have your room."

After Jill left that evening, Rachel went to the basement. The bedroom door was open, and Peter was sitting in his chair, reading.

"About the sleeping arrangements," she began.

"Don't worry," he said, turning a page and not looking up. "I'll find somewhere else to sleep when she's here. But it won't be the couch."

Rachel walked away without saying another word. And now, seven years later, she wished she'd said something then, or knew what to say now.

She shook herself out of her reverie. That work on the library budget was going to have to wait until morning. Rachel took a shower, turned off the lights, and went to bed. But she couldn't help pummeling the body pillow she'd been using since she started sleeping alone.

12

It'd been a tough night. An assembly line belt had failed near the end of Peter's shift, and nothing would do but that he would stay and repair it and make sure everything was operating properly.

When he'd called to let Rachel know he wouldn't be home before she left for work, she'd been as frosty as the mountain air. "You'll find bagels on the counter" was all she said.

As if working overtime was something he enjoyed, he thought as he got into the truck shortly after 9 a.m. So he wasn't as important as she was. Peter took pride in being the best mechanic in the joint, and management knew it. Knew it so well, in fact, that they had offered more than once to break one of their own rules and give him the day shift all the time instead of rotating him like everyone else. But Peter had said no. There were benefits to being one of the guys, no matter how much their lack of work ethic bothered him sometimes. He liked the night and overnight differential pay too.

But while he was a great mechanic, he wasn't much of a cook, and bagels didn't sound like enough for breakfast. Grits, eggs, sausage, and toast at the Bluemont Diner would be just the thing.

It wasn't until Peter took the turn out of the factory parking lot that he realized the quickest way to the diner would take him past Kara's place.

Well, so be it.

But as he made the final curve before the gingerbread house with red shutters, he saw a curious sight. A bus of some sort, not the old yellow kind Jill had ridden to school, was pulled up in front, lights flashing. A very pregnant woman was standing there with a small boy who tottered a little as he walked. The vehicle's door opened, and she helped the child up the stairs. Then the doors closed, and the woman began waving like crazy. She watched as the bus pulled away, then after it was out of sight put her left hand to her mouth.

No sign of the green sports car.

Peter pulled over to the side of the road in front of the house and got out of the truck.

"It's always hard when they go off to school, isn't it?" he said, walking toward the woman.

She turned around and smiled. She wasn't a pretty woman by his usual standards; dishwater blond hair carelessly pulled into a ponytail, crooked nose, brown eyes a little too close together. But the smile, well, it was like seeing one of those famous paintings.

"Oh, it's especially hard with Joe," she said, wiping her eyes but keeping the smile going. "He just turned ten, and this is the first year I haven't homeschooled him. You'd think I'd be used to it after two months, wouldn't you?"

"It's hard no matter what," Peter said. "I cried like a baby the day we dropped my daughter off at kindergarten. It was twenty years ago, but I remember it like it was yesterday."

The woman nodded. "Is there something I can help you with?"

Peter stopped and considered. He wasn't sure why he'd pulled the truck over.

"I...I mean, my...I wondered...I did some painting last summer for the lady who lived here. I was checking back on whether she needed any more work done."

"Ms. Lane?"

"Yeah, I think that was her name."

"She went back to live in the District again and rented the place to us. We moved in right after Labor Day."

Peter felt a thud in his heart, but not as bad as he would have expected.

"Well, I hope you're having another boy, since I painted that small bedroom blue," he said with what he hoped was a laugh.

"It doesn't matter, really."

"I guess as long as it's healthy, right?" Peter said, hoping to wrap up the odd conversation and head on down to the diner to lick his wounds over some greasy sausage.

The smile left young woman's face for just a moment, then returned. "We'll welcome this child, healthy or not, boy or girl."

"I meant no offense."

She closed her eyes and shook her head. "There's no way you'd know. Joe has special needs."

Peter wasn't sure what was bubbling up inside him. He shuffled his feet. "My wife…they told us not to have more kids…she had two miscarriages after our daughter. They didn't know why."

The woman nodded. "I think God has a special family planned for each of us. That's why I haven't had the test to see if this baby has special needs too. If he or she does, my husband and I will celebrate. If he or she doesn't, we'll celebrate that too. I'm sorry about the pain those miscarriages must have caused you and your wife. But you have her, and you have your daughter."

"And grandkids soon, I hope," Peter said with a crooked smile as he started to move toward the truck. "I'll be on my way. I wish you the best for you and your family."

The woman stuck out her hand. "I'm Chris."

"Gregory," he said, shaking her hand.

Instead of going to the diner and getting a grease fix, Peter headed home. "I dunno," he said to Callie the calico as he covered a couple of plain bagels with low-fat cream cheese. "It's not exactly that I expected to pick back up with Kara today, but I reckon it's better to know that temptation is out of reach."

Callie stretched, yawned, and rubbed against Peter's leg. Peter lifted the cat onto his lap and started petting her. Callie purred, then started licking a dab of cream cheese from Peter's idle hand.

Peter thought about the woman in Kara's house. She had the faith and the grit to make things work out. Rachel was like that too, more than he generally gave her credit for, maybe because he'd got used to her always making things work out. After she got over the initial shock of being pregnant, she threw herself into being the best wife and mother she could be. After they'd found out their family would be small, she'd started taking classes at the community college at times when he could be home with Jill, then later on the internet. She ended up with her library science degrees, even though getting them took a lot longer than she'd planned. While her job wasn't the Library of Congress sort she'd dreamed of in high school, what she did mattered to a lot of folk.

Rachel had grit when it came to him too. She'd stuck through it with him, and not just for Jill's sake, or Rachel would have been gone seven years ago. Maybe he had grit when it came to her too. Maybe that was why, until Kara, things with the other women had been light and easy, not letting them into his heart or soul.

"Whaddya think, Callie? Or you think there's more to why we stay together than it being too hard to change? You think maybe she's got some love left that she don't know about?"

Callie contemplated for a moment, then licked some cream cheese from Peter's nose. The sandpaper tongue tickled, and Peter laughed.

He kissed the top of Callie's head and lowered her back to the floor. He needed to call that counselor and schedule an appointment before his nap.

13

He went to a counselor yesterday," Rachel said as she looked into the gym's full-length mirrors at her form on the rowing machine, arms extended but not locked. In, out, in, out in measured strokes.

"Really? For what?" Lizzie asked, huffing and puffing as she bobbed up and down on the ab cruncher nearby.

"Our marriage."

"Do you think it'll help?"

Rachel reset the tension level on the rower and moved to a neighboring biceps machine.

"Don't know. I'm not going."

Bang! One hundred pounds of weights on the ab cruncher fell back into their resting place as Lizzie bolted up to the start position.

"When did all this happen? When were you going to tell me?"

"Pastor Doug recommended it when we met with him. I said no. Peter said yes."

"I don't understand how only one person can go to marriage counseling." Lizzie stepped away from the ab cruncher, face red and hair half out of her ponytail. "I'm headed for the shower. Are you almost done? Can we go for coffee?"

Rachel pulled up the biceps weights again. "I've still got forty minutes to put in on the elliptical. Call you later, okay?"

"You better," Lizzie said, squeezing Rachel's shoulders from behind.

Rachel took a swig from her water bottle and walked to the elliptical area. She keyed in the random program, set the timer for a thirty-five-minute sequence and a five-minute cooldown. But the dratted machine wasn't working right. After the warm-up, it didn't play back her heart rate or calories burned. Go to another machine? But then she'd lose the time she'd already put in. Better to stay where she was and let the management know about the problem.

Thump, thump, thump. Rachel hit her stride, legs and arms moving in perfect sequence.

Routine. Rachel loved routine, whether it was working out on the machines in the same order or digging in the dirt or cooking. You started out with a plan, and executed. It felt good. Change sometimes brought excitement and passion—she knew that firsthand, but she also knew it brought heartache and pain. Why couldn't Peter see that? Why couldn't he just let things be as they were?

Because maybe there is something here to be saved, wife.

That was what Peter had said at that meeting with Pastor Doug. *Because maybe there is something here to be saved, wife.*

Was there?

For the first time in her life, Rachel cleared the elliptical's program with half her scheduled time remaining and stepped off.

⸙

Supper finished, Rachel started taking the plates to the dishwasher. She wondered if Peter had noticed that she'd put on mascara and lipstick, and was wearing the emerald green ballerina-sleeved top he'd complimented her on the week before.

"Guess I'll watch the game. So, I'll be saying good night," he said.

Rachel rinsed the plates and put them in the dishwasher, then took a deep breath.

"It's unseasonable warm this evening. I wonder about a short walk," she said, almost whispering.

"Beg pardon?"

She swallowed hard and turned to face him.

"I wondered if you'd like to take a walk."

"Say what?" Peter frowned.

"It was just an idea. Enjoy the game." Rachel opened the door underneath the sink and brought out the detergent. She heard him walk down the stairs.

Cleanup done, Rachel went to her bedroom. This was the room that had sold them on the tri-level the year after Jill was born. Before they saw it, the real estate agent had warned them it was a dump. But they had enough in savings to put down twenty percent, and they figured they could fix it up and sell it at a nice profit in a few years when they'd need more room for Jill and the babies who were certain to come. The two of them had stood in this room that took up the whole top floor and looked out the big window. "I fell in love with you in those mountains," Rachel had whispered in Peter's ear, standing on her tiptoes and sliding an arm around his waist. "I want to wake up with both of you every day. This house is perfect for us right now."

But the plans for more babies turned into one miscarriage, then two. Then the doctors advised Rachel to have a hysterectomy when they found the cervical cancer. The little house was big enough for them after all.

Rachel was still looking out the window, remembering that day, when she heard Peter coming up the stairs. She spun around to find him in the doorway, wearing sweats, sneakers, and an apologetic smile.

"About that walk. Where did you have in mind?"

"The old trail?"

"Sounds good. Ready?"

⸻ ❧ ⸻

Back in the day, even with infant Jill on one of their backs, they could do the two-mile loop in less than forty-five minutes, Rachel taking two strides for each of his. But they had almost never taken it that fast. It was more fun to listen to the birds and the leaves and watch for wildlife, bumping bodies playfully.

This time, they walked purposefully with no chitchat, Rachel staying on the right side of the trail, Peter on the left, each carrying a flashlight. They stopped when Rachel's phone buzzed about ten minutes in. She looked at the display—Jill.

"I think we should stop," she said to Peter, showing him the screen. He nodded.

"Jill? I'm with Dad. Can I put you on speaker?"

"Sure. Where are you two, anyway? I can never find you any-more."

Rachel put the phone on speaker and looked up at Peter. She moved closer to him.

"I'm sorry about that, Jilly-Bean," Rachel said. "We're taking a walk on the old trail."

"Really? The two of you are taking a walk together?"

"Nothing so unusual 'bout that," Peter said, smiling at Rachel in that way that still made her toes tingle. "But we're sorry we keep missing you. What's going on?"

"I'm pregnant! I just couldn't wait any longer to tell you."

"Jilly-Bean!" Peter shouted, loud enough for any nearby or not-so-nearby deer or rabbits to hear. "That is fantastic!"

"Oh, sweetie!" Rachel said, feeling the catch in her throat. Almost involuntarily, she held out her hand. Peter took it.

"We couldn't be more excited," Peter said. "Your mother's

73

plumb near speechless, she's so happy." He squeezed her hand tight.

Rachel shut her eyes and tried to slow down her breathing. How strange, to find out near the very spot where she had become pregnant with Jill.

"Jill, your dad is one hundred percent right. We are so thrilled for you and Eric. The two of you will be wonderful parents. What did he say? When are you due? Have you thought about names?" Rachel threw out a rush of questions in hopes that she could regain her bearings while Jill answered. But Peter intervened.

"We are as happy and proud as all get out," he boomed. "We can't wait to be grandparents. Can we stop by and see you on our way home?"

"That'd be great! Please do."

"We'll be there in about thirty minutes," Rachel said. "Love you." She ended the call. When had Peter let go of her hand?

"I knew it. I just knew it," Peter said, rubbing his hands together. "Now there's some joy for our family."

"There is," Rachel said. "I just hope there aren't any problems."

"Wife, that's your parents talking. Always borrowing trouble. Can we just be happy and see what happens?"

"That's not my parents talking. That's experience." As soon as the words were out, Rachel wished she had them back.

"Dwelling on the past ain't going to do any of us any good, you know."

They were the last words either of them said, all the way back to the truck and on the drive to Jill's apartment. There, they were a unit, full of oohing and aahing, Fifth joining them, looking for a petting or twenty. Jill had been to the doctor to confirm the pregnancy and said so far, she felt great, no morning sickness at all. Rachel thought something still seemed a little off—Jill was talking fast even for her and didn't seem to be able to look her mother in the face. Well, an explanation would come eventually. They made plans for a celebratory supper—Jill's favorite, Rachel's lasagna and garlic bread—the following night.

On the way home, Peter's words about her parents kept coming back to Rachel. Had she really become as rigid and negative as they were? Hard to believe. But maybe there was something to what he had said. The way she had reacted to finding Peter at Redeemer was right about what Maarten and Mavis would have done, minus the shouting.

She wanted to be a grandmother the way the Grossmutter had been. Maarten's mother, even with her limited English and Rachel's limited German, had taught Rachel how to put out a garden, how to bake all manner of Christmas cookies, and how to love Jesus. Rachel had often wished the Grossmutter had met Peter, had been there to see his lazy smile, to meet Jill, to hug the grown-up Rachel the way she'd hugged her when she was little and had skinned knees and bee stings. Rachel knew Jill would be a better mother than Mavis ever was, maybe even better than Rachel was. But she also hoped the grandbaby would look to her for some love with and without words, the same way Rachel had looked to the Grossmutter.

"I have to ask you about something," she said to Peter as they entered the kitchen. "What you said when we were with Pastor Doug about there maybe being something worth saving in our marriage. What did you mean?"

"Well," he said after a few seconds, "we started out together with a bit of a storm. We've had more than our fair share of 'em ever since. But neither of us has ever mentioned divorce other than the one time years ago. To me, that says there's still some love and hope somewhere. What do you think?"

What did she think? Rachel wasn't sure. She sat down at the kitchen table, rubbed her eyes, and stared ahead. She didn't trust herself to look at him, not just then. "I guess my thinking has never got past that we pledged that no man would put asunder what God had joined together."

"Do you remember loving me?"

Rachel closed her eyes. What to say? "Yes, I was remembering when you stood in my bedroom doorway this evening." "Yes, whenever I see Jill." "Yes, every time I walk into church and remember our wedding and how scared I was, but how sure I was that you had enough courage for both of us." She decided to be brave.

"Yes," she said. "Every day of my life. That's why it hurts so much."

"Do you still love me?"

"I don't know."

"Do you want to find out?"

"I don't know."

"That's fair," Peter said. "I do love you. I've thought a lot about it the past few weeks. Thought about nothing much else, if you want the facts. But our history shows we can't fix it alone. I think that counselor can help me understand the things I done that got us off track, and what I need to do now. Would you please come with me?"

"Not just yet." Couldn't he see that it had taken them a long time to get to where they were, and that he was changing far too fast for her to believe?

He nodded. "If you change your mind, you'll be welcome to join me anytime." He started down the stairs to his room, then turned around.

"Next week is my last one on graveyard. I'll be going to days for three months after that."

It'd be the Christian thing to do, Rachel thought. And it'd be good for him, and a whole lot of other people. Maybe it'd be good for her too.

"Then I guess you have your work cut out for you next week."

"Say what?"

"That's not a lot of time to fix the sanctuary roof and paint and carpet."

He gave her that grin that had captured the heart of every girl in Gilroy County High School back in the day. It still made her tingle.

14

I t's a right beautiful thing, to name the baby after your brother Daniel if it's a boy," Peter said the next night as he took a third piece of garlic bread. "But what if it's a girl?"

"We're still talking on that one," Jill said. "We both, Eric especially, like Rebecca. But I'm also fond of Monica."

"I wish you'd known your Grandma Gregory. She'd be proud of you, and right pleased that you'd consider naming a baby for her."

"I wish I'd known her, and your daddy too. You never talk much about them."

It was a true fact; he didn't. But Peter wondered about the glare Rachel gave Jill. It almost looked like a warning.

"Well, you know about how Mama and Little Sister passed. I was just four. I remember her singing and laughing all the time, and tickling me," he said. "I don't favor her in looks. She was tiny with blond hair. Her and Daddy used to like to put on the player and dance in the kitchen. Daddy loved her to distraction."

"And then he died in the hunting accident. That must have been hard."

Peter noted another one of those dagger looks pass from Rachel to Jill. He wasn't sure what was going on, but he was grateful Rachel knew this topic was off-limits.

"One of the hardest things ever, and that's about that."

"Jill?" Rachel placed her left hand on her daughter's right hand. "You look a little peaked. Are you feeling all right?"

"I'm sorry. Haven't been sleeping very well, I guess. Still no morning sickness, though. We're not that long past the October 15 deadline for extended tax returns. Not a fun time for accountants like me, and I'm still kind of recovering."

An uncertain silence settled over the table. Someone has to say something, Peter thought. The best he could come up with was: "I heard a rumor there's apple pie for dessert. Or should I say, I smelled a rumor."

Rachel laughed. "Right you are. There's also homemade cinnamon ice cream in the freezer for those who feel like indulging. Would you mind getting it?"

"I'll get it, Mother," Jill said, springing out of her seat. She disappeared down the steps to the basement level.

"I don't care how hard she's been working," Rachel whispered. "I've never seen that child eat less in her life, and right now she needs to be eating for two. Something beyond being pregnant is up, and has been for a while."

"Shh," he said, pointing downstairs.

Rachel was right, Peter thought. This wasn't like Jill at all. The child couldn't keep a secret to save her soul. When she was ten or so, she had come home with a troubled face and showed them the candy bar she'd shoplifted on a dare. He and Rachel had been by her side when she took it back to the grocery store manager and apologized. No, secrets were not part of Jill's DNA.

Rachel stood, but Peter shook his head. "I'll go."

The laundry room where the freezer was kept was dark, but the light was on in Peter's small bedroom to the left. That was where he found Jill, sitting on his bed next to the nightstand, holding something in her hands.

"You found it," she said.

When he joined her, he saw what it was—that happy birthday card she had made him so many years before. Ever since he had come across it, he'd kept it where he could see it, a reminder of his part in getting his marriage into such a mess.

Peter swallowed hard. "You know we kept all the things you made when you were a kid. I suspect you and Eric will do the same."

He watched as she closed her eyes and moved her lips ever so slightly.

"No, I mean you found it in the stack of papers in your closet. In with her magazine articles. Where I put it."

Peter's heart seemed to be stuck in his throat and in the pit of his stomach at the same time. "Say what?"

"I put it there. After I went to her house."

Wherever that heart of his was, it was running like a racehorse.

"Am I going to have to eat pie all by myself?" Rachel called from the kitchen. "What are you two doing down there?"

Peter looked at Jill. She shook her head.

"Go on, wife," Peter shouted. "Don't wait on us."

Then he turned back to Jill, took the card from her hands, and placed it back on his nightstand. For the first time in days, Peter wished he had a cigarette.

"How did you find it?"

"You've had the same hiding places forever. I know all of them, and so does Mother. I showed them to her. Mainly, she thinks they're your business. I don't. I think it's horrible the way you keep this stuff, like trophies or souvenirs or something."

Oh daughter, Peter wanted to say. How wrong you are. They are memories of women who cared for me and showed it, not just physically. But this wasn't the time.

"You went to her house. How did that come to be?"

Jill walked over to the window.

"Remember in August when my car had that funny rattle to it, a couple weeks before I went to see Eric? You said you were taking a day off and would take a look if I came over at lunchtime. I left work a little early and took the scenic way. And that was when I saw you—carrying her into her house."

Peter knew that day. It was already in the eighties when Rachel left for work that morning and when, fifteen minutes later, he left for Dulles to pick up Kara, who was returning from California. The truck's air conditioner was useless that day, but neither the noise of the traffic nor the heat through the open windows had kept Kara from sleeping all the way to the Valley.

He put her bags in the house, and then came back to the truck, opened the passenger door, and tried to wake her. She gave him a sleepy smile and said, "Carry me." And he did it, her five-eight frame somehow fitting as comfortably into his arms as Jill had when she was a baby. He put her on top of her bed, got a glass of water for the nightstand, and was home in time to meet Jill.

The next week, Kara dumped him.

He sighed.

"You love her," Jill said.

Peter wondered how many men in the history of the world had had a conversation like this with a daughter. Very few, he hoped.

"You love her," Jill said again.

"I did. But it's in the past. She ended it soon after that day."

Jill pressed her forehead against the window. "Because I asked her to."

Peter's throat tightened like someone was suffocating him. He stood up and went to the window. He took Jill by the shoulders and spun her around to face him.

"You did what?"

Jill's closed eyes squeezed tighter. "While you were looking at the car, I came inside and found your stash. That old birthday card was in one of the albums in the living room, and I found it and stuck it in with her stuff to remind you of what I always thought deep down was most important to you—Mother and me."

Peter thought about asking Jill about his other hiding places, then decided against it. He'd never need one again anyway.

"I went to see her on the way back to work. I woke her up. I told her who I was and that she scared me, because I'd never seen you look at a woman other than Mother or me with such tenderness. I told her to go away and leave our family alone. And then, when I got back from Vegas, she had mailed me a note. It just said, 'It's done,' and the letter K. It's been on my soul, Dad. You were wrong, really wrong, but so was I. I should have come to you, not her."

Peter released his grip on Jill's shoulders and put his shaking hands on his face, then took a deep breath and removed them.

"I'm not sure what I would have done if you'd come to me instead of her, to be honest. It was maybe better this way. Her and me, well, that was playing with fire. After I found your little card, I put it here on the nightstand to remind me about what I lost and what I want. I thank you, Jilly-Bean."

As Peter reached to hug his daughter, he looked up the stairway. Rachel was standing there, wiping her eyes with one hand and holding the ice cream bucket in the other. She nodded, put a finger to her lips, and turned back toward the kitchen.

Shaking, Rachel cut three pieces of pie—one large, one medium, one sliver—and opened the container of cinnamon ice cream. Playing with fire, indeed. Somehow, the idea of him carrying a woman in his arms hurt her more than anything else she had ever imagined him doing with someone else. It was intimate. It was gentle, not full of lust. It was the Peter she loved but that she hadn't thought any of them had known.

She jabbed the scoop into the ice cream bucket. The one thing she thought she had had that the others hadn't had was gone. He had loved another woman—loved her deeply, it seemed, not just bedded her.

Rachel heard them coming up the steps, pasted on a smile, and turned. "I was beginning to think I'd have to eat all this pie by myself. I do hope the two of you solved the problems of the world or at least Gilroy County, given how long you were down there."

"We did," Peter said as he walked behind her to his chair. "The world is now a safer place for eating the best homemade pie and ice cream there is."

Peter and Jill both had second pieces of pie and chattered away about the baby, plans for Thanksgiving as always with Shoe, and what time Eric would be back on Christmas Eve. Rachel picked away at her sliver of pie. The first heat of anger past, she supposed there was something to be said for Peter owning up to what had happened. Maybe that counselor was doing some good. Now, Rachel began to dread what would happen when Jill left. The two of them would need to talk, she knew. Lord, walk with me. Hold my hand and my tongue where needed.

Jill thanked them for supper, promised to keep them posted on Eric's plans, and left for home.

"I wonder about some decaf in the living room before we turn in," Peter said as Rachel loaded the dishwasher. She nodded. He poured the cups and went into the next room.

As usual, he sat in his recliner, Rachel on the couch.

"That's some young woman we've raised," he began.

"I'm glad you think so. I was a bit surprised you weren't angry with her about breaking up—" Rachel took a deep breath. "—what seems to have been the love of your life."

She closed her eyes, not wanting to see his face and whatever it registered. She heard him exhale slowly, like he had when he and Jill were talking.

"Wife," he said, "that next-door neighbor from back in the day? I never more than kissed her. That was wrong, I know. But it hurt us worse that we never talked it out, that you believed I was in her bed and that me and you left it at that. When the next fight came, I told myself that as long as you thought I was catting around, I might as well do it. I'm sorry."

"But what about this one Jill saw you with in the summer? Did you just kiss her too?" Finally, Rachel opened her eyes.

"No."

"And you loved her. You said so." Rachel did her best to keep an even tone, but it was hard to keep her voice from cracking. She felt her face go from red to white and saw Peter's do the same.

"Yes. I loved her. I don't see her anymore. If it puts your mind more at ease, she's moved away. Is there anything else you want to know about her? Because this is the time to ask."

A zillion questions crossed Rachel's mind: Is she prettier than me? Younger? What was it about her that made her different, that made you love her? Then she decided knowing would be opening Pandora's box even wider.

"What's done is done," she said as casually as she could with her heart in her throat. "No, I don't have any more questions about her. And now, Grandpa, when's your next counseling session? I do believe I'd like to go along."

15

"I must say, Shoe, that saw took its own sweet time getting here," Peter said as he walked into the hardware store office. Shoe was seated at the computer, an aggravated look on his face as he hit the keys hard.

"Didn't it, though?" Shoe said. "Back-ordered and mis-shipped and then back-ordered again. But it's here now, in the box under the stairs."

Peter wound his way out of the dingy office past the paints and varnishes to the stairway that led to Shoe's living quarters.

He cut through the tape on the box with his pocket knife. It was a beauty. Squeaky clean gray tool with a bright red control. Peter was careful as he thumbed the blade. He wondered if that was the one that had come with the saw or if Shoe had substituted it with a better one and retaped the box. Wouldn't be the first time.

Peter closed the box again, hoisted it under his right arm, and returned to the office.

"It looks perfect and worth the wait. I thank you. The wife will be thrilled. She's been waiting on me to redo the bathroom tile."

Shoe cleared a pile of magazines off the battered green couch next to his desk. "Still trying to stay away from temptation?"

"It's not so much about the temptation these days. It's about the rebuilding. It's coming slow. Can't say as I blame her. But it'd be easier if I knew she was committed to it too."

"Have you prayed on it?"

"I been a couple times to this woman counselor Pastor Doug knows. Rachel says she'll start coming along. I'm happy about that, but it's gonna be even harder with her there than it is now."

Shoe nodded. "That's good. But I asked if you'd prayed on it."

"Figured I'd get started back on that later if things get better with the wife."

Shoe sighed and moved to the couch.

"God don't want you to wait till things are tied up in a pretty bow. You know I know about that firsthand, from the accident. It's a true fact the Almighty loves you today, just like yesterday, just like tomorrow."

"You don't know about everything—"

"I don't need to. Our Lord does, and He forgives you."

He watched as Shoe bowed his head and closed his eyes.

"Lord, You heard what Peter said. You know what's in his heart, better'n anyone. He's a good man, Lord. I've knowed him all his life. He's made his mistakes. But he loves that woman, and sometimes, she's a mite difficult to love, just like all of us. You put them together, Lord. Now they need Your help in getting back to where You want 'em. Lord, I call on You to help Peter get back in conversation with You." Shoe raised his head and looked at Peter. "Anything you wanna say, son?"

Shoe's wrinkled baseball mitt of a face looked so relaxed, as if he'd just had one of those facial things Rachel and Lizzie and Jill were always talking about. Come to think of it, Shoe's face almost always looked that way, unless he was working on the computer.

Peter coughed. "Well, yes, there is."

"Then go on and say it."

"God, I do get lonely—not just for Rachel's love, but for Yours. If Shoe is right and You do love me, I'd appreciate You pounding that into my thick head somehow."

"In Jesus' name, we ask all these things," Shoe said after a few seconds. "Amen."

Peter stood up and stretched, passing his palm in front of his face. "Well, that saw ain't gonna walk itself home. Thanks for everything."

Shoe stood up too. "Now I gotta ask you a favor."

"Anything."

"Come to church with me tomorrow."

Peter wished he hadn't said "Anything" quite so quickly.

"Rachel don't want me at Redeemer when she's there. I told you about the hissy she threw at first when she found out I was doing the insulation."

Shoe shook his head. "God don't care about hissies. The Almighty wants us to worship and get along with our neighbors. If you don't want to come with me, ask Rachel about coming with her."

"Maybe another time," Peter said, picking up the saw box.

He was waiting in the kitchen, face shaved, hair combed, dressed in a red polo shirt and blue slacks when Rachel came down from her room the next morning. Black slacks, tan shirt, black blazer. She had the green scarf around her neck, and Peter thought she looked like she could have walked out of one of those fashion TV shows she and Lizzie liked to watch.

He squirmed a little as her eyes narrowed. "What are you up to so early on a Sunday? I told you I was planning to make breakfast after church today, not before."

"I thought I might go with you."

Her eyebrows shot up. Then she closed her eyes and bit her lips. He was close to calling off the whole thing when she gave him a tentative smile.

"I'd like that. Would you drive?"

They didn't say anything in the time it took to get to Redeemer. He got out first and came around to her side to open the door, just like always.

"Thanks," she said.

"I thank you," he said. "Are you ready?"

"Yes. Are you?"

"Ready as I'm gonna be. We been through worse. Remember the day we came here for our wedding and you ended up in tears on account of the way your folks talked to us? I don't think anything like that will happen."

Peter was ready for whispers and buzzing and pointing as they stood in the threshold. But there weren't any. Becky, stationed by the door, held out her right hand and said how-do. Pastor Doug nodded from the front where he was getting things ready and waved as if it was the most natural thing in the world to see them come to services together. Some other acquaintances did the same.

Then Jill, who was ushering, saw them. She pressed her fingers hard against her mouth, then hugged them both without saying a word before going to help a woman with a cane who came in just after them.

Peter started to get into the back row, but Rachel kept walking. He scurried to join her. What in the world? She was going to sit in the third row! Then he realized it must be her usual spot, as Lizzie was already there. Rachel tapped Lizzie's shoulder. Lizzie looked up with a bright smile, then, when she saw Peter, whispered, "Praise be!" and slid over.

There was a lot of talk about Jesus and such, and a lot of praying. It felt good. Peter was surprised just how good. He didn't understand everything Pastor Doug said, but he knew he wanted to, and that was going to require coming regularly.

When services were over, Shoe came over to envelop them both in a big old bear hug. He whispered in Peter's ear, "God and I were with you when you walked out that door years ago. We're both real proud to be with you today, son. Welcome home."

"I'll call you when the food is ready, all right?" Rachel said as they walked into the kitchen from the carport after services.

"All right," Peter said, heading down to his room.

In her room, Rachel changed into a pair of sweatpants and a faded T-shirt. Then she curled up into a ball on her bed, hugging her knees and rocking.

What a morning! "Please let Peter find You again" had been a part of her daily prayers for so many years that it was rote. In fact, she'd prayed it as she was dressing for church. And then, there he had been, asking to come along. A gift from God.

At church, she hadn't heard or seen anyone clucking about them. More gifts. And Jill had had the good sense not to ask questions on the spot, though Rachel knew she'd have plenty the next time they talked.

"I guess everybody's happy when someone comes back to church," Rachel said out loud. "I'm happy too. It felt good, having him next to me, all cleaned up and handsome, him focused on You, and me focused on the both of you. Even if it doesn't last, today was a treasure. Thank You."

Rachel got up. But she stopped when she caught a glimpse of herself in the full-length mirror on the back side of her door. She went to the closet and took out the orange-red V-neck sweater Jill and Eric had given her for her birthday the year before, and her nicest pair of jeans. She opened a drawer, looking for her brown-checkered scarf; she didn't wear it often. When she picked it up, she found she had wrapped it around an empty bottle of White Linen cologne. She held the scarf to her nose. A faint scent was still there.

"Peter? Ready when you are," she called. The table was set with a green cloth and fresh place mats and napkins in rings, a squat candle burning in the middle. Fried eggs, biscuits, and sausage gravy were steaming on their plates.

"My," he said as he took his seat, still dressed in his polo shirt and slacks. "It's been some time since we ate like this."

"It's a special day, and I wanted to have a special meal. And it's not so bad, turkey sausage instead of pork. Would you like to pray?"

"I would," he said, folding his hands together. "Lord, thank You for this food we are about to eat. Thank You for a beautiful day and a great service. Thank You for new beginnings. And Lord, thank You for good-smelling women who cook like angels. Amen."

He noticed!

"I have to ask," she said as they placed the napkins in their laps. "What made you decide to come today?"

Peter put his right elbow on the table and rested his chin in his palm. "A lot of things. Thinking about the past with the counselor. Getting to know Pastor Doug. Talking with Shoe about some things yesterday when I picked up the saw. Told him I was lonely, not just in my head, but in my soul."

Rachel knew that feeling.

"What'd Shoe say?"

"We prayed. He told me God loves me even as bad as I've been. Then he asked me to go to church with him today."

"But you didn't. You came with me. Why?"

"Because I remembered you being shockedlike that day when you saw me with the insulation. I wasn't going to surprise you that way again."

"And if I had said no when you asked?"

He leaned forward, his face about a foot from hers. After a few seconds, he pulled back and picked up his knife and fork.

"I would have stayed home today. But I would have talked with you about it again this week. If you still said no, I would have started looking for a church of my own. I'm thinking I need to get to know God again, maybe even more than I need to get to know you again."

"Getting to know the Lord isn't easy," Rachel said as she poured orange juice. "He's always there, that's for sure, but parts of us get in the way. Pride and wrath for me. I've always put the wrath out there; people can't hurt you if you push them away first. I guess you above everyone else know that."

"I also know that under that prickly chestnut burr you've got a sweet center."

Rachel choked. "Funny you'd compare me to a chestnut tree. Remember when we planted the one out front before we knew it'd be sterile, just like me?"

Peter shook his head and took one of her hands. "I meant no harm. We have a beautiful daughter. What happened later, well, you licked the big C and you're here today."

Rachel withdrew her hand and patted his. "Yes, I am here today. And this food isn't going to get any prettier. Let's eat."

She spent most of the afternoon raking the lawn and pulling up the remaining plants in the vegetable garden. They were past production, and the first hard frost wouldn't be far off. About three thirty, Peter came outside. Someone on the night shift had called in sick, and the boss had called him to cover. Rachel walked with him to the truck and waved him off, watching until she could no longer see him driving down Marshall Road.

In the evening, she fixed herself a light salad and brought out her Bible, reading Luke 15:22 again and again: "But the father said to his slaves, 'Quickly, bring out a robe—the best one—and put it on him; put a ring on his finger and sandals on his feet.'"

The prodigal. The father. The brother. Who would she be?

Just before she went to bed, Rachel took a small envelope out of the bottom drawer in her jewelry box. She took it to the kitchen table and placed it on a piece of paper and wrote, "Thought you might want this. There's ham for a sandwich in the fridge if you need a snack. See you at breakfast. Welcome home."

16

She wasn't in the kitchen when he got home the next morning, which was odd. No food on the table either.

"Wife, I'm home," he shouted up the stairs. "Long night. You up?"

Rachel came out of her room and stood at the top of the steps with a big smile. Had she done something different with her hair? "Good morning. I'll be down in just a second. Are you just coming home?"

"Yes, barely," he muttered. "I'm going to change. Be there in a bit."

He sat on the bed and eased off his work boots, then started rubbing his aching arches. It had been a long night, a lot longer than even the sixteen hours on the clock showed.

The belt he'd repaired a while back with spit and baling wire was still holding, but now something was off with the timing mechanism. They'd had to shut down the whole line an hour before he was supposed to leave. It took him five hours to come up with a temporary fix. He'd waited three more hours for the manufacturer's expert to arrive so he could fill him in on the situation. Most of the other guys were less than worthless, if you wanted to be honest about it. They had a real knack for sneaking off for a smoke and Lord knows what else when he needed them most. Not that he'd tell the boss. Peter was no snitch. But he sure wished the boss would notice. There'd been rumors they were going to bring in some inmates from the minimum-security prison over at Coffeewood on a work release program, and Peter didn't think they could be any worse than the current crew.

He unbuttoned his stiff-with-dried-sweat chambray shirt and tossed it toward the hamper—and missed. It figured. He'd pick it up later. Right now, he was too cranky and sore from crawling around under the line to deal with much of anything. All he wanted to do was eat and fall into bed. He didn't have enough energy for a shower, although he knew he needed one. He could barely stand his own body odor, and that didn't happen often.

Peter stood up and undid his jeans. Dirty and greasy. No second wear on this pair. He threw them toward the hamper, missing again, and took sweats out of the dresser. When he turned around, he saw a big dark grease spot where he'd been sitting on the bedspread. He halfway wished he was still a swearing man.

Well, the spread would have to be washed too. Peter rolled it into a ball and put it on the floor. Then he pulled on his sweatpants and sweatshirt and joined Rachel at the table.

"Hello!" she chirped. "Is something wrong? You were down there forever."

"Nothing that ten or so hours of sleep wouldn't cure. It was a real mess. First, the—"

"You didn't even see it," Rachel said in an injured tone.

"See what?"

She sniffed. "You talk about how maybe there's something to be saved in this marriage, so I take your ring out of mothballs and leave it for you, and you didn't even notice."

"I don't have the slightest idea what you're talking about, wife."

Rachel reached over to a piece of paper that was standing against the napkin holder and handed it and an envelope to him.

He opened the envelope, and there it was, the wedding ring he hadn't seen for a year.

"Where did you find it?"

"I had it all along in my jewelry box," she said with a laugh. "I thought it'd teach you to take better care of things instead of leaving it in your pants pockets and me fishing it out when I did the wash. I guess it tells us both something that you didn't miss it."

Peter could feel his face going red. He was so dog-tired it wasn't even funny. He'd tried to tell her that, but she wouldn't listen. And what gave her the right to hide something that was his? Whatever. He picked up the ring.

He couldn't get it past the second knuckle.

Rachel laughed again.

"Put on a little weight, have we? Mine still fits as perfectly as the day we bought them."

That did it.

"Yes, wife, everything about you fits perfectly. That's because you never change. Not one bit. You're still nursing the same hurts and grudges you've held for years against me, your folks, and your-self. And now, I'm going to get some breakfast somewhere that they won't care that my wedding ring don't fit." He put the ring in his pocket and grabbed the truck keys.

It took Peter twenty minutes to get to the Bluemont Diner, and by the time he got a booth and started to read the menu, he had calmed down some. He pulled out the ring again and tried to put it on. It was no good. So maybe he had put on a pound or two since he wore it last. So what?

"Long time no see."

Peter slowly looked up. An Amazon with short blond hair stood before him. Her pin said her name was Suzanne. Beyond being his waitress, he had no idea who she was.

"You don't remember me, do you?"

He gulped. "Um, well, of course I do, Suzanne."

"It's Su-ZAHN," she said, an irritated tone in her voice. "But you always called me baby."

That was no help.

"Well, Su-ZAHN," he said after a minute or two, "you're looking great. Ain't changed a bit."

She stared at him intently enough that he started to squirm. "My hair was brown and it was in a long shag. I weighed about twenty pounds more then, which seems to have ended up on you."

What was it with women and his weight this morning? Peter searched his memory for some form of Su-ZAHN and came up blank.

"You're right," he said finally. "I don't remember. I'm sure that you're a wonderful woman and that I treated you like pond scum at the end. I apologize. Now, can you tell me what a man has to do to get some eggs and coffee?"

"If that man is you, he has to go to another restaurant," she said, and turned away.

Peter sighed and stood up to leave for home, but not before he moved the ring to his wallet.

A rap on the bedroom door made him start. What time was it? He wasn't sure, what with the room-darkening shades. "Yes?" he called out.

"It's after eight. Just thought you might want something to eat."

Peter snapped on the reading lamp by the bed and looked at the clock. She was right. He'd slept through the whole day! Then he heard his stomach growl.

"Be there in a minute." He hit the bathroom and smoothed down his hair a little, peering into the mirror. Had he got fat? Well, nothing he could do about it right then.

"I thank you for the knock," Peter said as he walked up the

steps to the table. Rachel was standing by the microwave, her back toward him. "Last night was real hard for me. I kind of took it out on you. Sorry about that."

"I'm sorry too." She nodded and brought out something that smelled delicious. "It's eggplant lasagna. No-fat ricotta and no-salt tomato sauce. I froze a bunch to take to work for lunches. I know it's not your usual thing, but it's quick and it's healthy."

"I'm sure it'll be wonderful," he said. Then Peter bowed his head and prayed silently. *Lord, I apologize to You and to Su-ZAHN and mostly to Rachel for today. Thank You for the chance to do it better tomorrow. Amen.*

"You saw the appointment with the counselor on the calendar, right?" he said as he opened his napkin.

"Yes," Rachel said. "Five o'clock tomorrow. I'll be there. Will we have to talk about today?"

"Not if we don't want to. I think we both know we spoke too fast and too hard. But I think that's better than the freeze-out, don't you? Maybe we're making progress."

"Maybe," she said, going toward the stairs to her room. "I've got some reading to do. See you at breakfast."

He took a forkful of the lasagna, and was surprised to find it tasted great.

17

Rachel hated being late to anything, but it couldn't be helped. The library board had called an emergency meeting at two to discuss the budget. She scooted out as quickly as she could, but it still was a few minutes after five by the time she reached the counselor's office.

It was in one of those fake Georgian office buildings, two-story, tan fake brick, multipaned windows for each of the eight tenants. The wooden directory listed an accountant, a travel agent, an attorney, an insurance agent, a real estate agent, a financial planner, a "ceramics research" outfit that everyone in town knew was a front for the CIA, and Marsha Miller, Licensed Marriage and Family Therapist.

When Rachel opened the first-floor office's entrance, she heard laughter—Peter's and a woman's. It stopped when she closed the door. An older woman entered the hallway. "Rachel," she said with a smile and extended her hand. "I'm Marsha Miller. I'm happy to meet you. And I think it's safe to say Peter is delighted you've chosen to join us."

Rachel nodded and shook the woman's hand. She was slender and tall—very tall, maybe five foot ten. Frizzy sandy hair that she wore down to her shoulders, way too long for a woman in her sixties. And those big hippie eyeglasses could have used an update too.

She followed Marsha Miller into what looked like a study. Shelves and shelves of books. A tidy light honey wooden desk. A small table with four chairs, made from the same type of wood, nearby. An overstuffed navy and yellow-striped recliner opposite a couch covered with the same fabric as the chair. Peter was seated smack in the middle of the couch, and rose as they entered.

"I thank you for coming," he said with a nod of the head, then settled into the far end of the couch. "I was just telling Marsha about the latest doings at work. They announced today that they're going to be bringing some of those inmates to help on the line. As hard as we need them to work, I said they may wish they were staying in their cells instead."

Rachel didn't quite see how that had merited the guffaws she'd heard, but she smiled to be polite, then sat at the other end of the couch.

Rachel looked at the therapist. The therapist and Peter looked at Rachel.

"Shall we pray?" Marsha asked.

Rachel looked at Peter, then nodded.

"Heavenly Lord, we thank You for Rachel's presence today and for the many gifts You share with each of us every day. Lord, You brought Rachel and Peter together many years ago for a purpose. We ask that You help each of us to listen, to share, and to love so that with Your help they may rediscover that purpose. In Christ's name, we pray. Amen."

Rachel wondered what came next. The therapist and Peter both remained in prayer, heads bowed, hands folded.

After two or three minutes, Rachel couldn't wait any longer: "How does this work, Ms. Miller?"

"Please, call me Marsha. It works the way you and Peter want it to work. Typically, Peter shares some thoughts about where he believes his relationship with you is, and where your marriage is with God."

Rachel snorted. "I'm sure he's given you an earful about me."

The therapist looked at them both.

"I ain't said much about anything you have or haven't done," Peter said. "Mainly I talk with Marsha about the stuff that I need to work on."

Marsha, Marsha, Marsha. Wonder how cozy he's been with her. Then Rachel shook herself, hard. Why did that jump into her brain so quickly? This woman was a professional, just like her. She had a code of ethics she was supposed to follow and, after all, she was a Christian marriage counselor.

"Rachel, would it be helpful if I told you a little about myself and my background?"

Rachel nodded, grateful.

"You know I know Pastor Doug. My grandson and he have been friends since before they could walk."

Her grandson? Rachel started doing some math, but Marsha beat her to it.

"I'm sixty-seven. My oldest daughter is fifty-two, and her son is thirty."

So that was why…

"I went to UVA when my daughter did and majored in psychology. I worked in a halfway house for battered spouses for many years. My husband retired from pastoring when we were fifty-five, and then I went back to school and received a master's in marriage and family therapy from Virginia Tech. I've been in private practice here for seven years and teach one of the pastoral care courses at the seminary. Any questions?"

A mother at fifteen. A pastor's wife for probably decades. She'd had a hard row to hoe. Yet she talked about it without any shame.

Rachel shook her head.

"All right, Rachel. Now, Peter has shared with me his reasons for entering counseling. I'd like to hear yours. We can ask him to leave the room if you like."

Rachel breathed deeply. Why was she here?

"He can stay," she said, looking at Marsha. "For me, mainly, because we found out we're going to be grandparents and I think we both want to set a good example. We're rightly proud of the job we did as parents, regardless of the distance between us much of that time. And, I guess because I'm not sure what I think I know about him is all correct. I heard a story recently about a kindness he'd done for someone a few years ago. I felt bad that I didn't know anything about it."

Marsha nodded. "And what would you hope to get out of our sessions? What would success look like to you?"

Rachel closed her eyes and thought for several minutes. Then she opened them, and looked at Peter.

"What did you say success would look like?"

He returned her gaze. "Love. Trust. Devotion. Honesty."

"And a place back in my bed?"

"A place in your heart and soul first. After that, yes, a place back in your bed. When you're ready and not a second before."

"Let's circle back," Marsha said. "Rachel, what would success look like to you?"

"To be honest, I don't know. It kind of shamed me, the way I reacted when I found out Peter was helping at church. It wasn't very Christian of me. I prayed for years that he'd find a relationship with the Lord. I don't know what to do now that that prayer's been answered."

Peter rose and walked to the window.

"Why do you think you need to do anything?" Marsha asked.

"Because if God's forgiven him, then I need to figure out a way to do that too. And that's hard."

"Why is that hard?"

Good question, Rachel thought. Everything she'd ever learned in Sunday school or Bible study or prayer group said she should be killing the fatted calf and welcoming Peter as her husband and brother in Christ. She kept spending time with Luke 15 and sometimes she felt grateful, other times not.

"I've gotten used to the way we are, more like roommates. It took me a long time to get there because, believe it or not—" Rachel shifted on the couch. "—I loved him more than life itself at the beginning, when Jill was being born and we had hope for the other babies. Later, we were at least friends, but that changed when Jill went off to college. It wasn't all him. It was me too, but it was bad. It took a long time to reach a place where my heart and soul were scarred over."

Peter turned around. Rachel couldn't quite read the look on his face. Then his blue eyes flashed.

"You're scared to love me," he said.

She nodded. Please God, let him come back and sit on the couch and hold my hands and tell me it's okay that I'm scared, that he'll take care of me.

Instead, he folded his arms across his chest. "I'm scared too. It hurt to get pushed away over and over. You know better'n anyone else on this planet that there's a lot of good to me."

Marsha coughed.

"I'm hearing a lot of pain in this room," she said. "I'm hearing that you loved each other very much in the early days of your marriage, but that you've both established patterns to shield yourselves."

Peter came back to the couch and sat as close to the end as he could.

"I'd say that's a pretty good assessment," Rachel said.

Peter nodded.

"I'd like you both to think about something. I don't suggest this often, and almost never this early in a counseling situation. But I wonder how you'd both feel about a controlled separation."

Peter raised his eyebrow in that way that always gave Rachel shivers. "Controlled separation? We're here to figure out how to fix our marriage, not end it."

Rachel nodded. "If I were going to leave him, I would have done it a long time ago."

"A controlled separation is more of a time-out rather than an initial step to divorce," Marsha said. "Sometimes, couples find that living apart for a specific amount of time with scheduled contact periods helps them to determine their true feelings for each other."

How could getting away from the situation entirely help? Rachel's thoughts were interrupted by the clicking of Peter's boots on the wooden floor.

"I'd just ask that you think about this," Marsha said. "It might give each of you some space away from the busy day-to-day to think about why you fell in love, why you've stayed married, and what might be used to build a stronger marriage going forward. And now, before we end, let's pray."

Rachel bowed her head, but didn't hear Marsha's words. She was trying to think back to the last time that she'd gone a single day without seeing Peter. Not since the day she'd told him she was pregnant. More than half her life. She couldn't imagine it.

"What did you think?" Peter asked as they walked to their vehicles.

"It's different than I expected," Rachel said. "I thought there'd be a lot more finger pointing."

Peter nodded. "But maybe this is good. Maybe we've had enough of the other."

"Maybe. But I'm not keen on this separation thing. I think it'd send the wrong message to folk, especially Jill and Eric."

"The wrong message? How?"

"You moving out and all, it would say to the world that it was over between us."

"Why do you—" Peter stopped. "As you wish. See you at home." He got into the truck.

Why do I what? Rachel wondered. Why do I care what the

world thinks? Why do I think he'd be the one to move out? She hit the button to unlock the hybrid and got inside.

18

Rachel heard the door open and cold air whoosh in just as she put the last cookie sheet of pfeffernusse in the oven. Baking the Grossmutter's recipe for the little spice cookies on Christmas Eve was a family tradition.

"We're heee-re!"

She smiled; then, after turning around, had to laugh. Jill and Eric, cheeks red, were hand in hand, both with Santa caps on their heads and beards on their faces.

"Have you been naughty or nice?" Eric said, wagging a finger at her.

"Now, what do you think? Come here, both of you!" The three of them hugged, arms and shoulders and cheeks tangling, caps and beards falling to the floor. Rachel was the first to break away.

"Let me look at you! Don't they feed you in the Marines?" Her six-foot-six son-in-law was even more of a string bean than when she'd seen him last. As always, his blond hair was buzzed short, his posture ramrod stiff, and his freckled face split in a wide smile.

"Nothing like your cooking. That's why I keep Jill around,

Mom. She's my connection to the best cooking in the Commonwealth of Virginia. Speaking of, okay to have a cookie?"

Rachel pointed to the cooling rack on the counter. "I can't say no to the father of my grandchild. Be careful, though. I just dusted that batch, and they'll be a little messy."

Eric grabbed a couple of the warm bite-sized cookies, giving one to Jill and inhaling the other. "Mom, doesn't she look great? Even more beautiful, if that's possible."

Jill smiled and gave Eric a hug. "Mother, you're not going to believe this. The whole time we were waiting for his luggage, he was telling people that we're expecting. One lady tried to give us twenty dollars!"

Rachel laughed. Without Eric's news broadcasts, you'd never know five-foot-eight Jill was three months pregnant. She barely had what those girls in Hollywood called a "baby bump."

It had been an easy pregnancy so far. Jill hadn't even had morning sickness. So different from Rachel's own; all three times, she'd been sick as sick could be starting in the first month. With Jill, by three months, she was having trouble zipping her jeans. A month later, at her wedding, she'd looked like a stork herself—legs and chest still skinny, belly sticking out to there.

"Mother?"

Rachel gave a little shake. "I'm sorry, Eric. What did you say?"

"I'm going to take my bride home and get unpacked and take a nap. When do you want us back?"

"How about six? That way we'll have time to eat and talk before services at eight."

"Per-fect!" Jill sang out. "That gives us four hours. Want us to bring anything for supper?"

"Thanks, but I think we're good. I'll put the prime rib in around four, and start the twice-baked potatoes around five. I've got everything I need for them, and your dad's picking up brussels sprouts and rolls."

"Great! Let us know if you think of anything. Love you, Mother!" Another group hug, and they were out the door.

The timer went off for the last batch of pfeffernusse. Rachel took them out of the oven, moved them to the cooling rack, then sifted powdered sugar over the tops.

One of the Christmas cards taped to the carport door fluttered down, and Rachel went to reattach it. Having the cards up was a cheery reminder of just how many people she and Peter, a couple of only children, had in their lives. Eric's folks, retired military, always sent a big, showy card from Florida, asking the Gregorys if they wouldn't please come down for a visit this winter. They wouldn't, of course. Peter had never been on a plane in his life and swore he never would, and Rachel couldn't spare the time from work for them to drive down and back. But she liked that the Stantons always asked. The standard hardware store card plus a personal one from Shoe. An old-timey card with real lace and velvet from Lizzie. A beautiful shot of the University of Virgini from Lizzie's son, Jack, who was finishing his degree in some science field. More from the library staff, county board members, Peter's coworkers, neighbors, and friends at church. Rachel opened the front of the smallest, most unassuming one, the kind that you got a dozen of in the mail from organizations that wanted donations.

"To Rachel on the anniversary of our Savior's birth," the spidery handwriting inside read. "From your parents, Maarten and Mavis Grossman."

The ringing of the phone interrupted her reverie.

"Hey, it's me. Sorry to say but they're clean out of sprouts. What's your pleasure?"

It didn't take Rachel but a second. The Grossmutter's green beans and bacon would be a perfect substitute.

"Pick up a couple pounds of green beans, if you would. And some bacon. Don't forget the rolls, okay? I didn't have time to do dough."

"Got it. Kids get in?"

"Yes. They stopped over here on the way to the apartment. Eric's lost some weight. They'll be back around six."

What a change, Rachel thought as she hung up the phone. Six months ago, he wouldn't have bothered to call, just would have come home empty-handed or forgotten to go in the first place. "Maybe you can teach an old dog new tricks," she said to Callie the calico as she walked to her bathroom to shower before preparing the roast. She shook her head as she stepped on yet another loose tile. When was he going to fix that floor?

Shower done, Rachel slipped into the ancient oversized jade green chenille bathrobe she always unpacked with the Christmas decorations and picked up the hair dryer. Then she realized she'd turned the oven off after the last sheet of cookies. It needed to be preheated for the roast. Better to turn it back on before the hair. She hurried down the stairs and into the kitchen just as Peter was coming through the door. He put the grocery bag on the table, then stood and looked her up and down. His leather jacket was the same jet black as his hair, which needed a trim. The ends curled up around his ears.

"Green always was your color," he said thickly, as if something was stuck in his throat.

"This? Are you kidding? It's so old. I should just get rid of it, but it's so comfy and Christmas-y." She couldn't remember the last time he'd seen her this close to naked. "I don't even remember when or where I got it."

Peter took a step toward her. They were still six feet apart, but it felt a whole lot closer to Rachel.

"You got it from me, the Christmas after we got married. You were bigger'n a house, and so embarrassed about covering yourself even when you were just getting out of the shower. I mail-ordered it from a maternity store Doc Jones knew about. It cost fifty dollars, and that was a lot of money for us then. You were so ticked, you said you'd have to wear it forever. I said that'd be all right by me, because you looked like an elf in it."

She shoved her hands deep into the robe's ample pockets.

"You're right. I remember. I probably didn't say thank you then. So I say it now—thank you for this beautiful robe, and the compliment."

Peter took a step forward.

"Rachel—"

His cell phone rang, loudly. It was "Jillian's Song" from that soap opera she and Lizzie had loved so much in the day, the one about the dysfunctional Irish family in New York City, that there'd been no question what their daughter would be named.

"Wonder why she's not calling the landline," Peter said, pulling out his phone.

"Your timing could have been better, daughter," he said with a short laugh. Then his face went white. "Oh God," he said. Silence. "Oh God. Is—" he looked at Rachel and cut himself short.

Oh Lord, please let them be all right. It's Christmas Eve. She ran her fingers through her hair, still wet.

"'Course we know where it is," he said. "We'll be there in twenty minutes." He closed the phone without a "Love you" or "See you soon."

"What is it? What's going on? Are they hurt? Was there an accident? Where—" she couldn't stop talking. If she kept talking, she wouldn't have to listen.

Peter placed his rough hands on either side of her face and kissed the top of her head.

"They're at the hospital."

"What happened?" she screamed, tears coming to her eyes, her heart beating hard.

"They're at the hospital. Just get dressed. I'll tell you on the way over."

19

It was cold out, crazy cold for Christmas Eve in the Shenandoah Valley, maybe twenty-five degrees. Not even 4 p.m., and almost as dark as dusk. Peter cranked up the heat in the truck as high as it would go. It was the least he could do, have the thing warm when Rachel heard the news.

He put his arms over the steering wheel and put his head down. "Please, Lord," he whispered. "It's a hard blow for all of us. Help us—"

He heard the passenger side door open. Rachel jumped into the seat.

"They're dead."

Peter turned his head and held out his right hand. "No, they're not dead."

She shook her head, refusing his hand. "She's losing the—"

He nodded. It would have been cruel to make her finish the sentence.

Rachel curled into the door.

"Nooooo!"

Peter backed the truck out of the carport and sped down the four-lane to the medical center. He remembered the drill all too well from Rachel's miscarriages. There wouldn't be a lot to do once they got there, other than to love Jill and Eric. He coughed.

"Eric said she told him she'd been spotting for several days but didn't want to worry anyone."

"Nooooo!" Rachel shrieked again, staying by the door and waving her left arm at him. "Don't tell me. Don't tell me!"

Hey! He wanted to shout. She's my daughter too! I'm pained for her—and for Eric and for us too. Those angels we lost—they were my angels too! This isn't only about you.

But he kept his mouth shut until they arrived at the emergency room entrance.

"You go on," he said, putting the truck into park. "I'll be there directly."

He watched as Rachel raced toward the automatic double doors, practically running down a young couple who were walking in, the woman cradling her wrist. They were laughing as they went. Peter shook his head.

Wish that just one of our visits hadn't been so hard. Just one. Maybe a sprained ankle or poison ivy or something. But no, the Gregorys only come to the ER when they're losing angels.

The world started to go black, punctuated by fireworks. He put the window down, gasping for air. Lord, I beg you. I need just a little of Your strength. Both of us falling apart ain't gonna do anybody any good.

After a few minutes, he was breathing better and felt good enough to drive into the garage and then walk to the ER.

"Jill Stanton?" he asked the receptionist. "I'm her dad, Peter Gregory."

The woman nodded and pointed. "Second set of curtains on your right."

When he parted the curtains, he was surprised to find Jill sitting in a chair instead of in bed. She looked a little peaked and her eyes were closed, but she was dressed, with a cup of what looked like orange juice on a cart next to her. He whispered to the nurse that he was her dad. The nurse nodded and left.

"Jilly-Bean?" he said. "It's Dad. I love you. I'm so sorry." He sat down in the chair next to her and rubbed her hand.

She nodded, keeping her eyes shut. "Love you too, Dad." The words seemed to come a little slow.

"Where are Eric and your mother?"

Her eyes fluttered open. "Doctor Kidder wanted to talk with Eric about how to take care of me. It's all done. I'm going home."

Going home? Rachel had always stayed overnight with her miscarriages. What were these fools thinking? Peter started to get up to find that crazy doctor, but then thought better of it.

"I'll just stay by you, if that's all right?"

"Please, Dad," she said with a weak smile. "Maybe sing me a song?"

All he could think of were Christmas songs, all wrong. "Hark! The Herald Angels Sing." "For Unto Us a Child Is Born." "The Little Drummer Boy." "Lo, How a Rose Ere Blooming." All about the beautiful baby.

Then he heard her, softly, words slurring a little:

Jesus loves me! This I know, for the Bible tells me so.

He choked on the next line, but got it out anyway:

Little ones to Him belong; they are weak, but He is strong.

Together, they sang the refrain:

Yes, Jesus loves me! Yes, Jesus loves me!

Yes, Jesus loves me! The Bible tells me so.

Jill took his hand and smiled slightly. Her eyes closed again.

They sat like that for what seemed like hours, but it must have been only fifteen minutes or so. Peter was in awe of his daughter. It wasn't just the drugs that made her so calm, so unlike when her mother had been in the same situation. *It's confidence,* he thought. *Confidence she's loved by all of us. Confidence she's loved by God. He gave us the angel we needed. It's okay that He took the other ones, including my grandbaby, Home so quick.*

He released her hand when Eric stuck his head through the curtain and motioned Peter outside.

"This is Jill's dad, Peter Gregory," Eric said. "Dad, this is Jill's doctor, Doctor Kidder."

Doctor Kidder, a blond woman about Rachel's size, had a pair of glasses on top of her head. She had the kind of smile lines around her mouth and eyes that Peter had seen on other happy people her age. She shook Peter's hand. "Mr. Gregory, I'm so sorry for your loss. I've just been telling Eric that Jill's ready to go home. She'll need to rest, but she'll sleep better at home than she would here."

"Are you sure, Doc? Because the wife and me, we been through this before, and she always needed to stay after…"

"Mr. Gregory, your wife had the same concerns when we talked a few minutes ago. But Mrs. Gregory's miscarriages were much later in her pregnancies and very close together. They both required additional medical care. I understand she had a hysterectomy after the second one? How hard it must have been on both of you."

Peter nodded. "You don't know how hard. But what about Jill?"

"Jill was barely three months pregnant. She's a healthy twenty-five-year-old. Given the family history, I've been monitoring her carefully all along. Mr. Gregory, sometimes things just happen. I wish I could tell you why Jill lost the baby, but we don't know. I can tell you that 85 percent of women who lose a child at this stage go on to have normal pregnancies and births."

Peter looked at Eric. "You're less than twelve hours off an international flight and jet lagged. Maybe it'd be better to stay here—or all y'all could come stay with us?"

Eric shook his head. "Thanks for the offer. But I can't think of anywhere either of us would rather be than in our own bed and together. I'll call you and Mom if we need any help, but I suspect we'll both just sleep clear through the night."

That was when Peter remembered. "Rachel! Where is she?"

"In the chapel up on the second floor."

"I'd best go find her." Peter turned back to the doctor and nodded. "Doctor Kidder, I thank you for the care you give my little girl. Bye now."

The white, antiseptic hallways were deserted. Seemed everyone else in the county was off getting ready to greet the Baby Jesus or Santa Claus or at least at home with their families, eating or fighting or opening gifts. The Gregorys were out of step as usual.

Peter hated the loud click-click-click noise his boots made. Weren't people supposed to be quiet in hospitals? How could a man do that with those linoleum floors? He was relieved to find the final hallway to the chapel was carpeted. He opened the door and stepped inside.

It was a quiet, calm, dim place with about a dozen maple chairs arranged in two columns, facing a table lit by a couple of candles. Rachel was seated in the front row, the only person in the room.

"I hate you," he heard her say.

How can she blame me for this? Peter thought. The doctor just said we don't know why Jill lost the baby.

"I do everything You want," she continued. "I keep the commandments. I do Your work at church. I tithe. And what do You give me? A diseased body. A man I made the mistake of loving even more than You, only to be betrayed. Now, I envy the trusting relationship he has found with You. A daughter You make suffer the same way You made me suffer. Your book and Your words tell me You love me, that You are a forgiving God. It's all a lie."

Peter breathed in, so deeply that Rachel turned around at the noise. She stared for a moment, then stood up and walked toward him.

"It's time to go," she said.

Peter looked at his watch. Almost 7. Church of the Redeemer's Christmas service would start in an hour or so.

"I'm sorry."

"Sorry about what?"

"About eavesdropping on your prayer. About the things I've done that seem to have hardened your heart to the Lord. About the baby."

She nodded. "Where's Eric?"

"Took Jill home. Doctor said it was all right."

She nodded again.

"I wonder if maybe you'd like to get some drive-through before we go to services. They're always open, even on Christmas Eve."

"I've had enough of God for a while," Rachel snapped. "Just take me home—please."

Peter pulled into the carport, and they silently entered the kitchen. The hope and anticipation and joy and, yes, love, that had been in the air just a few hours earlier had vanished. The room felt as empty as the hospital halls had.

"I think I'll just go to bed," Rachel said. "There are fixings for a sandwich if you've a mind."

"But it's not even seven thirty. What about all that food you had started? Are you sure you want to go to bed?"

"I'm tired and sad and worn out, and I'm a little surprised you aren't."

Could she really believe that?

"I'm tired and sad and worn out too. We lost our first grandchild today. But I believe the Lord will help us through this valley, and I'm fixin' to show Him that by going to the service. Won't you please come with me?"

Rachel shook her head. "Good night."

He watched as she went up the steps and shut the door to her bedroom. He waited until the light went out. Then he went to her door and knocked.

"Wife, I'm going to go over there now. And I'll"—he hesitated—"I'll pray that the Lord will provide some healing for you."

He heard light footsteps. Peter wondered if she was going to ask him to wait while she got dressed. Then he heard her lock the door.

20

Church of the Redeemer's parking lot was packed. A good thing, Peter thought. He liked that so many people wanted to be to-gether to celebrate Jesus's birth. He wondered what Rachel would have said. Probably, she would have griped about how some people thought coming to see Him twice a year was enough.

Peter shook his head as he circled the lot for a fourth time. Or maybe she'd feel blessed for seeing all the vehicles too. He was working on forgetting about years of reacting to what he knew she'd say before she said it. He understood she had to lash out at someone tonight. Still, Peter was a little surprised it was God rather than him.

He drove around the corner to the rectory and parked the truck behind Pastor Doug's sensible black sedan. The pastor wouldn't be driving anywhere tonight anyway. "Better hustle," Peter said out loud to no one. He entered the chilly night, stuffed his hands in his jacket pockets, and walked to the church entrance.

He stood in the vestibule, stamping his feet. The sanctuary was as pretty as he'd ever seen it. Pink, white, and red poinsettias abounded. The choir members were wearing red and green and were singing "O Come, All Ye Faithful" with all the joy and talent anyone could ask for.

Peter glanced up at the roof right above the tree. He was pleased with his work. You couldn't tell it'd been patched at all.

"Merry Christmas, Peter," Shoe whispered, handing him a bulletin. "It's crowded, but I'll find you a seat. Are the others on the way?"

"It's just me. Tell you why later."

Shoe nodded and led Peter to a row of benches that had a tiny space at the end. "Sit friendly, please," he said to the folk already seated there. Everyone moved down a couple of inches and made room for Peter.

The readers were all good, Peter supposed. Pastor Doug, who appeared uncharacteristically comfortable in a black suit that looked like it was fresh off the rack, read from Luke 2 about Jesus's birth and how all the angels sang. And the choir and the congregation did a nice job of singing all the songs. But Peter spent most of the service in prayer.

You've put me in a mighty odd position, Lord, he prayed. Who'd have ever thought I'd be in Your house on Christmas Eve, and it'd be Rachel and Jill and Eric who'd be at home? There's got to be a purpose here, but I ain't smart enough to figure it out on my own.

The children's choir moved to the front to sing "Away in a Manger." Ranging in age from about four to ten, they were dressed in white robes and wore serious faces, intense and maybe a little nervous about being in front of so many people. Except one of the youngest. She wore the world's biggest grin and waved to folk Peter supposed were her parents and grandparents. She was half a measure behind through the whole song, her clear, high voice going off in its own direction. There were smiles all around the church, especially from Peter. Make the hair black instead of blond, and it was Jill, the last time he'd been to a Christmas service.

My little girl, Lord…hold her close to You, please. She's got a faith in You that could move mountains, and she's gonna need it, especially once Eric goes. And about Rachel, Lord, we've had so many conversations about her, I'm not sure what else to ask, except I hope You didn't take her too serious today.

The song ended, and the special collection for the local homeless shelter began. Peter pulled out his billfold, placed a twenty-dollar bill in the basket, and started to pass it. Then he reconsidered, and pulled out another twenty. Pastor Doug had said something recently about giving till it pinched, and he was right. Peter had so much, really. A rekindled relationship with the Lord and His people. A wife he loved to distraction, whether she believed it or not. The world's best daughter and son-in-law. The heart and blood pressure rate of a man twenty years younger. A house that was paid in full, with money in the bank. A job that paid all right for a blue-collar guy with a high school diploma. Friends like Shoe and Pastor Doug.

He looked around at the faces. Lizzie, two rows over, sitting with her son, Jack, who was up from Charlottesville. Becky the receptionist on the outside of the front row. That Connor Newman fellow who kept asking Peter to serve on more and more committees. A lot of faces he recognized but didn't know, and many he'd never seen before.

The lights dimmed further, almost out, and the strains of "Silent Night" began. There was a rustle in the congregation, and people started taking small white candles out of their pockets and purses. Peter remembered seeing the candles in wicker baskets when he came in, but he hadn't gotten one. No matter. He could sing without it.

Then he felt a nudge at his back and turned around. It was that young woman who was living in Kara's house now, infant in a sling across her chest, her little boy on one side and a guy who was probably her husband on the other. She was holding a lighted candle in one hand and an unlit one in the other. "For you, Gregory," she whispered. "Our Savior is born. Merry Christmas."

How could he have thought she was less than beautiful when

they met? Her face shone with love the way Mary's must have on that night in Bethlehem. For a second, he wondered if the baby had special needs like her son. And then it hit him:

Lord, everyone has special needs, and You take care of them all when we bring them to you.

He nodded and accepted the candle and lit it from the woman's. Then he turned and lit the candle of the person next to him.

His plan was to leave church silently. The miscarriage was Eric and Jill's news, and Peter figured it was best to let Rachel explain her absence as she liked.

But Shoe grabbed him as soon as the sending forth and music were done. "Is everyone all right?"

Right then, Lizzie and her son came up. Then Pastor Doug. Then Connor. Then Becky. So he had to tell. It seemed like half the church was there, shaking their heads and sighing.

"Jill and Eric are at the apartment resting. And Rachel, this hit her pretty hard. She was too wore out to come tonight," he finished.

"We should pray," Pastor Doug said, extending his hands to the people to his right and left. The circle grew and grew.

"Heavenly Father, we thank You for the gift of Your Son, whose birth we joyously welcome tonight. We know You welcome the return of Jill and Eric's baby to You on this holy night. We lift up Jill and Eric and Rachel and Peter's sorrow, and ask that You bless them with the knowledge that You will show them the way through this valley. In Jesus's name we pray. Amen."

When Peter got home a half hour later, he could tell by the headlights that there was a note tacked to the door from the carport into the kitchen. He took his small flashlight out of the truck's glove compartment to read it: "There's a chicken salad sandwich for you in the fridge. I put away everything we were going to have for supper. Please don't wake me." He took off his boots and carried them inside.

The sandwich was delicious. Peter hadn't realized just how hungry he was. He put the plate in the dishwasher as quietly as he could, and started for the stairs to his bedroom. Then he reconsidered and climbed the steps to Rachel's room.

The door was open, so he walked in as much as he dared. She was lying so that she was facing the door, backlit by the full moon. She had put the green robe back on; her arms were wrapped around a body pillow. He could see the dried tear tracks on her face.

"Aw, Rusty," he whispered. "Sleep in heavenly peace, my love."

21

Are you one hundred percent, absolutely sure, this isn't too soon for Jill?" Lizzie said as she walked into the Gregory kitchen after rapping once on the door, for years the women's signal when they arrived at each other's homes. "You and I could have just gotten together at my place. It's been less than a week."

"I asked, believe me," Rachel said. "More than once. As a matter of fact, I thought it might be too soon for me. But she wanted to do it. Said she thought it'd be good for both her and me to laugh, and who better to do it with than you?"

Lizzie nodded, and put down her overnight bag. "I guess there's something to be said for tradition when it comes to healing. Have Peter and Eric already left?"

"They have. It's four-plus hours, you know."

"Jack's awful sorry he had to get back to Charlottesville. You know how much he's always enjoyed the he-man hunt."

Rachel wondered about that. She suspected Jack had found last year's hunt, the first after his father's death, to be too emotional, and she couldn't blame him. Then again, maybe Jack figured it'd be good for Eric and Peter to have some time alone.

The he-man hunt had been going on almost as long as the slumber party tradition, which dated back to the December 30 when she and Lizzie were high school freshmen. That first time, it was just the two of them, camped out in sleeping bags in Lizzie's parents' family room, playing popular music, eating popcorn, and doing all sorts of other activities Rachel could never do at home.

The sleepover moved to the Gregorys' when Rachel and Peter married. The following year, Peter announced he wasn't going through what he dubbed "she-woman sharing" again. Instead, he said, he was going to hunt in West Virginia—and to face down some demons. The comment had given Rachel pause, since he was headed for the same area where his dad had died, and the accident was the one topic Peter refused to talk about with her. Busy with Jill, who was just starting to walk, she had let it go.

He came back peaceful and quiet, and so a new tradition was born. A couple years later, Lizzie married John, who went hunting with Peter. Jack joined the women until he was old enough to go with the men. And everyone knew when Jill was serious about Eric: when she was a college sophomore, he became the first boyfriend she'd ever asked to have invited to the he-man hunt.

As Rachel was filling the huge popcorn bowl to the brim, Jill arrived and joined Lizzie in the living room. When Rachel came in, the other two were busy laying out photo albums and board games and trays for supper, which always consisted of lasagna, using Lizzie and Rachel's calorie-laden recipe from junior high home economics; from-scratch Italian bread; and eggnog. Lizzie was the only one who ever drank more than half a glass of the stuff, but it was part of the tradition.

An hour later, Jill and Lizzie declared they were so stuffed they couldn't have another bite of lasagna or slice of bread if they tried (and then both proceeded to do just that). Rachel shook her head, but said nothing. It was their business if they didn't want their clothes to fit come the new year.

Next up: manicures and pedicures. Jill trimmed and buffed her mother's nails, and sighed. "Mother, I wish I had your nailbeds.

They're nice and long, and your hands are so small. Are you sure you don't want some polish?"

Lizzie chortled. "You know she's never worn polish on her fingernails. First, her folks wouldn't let her. She cheated and wore it on her toes, though, just like she does now. Then when you and Jack were kids, we neither of us had the time or money to keep up our nails, ourselves or getting them done."

Rachel nodded.

"But Mother, it's not like you're strapped anymore," Jill said in a gentle voice. "Getting a manicure when you and Lizzie have your pedicures could be a little treat to yourself."

"It just seems like a waste," Rachel said. "With the amount of time I spend on the computer, I doubt a manicure would last a week. A pedicure lasts a good month."

"Suit yourself," Jill said with a grin. Then she unzipped her backpack and pulled out a photo. "Here," she said, passing the photo to Rachel. "This is my absolute favorite picture of us from when I was little. I found it when I was looking for some of the baby pictures of me back at Thanksgiving. Do you remember it?"

Rachel stared at the photo, stroking it with her fingers. It was of a picnic along the old trail during the dog days of summer. Toddler Jill was standing in what she thought was a ballerina pose. Lizzie, loose blond hair blowing across her face, was sitting cross-legged, cradling baby Jack and smiling at John, who was behind the camera.

But John had snapped the picture earlier than Rachel and Peter expected. Instead of being seated next to each other and smiling for the camera, they were on their knees, bodies facing and touching. His left hand was on her back, playing with her braid. His lips were on her forehead. And not even the print's age had faded the smile of joy and love on Rachel's face in profile.

"I had forgotten all about this," Rachel said. "I was pregnant that day. I didn't know it when John made the picture. Didn't find out for another month. Lost him three months after that."

Jill moved closer to her mother. "It would have been Daniel?"

Rachel nodded. "Then the next year, Michael."

God, what happened? she thought. I was twenty-one when John made that picture, younger than Jill is now. A toddler to take care of. But I look so in love with my husband.

Rachel carefully placed the photo on the end table. "Now, as I recall, I was the Yahtzee grand champion last year. Who's brave enough to take me on?"

For the next five hours, they ate popcorn, giggled a lot, talked even more, cried a little, and made lists of resolutions for the year to come. Mostly, they were the same: Exercise more. Gossip less. Pray more. Jill resolved to text, email, or speak with Eric every single day, and Lizzie pledged to be more open to the men who were beginning to ask her out on dates. Rachel added resolutions to leave work on time more often and to be less critical of people like Connor Newman, "even when they're complete idiots."

Finally, at midnight, they agreed to call it a night. While Lizzie used Rachel's bathroom to wash up and change into her pajamas, Jill and Rachel spread out the three sleeping bags.

"Jill, I wonder if you'd do something for me tomorrow before the men get home," Rachel said.

"Of course! What?"

"I think I'd like to try a manicure. Nothing too fancy or bright, maybe that pinkish-brown color you showed me."

The only answer Jill gave was a hug.

22

"You might want to ease up a little," Peter said. "Speed trap around the curve as we come into Big Pine. They've got me a few times."

Eric grinned. "Thanks, Dad."

Big Pine meant about another half hour to Springs Resort State Park. Peter leaned back on the passenger side and closed his eyes. Eric was the one person he trusted to drive his truck. Rachel didn't like driving anything bigger than the hybrid, and Jill was always busy doing something while she was behind the wheel—talking on the phone, eating, doing her makeup, you name it. She didn't do it when he was in the vehicle with her, but he'd noticed enough times when she was pulling up to their house. Peter didn't much like it and had told her so. So, they'd reached a truce—when they were together, he drove.

Eric was another story entirely. The boy focused on the road ahead, got the big picture, left himself an out, all those things they teach you in school. Peter could rest easy with Eric driving.

He-man hunt would be different this year. But different wasn't always bad. Peter suspected Jack would come back next year, or the next. He'd keep asking. That was all you could do. He missed John himself, had cried like a baby at the funeral. First time he'd done that since—

"Dad? We're here."

Peter yawned and rubbed his eyes. "Good deal. Let's unload."

He opened the passenger door to a gust of mountain air and sucked in his breath. That first blast always knocked him back. Springs was about 1,700 feet higher than Lyman. His daddy had always called it a thin place, and Peter guessed he'd been right about that.

Peter watched as Eric reached behind the seat for the backpack that held his clothes and such and strapped the pack on.

"Gotta leave the cammies and jackets in the flatbed, otherwise the smells will keep the deer away," Peter said with a chuckle. "Guess I forgot to remind you, sorry."

Eric laughed. "Will do. I can lead a battalion on a mission and brief generals, but I've still got a lot to learn from you. Why don't you go ahead and check us in? It'll take a few trips to get all the gear that does go inside with us."

Peter entered the resort lobby. They'd refaced the brick on the big fireplace, but other than that, things looked the same as they had when he came here for the first time back in 1987 with his daddy and Shoe. A large room to the right held a huge wood-burning stove, a bunch of tables and chairs, and two overstuffed green leather sectionals. To the left of the entrance was a small shop with cards and such. A wood-burned sign pointed the way to the dining hall.

Straight ahead, a woman was seated behind the front desk, her nose in a book. She had the look of a crow, dressed in black, black hair, black nail polish, big black glasses on her angular face. It didn't appear she heard him come in, despite that bell thing that went off when he opened the door.

Peter coughed. She still didn't look up.

"Miss, if you don't mind—"

She sighed and kept on reading. "The lodge is full. Tomorrow's the last day of deer hunting season."

"I know. That's why I made a reservation six months ago.

Gregory. Peter Jackson Gregory. Two beds, one night. I used your website."

"Do you have a confirmation number?"

"Sure do." He fumbled around in his jeans pockets, then his jacket.

The bell thing went off again, and Peter turned to see Eric walking in.

"What's up?"

"She can't find our reservation."

"You don't have a reservation," the woman said, turning a page.

Peter knelt to open his pack. The paper he wanted was right on top, folded into quarters. He dropped it onto the woman's book. If she disliked it here so much, why didn't she get her another job?

She opened the paper, gave a snort, and waggled a finger at Peter.

"You don't have a reservation. You had a reservation. For last night."

Peter grabbed the paper. Sure enough, she was right—December 29. How in the world he got that wrong, he didn't know. There wouldn't be a motel room for fifty miles. The best they could do was to hang up the idea of hunting, and pray there'd be a room in Lexington back on the other side of the mountains. Otherwise, it was going to be a very long night back to Lyman and the Stantons' apartment.

"Sorry, Eric," he said, shaking his head. "I messed up. We'd best start back."

But Eric moved toward the desk. "Ma'am? What is it that you're reading there?"

The woman looked at them for the first time. "*Rocket Boys* by Homer Hickam."

Eric nodded. "He's from near here, isn't he?"

"Over to Coalwood. My granddaddy graduated Big Creek High with him."

"Is that so? My granddaddy served with him in Vietnam. Mr. Hickam gave him an autographed copy of *Rocket Boys* when it first came out." Eric stuck out his hand. "I'm Eric Stanton, ma'am, and this here is my father-in-law, Mr. Peter Gregory. We're pleased to make your acquaintance."

A big smile broke across the woman's face, and she pushed the glasses up from the end of her nose. Peter was astonished to see how pretty that smile made her. "I'm Lucy, Lucy McDermott. Whereabouts are you from?"

"Everywhere. I was a military brat. My wife and her folks all live over to Lyman. The girls are having a hen party tonight, and we were hoping to get in some bow hunting before I head to the desert next week. I'm a Marine. Too bad about the misunderstanding about the reservation."

Lucy frowned. "It'd be a long drive to Lyman tonight. Could all y'all wait in the game room a bit?"

The men looked at each other, nodded, and moved into the next room, where they sat down at an old whiskey barrel with a top that now served as a checkerboard. Eric started setting up.

Eric had already beaten Peter twice when Lucy came rushing into the game room, arms full of sheets, blankets, and towels.

"I got something if all y'all ain't overfussy," she said. "How about bunking in here?"

The men looked at each other and nodded. Who would have thunk it? Peter thought.

"No shower, but there be restrooms yonder." She nodded toward the hall. "Thing is, I can't officially shut this room down till eleven. But everyone here is a hunter. I doubt anyone will be up past ten anyways."

"What a generous offer," Eric said, extending his hands to take some of the linens. "Are you sure it's all right?"

"Yep, I cleared it with the manager." She smiled toward Peter. "Other folk have had trouble with our website. He says to extend his apologies, and that all y'all will get a refund for last night. No charge for tonight, of course."

Eric toted in the rest of the gear while Peter divided the linens into two piles, one for each sectional. Then Eric went to the dining room and came back with hot dogs, hamburgers, and chips on paper plates. It wasn't the world's most nutritious supper, but it would do. As they ate, Eric cleaned Peter's clock at a few more rounds of checkers.

Peter was losing a game of cribbage big time when a group of a dozen or so hunters came in from supper in town. They were there with Big Joe, an outfitter from Pennsylvania who said he'd grown up nearby. The group had had a fine day, with three taking big bucks. Peter listened as they talked around the big wood-burning stove; he knew the spot they had hunted, and it was a good one, maybe better than the acreage he and Eric would be using. But then, the whole region was prime deer country. Firearms hunting hadn't been allowed since 1986, and some folk said there were so many bucks as a result that they were more likely to die from old age than from being harvested.

Peter nodded at Eric, and they put away the cribbage board and joined the group. The men swapped fish stories and deer stories and turkey stories and then, before anyone knew it, it was 9 p.m.

"Four's going to come awful early," Big Joe said, standing up and stretching. "I'd suggest we all get some shut-eye. Eric and Peter, good to meet you. See you at breakfast and if we don't, happy hunting."

As the men began leaving the room, Big Joe came over to Peter. "I didn't want to ask in front of the group, but was Willie Gregory your daddy?"

Peter did a double take, then nodded.

"Thought so. You're the spit and image of him. Saw him here many a time, and even hunted with him once or twice. You probably don't remember, but I was on the paramedic team that day. I'm sorry we didn't get here quicker."

"It wasn't your fault," Peter said. "It wasn't anyone's fault. It just happened."

Big Joe shook his head. "Well, I disagree, but as long as you're at peace with it. Happy hunting."

"What was Big Joe talking about?" Eric asked as he and Peter stood at sinks in the men's room.

Peter finished brushing his teeth. "You know my daddy died up here in a hunting accident back in 1987," he said, more casually than he felt. "Big Joe knew him a little, I guess. A lot of folk did. Daddy was quite the hunter, and this here was his favorite place."

"I know there was an accident, and you and Shoe were with him, and that he got shot. And that Shoe hasn't hunted since, and it took you a while to come back. But that's all Jill's told me."

"Not a lot else to tell," Peter said as he gathered his stuff and opened the restroom door. "We'd best be getting to bed ourselves if we want to be sharp in the morning."

"Must've been hard, losing him," Eric said a few minutes later, wrapping a sheet around one of a green sectional's curves. "When my Pops was deployed, I wasn't yet a teenager. I missed him like crazy and worried about whether he'd come back. But helping Mom keep my four brothers in line sure kept my mind occupied."

"I can see how it would. How are your folks doing anyway? This all has to be hard on them too, losing their first grandchild."

"It is. You know I'm going to spend a couple days down in Florida with them before I go back. I'd hoped Jill would join me, but she's just not up for that kind of travel yet. Now, about your daddy. You were what, sixteen?"

"That's right," Peter said, giving up on getting Eric to talk about something else—and on fitting the sheet into the sectional where he'd be sleeping. It would just have to hang loose. "It were just him and me. Mama went Home before I started school."

"That's when you went to live with Shoe, after your dad died."

"That's right."

"Here's the part I don't understand." Eric gave one of his own sheet's corners one last military snap, or as close to a military snap as a man could give on a sectional. "The guys were talking about that firearms hunting hasn't been allowed around here since 1986, but your father was shot the following year. What happened?"

Peter swallowed hard. "Daddy and Shoe had hunted here for years, and wasn't neither of them bow-hunting fans," he said slowly, beginning the story he and Shoe had been telling since 1987. "They figured the wardens would be soft on folk since it was the first year and so they decided to get in one more year with guns. Shoe was lining up his sights on a buck, and the buck heard something and took off. Shoe couldn't stop the shot. The bullet ricocheted and hit Daddy in the neck. No cell phones back then. We called on the CB radio for help, but it took a long time for them to find us. It wasn't anybody's fault. It just happened."

Eric nodded. "Even if it just happened, it had to hurt. It says a lot about your nature that you forgave Shoe and still love him so much and went to live with him and all."

"Forgave Shoe?" Peter looked at his son-in-law in disbelief. "I keep saying, it was an accident. Twasn't anything to forgive him for."

"Well, some might disagree, as Big Joe said. But thanks for sharing the story with me. I apologize if I pushed too hard."

"It's all right," Peter said uneasily. "Someday, your kids are gonna want to know about their families. You need to be able to tell them about their great-granddaddy, about how he was tall and strong and smart and funny and the best father in the world…"

Peter stopped for a second.

"And you need to be able to tell them that it was his sixteen-year-old son, cocky to be using his rifle for the first time on a real hunting trip, who killed him by accident."

23

Eric walked over to the other sectional and sat next to Peter. They both stared at the fire.

"I couldn't move," Peter said. "Daddy groaned and put his hand to his neck, then fell to the ground slowlike. Shoe went to him to try to stop the bleeding, and hollered at me to run to the truck and get on the CB for help. I did, but I wasn't real clear on where we were. I hadn't watched the road because I was too busy dreaming about getting my first buck's antlers mounted. We didn't have GPS in the day. It took them three hours to find us. Daddy never came to."

"And while you were waiting, Shoe said he'd tell them he fired the shot."

Peter nodded. "He said I had my whole life in front of me and he could carry it. Funny, he seemed so old then, but he was younger than I am now. The sheriff believed us. Shoe got a fine for using a firearm in a bow-only area."

"Then he took you in."

"Yep."

"And loved you like a son."

"Yep."

"Neither of you ever told anyone else?"

"Nope."

"Why are you telling me now?"

Peter got up to put more wood in the stove. He and Shoe had never spoken of it again. He'd stood up for John Davis at his wedding to Lizzie, yet he and John had never discussed it. He had often wondered if Rachel suspected, as there was a lot of talk around town after it happened, but she'd never pushed very hard to find out.

"I been thinking a lot about the old days, and I guess that's why," Peter said, stirring the embers. "I didn't think I'd ever be able to come back. But then time came for the hen party after Jill was born, and I knew I couldn't stand that much estrogen again for a night. I ended up coming here kind of in spite of myself."

"By yourself?"

"Yep. On the drive over, I thought about a lot of things—how much I missed Daddy, why Shoe done what he done, and how much I loved my new family. It started to clear my head."

"Did you hunt?"

"Not that first year. I just sat in a tree and thought. But when I gassed up on the way home, I talked with a group of bow hunters. They were telling me about how bow hunting just seemed closer to nature. When I got home, I picked up a cheap bow and some arrows and started practicing now and then. Later on, it turned out John Davis had an interest too. And after that, whether we got a buck or not, I always felt better when I got back home."

"You've had a lot of loss in your life, Dad."

"That I have, but a lot of joy too. Like most folk, I guess. And now, we'd best go to sleep."

Peter turned off the big overhead light and found the way to his sectional by the firelight. "And Eric?"

"Yes, Dad?"

"I hope you'll stand with me tomorrow when we get home and I tell the girls about this."

⁓ ∾ ⁓

They were up at four, in the truck a half hour later, and set up in their tree stands an hour before the hunting day started. The weather was perfect, Peter thought: clear, calm, in the mid-20s. The beech, dogwoods, and chestnuts would have been brilliant two months earlier. Today, their remaining leaves were a faded brown. There was a rustle now and then as squirrels and rabbits poked about. No sign yet of deer, but that was all right; he and Eric wouldn't head home until two or so.

Then he heard it—a deer call.

Peter looked down the hill where Eric was stationed. A doe was standing some yards away, looking perplexed and sniffing. Then she started, and raced away.

It was more of the same for the next several hours, neither of them getting off a single arrow. Peter looked at his watch. Noon. He thought his stomach had been rumbling. He put his glasses back in the pack, and pulled out of his vest some wheat crackers wrapped in a hankie.

While he was snacking, first one doe, then another, then a third ambled into view. But where was the buck? That many does, there had to be a buck nearby. Peter slowly took out his field glasses and scanned the area. Yes, there he was, taking it all in on a ridge above them. The does were ignoring him, intent on grazing. Peter watched them for fifteen minutes, trying to puzzle out what was going on in their deer brains. He could see Eric in his stand to the right, preparing to shoot.

Zing! Peter started at the noise of an arrow that fell just short of one of the doe. Eric's!

All three ran like lightning for the trees beyond him. Peter had to smile as they passed underneath, so graceful and in step. Then he picked up the glasses again and looked back up toward the ridge. The buck was coming, slowly. Hadn't he seen how the others had run? Minutes passed. The buck came into range and stopped, head tilted upward, nose quivering.

Peter came down the tree, making enough noise that he was sure Eric would hear him.

"Go home, you," he shouted in the direction of the buck, clapping his hands as loud as he could and pointing. "Go see to your women."

"Dad?" Eric came into view as well. "Dad, are you all right?"

The buck looked from one man to the other, then flicked his tail and ran.

Eric walked toward Peter, big grin on his face. "All that noise has probably made a few other hunters less than happy," he said when he got close. "Might be a good time for us to start home."

It was snowing lightly when the truck pulled onto Marshall Road.

"Well, here goes," Peter said after Eric turned off the ignition. "Would you pray with me first?"

They bowed their heads.

"All right," Peter said after they prayed, opening the passenger door. "Let's do it."

The house was a bevy of post-she-woman sharing activity. The dishwasher was humming, and Rachel was packing away the sleeping bags. Lizzie was in Rachel's bathroom primping—something about meeting people at a party in Old Town Winchester. When she came out, Peter didn't think she looked much different than usual, other than a bit of a sparkle in her eyes that had gone out when John died. She wished them all a happy new year, and left.

"It's a real shame you stopped for supper, because we've got scads of lasagna left," Jill said, walking to the refrigerator. "Are you sure you're not a teeny bit hungry? Plenty of Italian bread too. And—"

"Eggnog, right?" Peter said with a laugh. "There's always plenty of eggnog. Since it is New Year's Eve, we really ought to have some and drink a little toast. Shall we retire to the living room, ladies?"

Just as they had every year since Jill and Eric got serious, the foursome sang "Auld Lang Synge" off-key and shared goofy resolutions. Jill said she wouldn't wear plaid (since she didn't own any). Eric vowed not to enter the great state of Maine (since he had no plans to go there). Rachel pledged not to eat coconut (since it made her break out in hives). Peter said he wouldn't get on a plane (since he never had, and never wanted to). Then he broke with tradition.

"I'm going to resolve not to drink alcohol or smoke. I ain't had so much as a beer since August, and it makes for a clearer head. As for the smoking, well, I've pretty much already given it up too."

Rachel's ear-to-ear smile and single clap were even better than the chain saw she'd given him the week before as a Christmas present.

"And I'd like to declare a moratorium on secrets, starting with something I should have told you gals a long time ago." He drew in his breath. The smile Rachel had had on her face changed to a frown. She knit her brows and seemed to draw into herself.

Why were his thighs shaking so? Maybe the shaking would stop if he stood. Peter got up and looked out the window at the street light and snowflakes, coming down fast. He turned around and faced the women and Eric, arms folded across his chest.

"Me and Eric got to talking about some things up in the mountains, and well…you see, when Daddy died…well, twasn't Shoe's shot that bounced around and hit him. It was mine. Shoe thought it would be better if he owned it since I was so young."

A look went between Jill and Rachel, and he wasn't sure what it meant. Then Rachel shut her eyes and put her right hand in front of her mouth.

"Anyway, I told Eric last night when we were talking about hunting and such, and you should know the truth too."

Rachel got up and stood in front of him. For a moment, he

wondered if she was going to slap him—or hug him. But she did neither.

"Thank you. I've thought that for a long time."

Peter felt his face go white and his eyebrows shoot up. "What? Why?"

"Because Shoe's been getting you out of scrapes and trying to guide you to the right path ever since," Rachel said. "Look at how he got you back to church. Made sense he'd have done it for you then too. You were just a kid."

"It's in the way you look at each other, Dad," Jill said. "I know it was all an accident, but I've never believed you and Shoe would be so close if he'd fired the shot."

Peter narrowed his eyes. "So, the two of you figured all this out, and never let me in on it?"

Rachel looked at him intently, her jaw working. He could tell she was figuring the best way to say what she was going to say.

"Everyone in town and at school was talking about it the fall it happened. And you changed afterward. All of a sudden, you were all about drinking and smoking and girls and driving fast. It didn't take a genius to figure out something was on your soul. And as far as not letting you in on it, I asked you about it when we were first married. You made it clear that topic was off-limits and, after a few tries, I honored that."

"As for me," Jill said, "I first heard about it when I was ten. One of my teachers was talking with another teacher about what she thought happened and how it made you how you were. I came home crying and asked Mother. She told me what she thought had happened—" she looked at one parent, then the other "—and said, regardless of whatever I heard about you, whether it was true or not, to know that I had the best dad in the world, and she had the best husband."

The best dad in the world, and the best husband. By the time Jill was ten, he'd thought their marriage was on autopilot, in a zone where people didn't yell but they didn't love either, not really. He looked at Rachel. She bit her lips and nodded.

A hush fell over the little group, broken only when the nearby church's bell rang nine.

Eric stood up. "Dad and I have been up since four. If you don't mind, Mrs. Stanton, may we go home? I'm so tired that I could sleep until next year."

Peter laughed, grateful for the break in the tension, and the girls groaned. Rachel helped Jill gather up her things and take them to the car.

"How do you feel?" Eric said when the gals were out of earshot.

"Not sure. Relieved, I guess, but surprised that they kind of knew all along. Just proves it's hard to hide anything from people you love."

Eric smiled. "Amen to that."

Peter and Rachel walked with Eric and Jill to the carport and waved them off with shouts of "Happy new year!"

"Well, another year, almost done," Rachel said as they came back inside. "Any other resolutions you want to share, old man?"

"To trust in the Lord more. I wish I'd opened up to you when you asked. Maybe…well, I guess maybes and wish-I-hads don't get us nowhere now, do they?"

Rachel nodded. "I'll try to join you in that resolution."

"I say, wife, when Jill was ten, things were already different between us. Why did you tell Jill you had the best husband in the world? Just to make her feel better?"

She gave him another one of those looks he'd never been able to figure out, the kind where he felt like he was a puzzle looking to be solved. It seemed like she was going to say something, then she sighed and shrugged her shoulders.

"Happy new year, Rachel. Go on upstairs. I'll pick up and shut off the lights."

Peter went into the living room and picked up the four eggnog cups from the end tables. He took them into the kitchen, rinsed them out, and then put them in the dishwasher. It wasn't until he turned out that light that he realized a lamp remained on in the living room. He sighed, switched the kitchen light on again, and walked back to the other room.

Propped up against the lamp was a group of photos from she-woman sharing: Jill's crowning as homecoming queen, Lizzie and Rachel as cheerleaders, Rachel and Jill at some 4-H ceremony with blue ribbons galore. But it was a photo of a picnic that he picked up and held closer to the light. The best friends anyone could have asked for. A little girl who glowed with the same beautiful spark she had as an adult. And the woman who had held his heart then and every day since, even though he'd forgotten that for too long.

"Happy new year, love," he said under his breath as he put the photo back where he'd found it and turned off the lamp.

24

Of course I love Jill. But if I had it to do over again, I wouldn't have become a mother the way I did," Rachel said, squirming on one end of Marsha Miller's couch early one February evening.

She was convinced the words had to be said out loud, especially since Peter had told the truth about shooting his dad. But she hadn't wanted to say them without Marsha present.

"Getting pregnant changed everything, all my plans, all my dreams."

"Now that's—" Peter started.

Marsha put up a hand in Peter's direction. "Rachel, please go on."

Rachel looked out the window. The sun was gone, but the parking lights shone on old sheets someone had put around the saucer magnolias to protect them against the predicted frost. The poets could say what they wanted about April, but the gardener in Rachel knew February was the cruelest, most unpredictable month in the Shenandoah Valley.

"Who does your landscaping?" she asked. "They're doing a great job of watching after those magnolias."

Marsha didn't answer.

Rachel sighed.

"You know those things that get sent around in email? I got one last week that said, 'Don't put a question mark where Jesus puts a period.' I've spent the past twenty-six years putting a question mark after 'Forgive me' to the Lord, and He keeps putting a period after 'No.' I should think a loving God could have forgiven an eighteen-year-old good girl for two beers and a half hour of carnal pleasure. But He hasn't."

"What makes you think He hasn't?" Marsha asked.

"Well, most recently, Jill."

Peter started to say something, but Marsha again motioned him to stay quiet.

"Why?" Marsha asked.

Rachel shook her head. "Isn't it obvious? Scripture says the children will be punished for the fathers' sins. It's not enough that God punished me with miscarriages and cancer. Now, Jill is paying. God doesn't care how good a job we did raising her or how much I do for His church. He will have His vengeance. My parents always said my sins would be visited on my children and my children's children. I didn't want to believe it, but God's shown me it's the truth."

"Me, I always saw us getting pregnant as a blessing," Peter said. Rachel turned to look at him. He was leaning forward from the edge of the couch, his long legs splayed, elbows on his thighs, fingertips bouncing against each other.

"Why do you say that, Peter?" Marsha asked.

"You would have never married me otherwise," Peter said, turning toward Rachel. "You were out of my league—smart as a whip, ambitious. Sure, we've had our problems since then, a lot of them. But here we are, trying to work them out. We have a beautiful daughter, a great son-in-law, friends. No debt. Money in the bank. Where's the punishment in any of that? Maybe it's not the life you planned, but it's still a blessing. To me, anyway."

He moved closer to her on the couch, as if he wanted to hug her but wasn't sure he should. Rachel moved closer to her end.

"No, I was the one out of my league," she said. "I put you off for a year because I knew I wouldn't be able to keep your interest for long. I was right about that too. If I hadn't gotten pregnant, I would have just been another notch on your belt."

"Ah, wife," he said, moving away from her again and leaning back, arms folded across his chest. "You want to know how unlike the others you were? I can still tell you exactly what you wore: a white linen blouse that buttoned down the front, no sleeves. A denim skirt that hit you above your knees. Your red cheerleader sneakers. A silly outfit for a girl going on a hike, and you knew it and wore it anyway. All that hair. So beautiful when it was free."

Rachel pressed her right index and middle finger against her nose, hard. "How on earth can you remember that?"

"I remember everything about that night. I was working a dead-end construction job and living in a trailer. You were headed for college and out of my world forever in three months."

Rachel looked at her watch. "I guess it's time for us to go."

"We have a little more time," Marsha said. "Peter, how did you feel when Rachel told you she was pregnant?"

"I was thrilled."

"Thrilled?" Rachel's mouth hung open. "What was there to be thrilled about?"

"It meant you'd be in my life after all. I called you every day for weeks after we were together, and you wouldn't come to the phone. I asked Lizzie what was wrong, and you wouldn't tell her. Or she wouldn't tell me, anyway. I felt like a fool."

"I was the fool. If I'd been smart, I would have stood by my principles. And now, we're all paying for it, Jill included."

Peter set his jaw and clenched and unclenched his fists. Rachel waited for an explosion. But he placed the tips of his fingers together prayerfully for a few seconds, then turned and took her hands.

She wanted nothing more than to pull away, but couldn't.

"Let it go," he said. "Kind of like I'm working through on Daddy and me. So you got pregnant. We got married. We can't change that. Ain't we here in this room to figure out how to make it work today, not rehash the past?"

The past is what I know, Rachel wanted to say. But Marsha spoke first.

"I'm hearing quite a difference in the way the two of you remember that time, and the way each of you dealt with it. Peter, did you ever consider how frightened and disappointed Rachel was?"

He gave a short laugh. "I'm well aware of how frightened and disappointed my wife was—and is. That part went away for a while after we got married, and that's when I truly fell in love with Rachel, for her strength and faith, beyond her beauty and brains and being the mother of our daughter. I've dealt with frightened and disappointed for years now, and they don't faze me anymore. I know the real woman inside her. Kind and giving to a fault. Generous. Helpful."

Was that really how he saw her—kind, generous, helpful? They weren't words Rachel was sure she'd use to describe herself. She felt a bit ashamed and yet grateful.

"Rachel?"

She gave a start. "I'm sorry. Would you please repeat that, Marsha?"

"I asked whether you had ever considered what Peter's reaction was to your pregnancy."

"Can't say as I ever did. It all happened so fast. I mean, it didn't really matter what either of our reactions or feelings were. We had to do the right thing, and that was to get married."

Marsha looked at Rachel, then shifted her gaze to Peter, then back again.

"The two of you had a tremendous amount of upheaval when you were very young—getting married, becoming parents, buying a house, losing two babies, Rachel's cancer—all in the space of less than ten years. Did you consider counseling at that time?"

They looked at each other and shook their heads.

"We were too busy living," Rachel said. "It seemed like something important was always happening, and we just had to get through it all. I'm not sure either of us had much time or inclination to gaze at our navels and our marriage until we started coming to you."

Marsha nodded. "I wonder, have the two of you talked any further about that controlled separation concept I mentioned? It might help provide, as Rachel put it, the time and inclination to gaze at your navels and your marriage." She chuckled.

Well, I'm glad she thinks I'm funny, Rachel thought. "No, we haven't," she said.

Marsha rose from the recliner. "I think we've made some excellent progress today. Let's pray."

Peter and Rachel were quiet until they pulled into the carport.

"Peter?" Rachel asked.

"Yes?"

"You really were thrilled to hear we were going to have a baby?"

"Yes, I really was thrilled to hear we were going to have a baby."

"I wish you'd told me that before."

"I did. More than once. You just didn't believe it. But I'm telling you now again. Please believe me."

"Okay," she said. "I'll try."

25

Tomorrow's going to be busy," Rachel said to Peter one Saturday evening as they sat in the living room reading. "Church, then Mavis's birthday dinner, then supper here with Jill."

"And daylight savings time starts overnight," he said. "Maybe your time with your folks will seem shorter."

"Time with Maarten and Mavis never seems short."

They both laughed.

"I wish…" she said, and didn't finish the sentence. Too many wishes: That she wouldn't always leave her parents' house in such a bad mood. That her parents were positive, loving people. That Jill wasn't already talking about going to see Eric in Frankfurt in hopes of starting another baby. That the county wasn't having a budget crisis that was putting some of the library's programs in jeopardy. That her hair wasn't starting to have quite so much gray in it.

"If wishes were horses, beggars would ride," Peter said. "You can't control any of the things you worry about, wife. All you can control is your reaction to them."

"Sounds to me like you've been listening to Marsha a little too much, old man."

He laughed and stood up. "Maybe I have at that. I bid you good night. Don't forget to reset your clock. Spring forward, you know."

⁘

"Rachel? Rachel?" The call was accompanied by insistent knocking on her door. She rolled over and looked at her clock. Quarter of nine. Why was he bothering her? Her alarm was set for nine, which would be plenty of time to get ready and drive to services at ten. They'd agreed she'd leave from church for her parents' house, and he'd be on his own for dinner. "Yes?" she mumbled, rolling back over.

"Rachel! Are you feeling okay? Because if you are, we need to get going. Church starts in fifteen minutes."

She bolted up in bed. Fifteen minutes? Then Rachel realized she hadn't set her clock ahead.

"I forgot about daylight savings time. Go on without me. I'll see you there."

"Okay," Peter shouted. "See you there."

Why in the world was she so tired? Rachel wondered as she turned off the alarm. She'd gone to bed at eleven as usual. The day after the time change was hard for everyone, but this was ridiculous.

⁘

"Rachel? Rachel?" She felt like she was in that movie where the same thing kept happening over and over.

"What?"

"Rachel, it's eleven thirty. You missed services. And ain't you supposed to be at your folks' at noon?"

This time, Rachel didn't just sit up. She bounced out of bed and opened the door. She had to laugh at the double take Peter did.

"I don't know what's wrong with me. I don't feel sick or anything. Maybe it's because I'm just dreading going there so much."

"Would you like me to come along?"

Rachel looked him up and down. Dark blue khaki pants. Red

pullover sweater over a white collared shirt. Nicely polished loafers. Even Mavis and Maarten couldn't object to the way he was dressed.

"You don't have to."

"I know I don't have to. I'm offering."

"They won't like it. They haven't seen you since we were kids."

"Then maybe it's time. Go get dressed. I'll meet you at the truck."

❧

They pulled into the farmhouse driveway at 12:15 p.m. Mavis and Maarten were standing in front of the living room's large picture window. They seemed to be having what for them would have been an animated conversation that stopped cold when Peter stepped out of the truck and went around to the passenger side to open Rachel's door. After Peter helped her out, Rachel turned and smiled and waved to her parents. They moved away from the window.

"They got old," Peter whispered, as if he thought they could hear him.

Rachel giggled. "They're younger than they look. Mavis is sixty-seven today." She had an urge to grab Peter's hand, but resisted. They walked toward the rear of the house. Peter knocked and, after what seemed like years, Mavis came to the kitchen door.

"Hello, Mrs. Grossman," Peter said. "I'm Peter Gregory, your son-in-law. I came along to wish you a happy birthday."

Mavis frowned. "You're late."

Rachel started to speak, but stopped when Peter shook his head at her.

"Yes, Mrs. Grossman, we are late. Fifteen minutes late. We're sorry. We should have called. But better late than never. Is there any dinner left?"

"Yes."

"Then would you mind if we came in and had some?"

146

"Yes," she said, and walked back through the house.

"Yes she'd mind or yes we should come in?" Peter asked Rachel.

Rachel rolled her eyes. She felt like she was eighteen again, reckless and wild and strong with Peter by her side. "Let's go in. What's the worst they're going to do, tell us we're bad people? We already know they think that."

The kitchen counters were bare of food, which Rachel knew she was supposed to take as a sign she had let down her parents yet again. But somehow, she didn't feel she had. "Let's sing," she whispered to Peter as they entered the dining room.

"Happy birthday to you, happy birthday to—" they stopped as they realized Mavis and Maarten were in prayer. Rachel sat in her usual place, Peter next to her in a spot without a place setting. They closed their eyes and listened as Maarten beseeched God to forgive unworthy sinners such as the four of them and to, if it was the Almighty's will, give Mavis the gift of less back pain in the coming year. "Amen," he said finally.

"I'll be right back," Rachel said, rising. "I need to get a place setting for my husband and some food for the two of us."

"I thank you for welcoming the stranger, especially on your birthday," Peter said with a grin as he stood as well. "I apologize that we didn't let you know I was coming, but it was sort of an impulsive thing. And I apologize that I haven't been here for so many years. But that's going to change. I'll be coming along from now on. And now, Rachel, let's see to that place setting."

She managed to keep from laughing until they reached the kitchen. "Did you see their faces?" she whispered. "I don't think they know how to take us at all."

"They'll take us just as we are," Peter said.

They took part of the mountains of chicken, mashed potatoes, and corn out of the refrigerator. Even cold, the food was tasty, part of one of the more pleasant meals Rachel had had in the house since her marriage. It wasn't that Mavis and Maarten didn't complain about the weather, prices, and the state of the world. But somehow, with Peter sitting beside her, it was easier not to get defensive or argumentative.

After coffee and cake—with seven-minute icing, of course—Mavis stared at Rachel, an expectant look in her eyes. What was wrong? Rachel wondered. She and Peter both had complimented her on the cake and the meal in general. That was when she realized she'd left Mavis's birthday present, a silver-plated mirror, comb, and hairbrush set, in the truck.

"I'm sorry," she began, but then Peter coughed. "Hold that thought please, Rachel," he said. "If all y'all will excuse me, I'll be back directly."

Within minutes, he was back with the present in his hands. "Mrs. Grossman, it's been kind of a crazy day, I suspect because of the time change. Anyways, here's your present. I hope you like it, because Rachel takes a great deal of care in selecting gifts for you and Mr. Grossman."

Rachel watched as Mavis unwrapped the gift. Then, she heard the words she never remembered hearing come from her mother's mouth:

"Thank you."

⁓೨᧚⏽

"You had them eating out of your hand—at least, as much as my parents ever will eat out of someone's hand," Rachel said as they drove home. "How ever did you do it?"

"They're just people. They ain't always been kind to us, especially you and Jill, but they're just people, and people getting old at that."

"Are you kidding? These are the people who have told me for years that all my sins will be visited on Jill and her children. They're the people who said I was being punished for getting pregnant.

They called me every bad name that's in the Bible for a woman."

Peter nodded. "I know. I was there to hear some of those names sometimes. But they're your parents, and they're not going to be around forever. I'm not saying we need to spend every holiday with them. But the times we're with them, I'm going to treat them with as much respect as I'd give anyone else."

Rachel sighed. It certainly was a kind of crazy day.

26

"Here you go," Peter said as he returned to the scorer's table, two large soft drink cups in his hands.

"Ssh! Coach just put Kevin in," Shoe said.

Peter understood Shoe was excited his freshman grandson was getting a chance to pinch-hit, but it showed how far out of Lyman's reach the early-season baseball game truly was. 10-3 in the bottom of the ninth, with two out. That had never happened when Peter was the star pitcher. But he still enjoyed watching the Redbirds, and Shoe had roped him into helping to score for the past several years.

It only took one pitch, fast and inside. Kevin popped up. The game was over.

As the place cleared out, Shoe and Peter completed the final paperwork, signed their names, and put the forms in the box outside the athletic director's office. Kevin came by on his bike, and all three agreed that baseball was a game of inches and that he'd do better next time.

"That was good, that Kevin got in the game," Peter said as he and Shoe walked to the truck. "He's got some promise or he wouldn't have made varsity so soon. Could be the pick of the county someday."

Shoe laughed. "Oh, for a freshman he'll do. We'll see what happens next year when he's called upon in the clutch. Right now, his head's a little too full of how good looking and special all the girls think he is. That never seemed to bother you when you were playing."

Peter pursed his lips. It was the truth—sort of. He'd always welcomed female attention, back even in the grades, and there had been plenty of it. But he'd never taken his eye off his game—except to wonder why that cute little redheaded cheerleader wasn't among the admiring throng. In fact, she ignored him until chemistry class his senior year. Being that he was a Gregory and she was a Grossman, they ended up as partners.

"You're a pretty boy, Peter Gregory," she told him the first day of class. "I don't care that you're dating my best friend or that you generally slide by on charm and that lazy smile. I don't care that everyone feels bad about you being an orphan and all. You're bearing your share of the load at this lab table, and I don't intend to get out of here with less than an A."

They quickly learned to work as a team, handing tubes back and forth and recording results. They studied for exams together, and occasionally Rachel came along when he and Lizzie went to the movies or such. They never double-dated; Rachel said no to every guy who asked her out, other than to the big dances. She told him one day during chemistry that she wasn't going to waste her time with Gilroy County hayseeds when she had the whole world ahead of her. Peter thought she was being a mite judgmental. But he kept his mouth shut on that one.

Lizzie was a sweet enough gal, beautiful and not so smart—the way Peter generally liked them. But something inside him broke at his prom when they were on the dance floor and she started rubbing his buns, right in front of everyone. Across the gym, he could see Rachel put her hand over her face and then run off the floor.

Peter pulled away.

"Lizzie, this was never going anywhere, and it's done. Now. Get yourself a ride home with Rachel and her date, okay?"

Then he drove himself home and wondered why he'd done it.

The next Monday, finals week commenced. The chemistry teacher gave each table five unknowns. They'd have five class periods to solve them. Once they had all five solved, they had an A on the final and could stop coming to class.

"Rachel, about prom," Peter started as soon as they had their instructions.

"Hush," she whispered, eyes blazing with something, he couldn't tell quite what. "We are going to do this and get out of here and never see each other again. Understand?"

He nodded. "As you wish." He put on his goggles and picked up the first test tube.

By the end of class Tuesday, they'd solved four unknowns with minimal conversation. The fifth one was a different story. Wednesday came and went. Thursday came and went. At the beginning of class on Friday morning, they were the only ones in the room besides the instructor.

"I can't believe I'm going to get a crummy B on a final!" Rachel exploded.

Peter laughed. "Considering I expected to get a C in the course and we're both on track to get an A no matter what happens here, I can't see getting bent out of shape."

"You can't be serious!"

"I am."

Neither of them said anything for a couple minutes. Then Rachel grabbed the remaining tube and dumped the contents down the sink. They both burst into laughter and walked out, ignoring the instructor's calls after them.

He asked her out right then, for that evening. She said no. He called her every other week for the next year, after he'd started working construction and moved into the trailer. She was caught up in the whirl of a beautiful brainiac's senior year—National Honor Society, National Merit Scholar finalist, Student Council secretary, head of the young adults group at church, captain of the football/wrestling cheerleading squad. They'd always talk a bit about the books she was reading or about movies or the news. But she always said no to going out, that it would hurt Lizzie too much. For a best friend, Peter thought, she knew very little of Lizzie and how quickly she had moved on. Finally, he took Lizzie aside at the girls' graduation in May.

"I need you to tell Rachel you're over me," he said, arm around her.

Lizzie giggled. "I was over you an hour after you dumped me. You know how I am. Same as you."

Same as I was. I ain't had a date since. "Just tell her, okay? Tell her the next time I ask her out will be the last time, so she needs to say yes."

Lizzie pushed back the bright red graduation cap, face flushed. "Why do you keep asking, anyway? It's not like you don't have the pick of the county."

Peter swallowed hard and looked at the toes of his scuffed work boots.

"Because for me, she is the pick of the county."

He felt Lizzie reach up and kiss his cheek. "Consider it done. One favor?"

"Yes?"

"Take care of her. She's more fragilelike than us." Then Lizzie disappeared into the crowd of graduates and well-wishers.

The next day when Peter called, Rachel said yes.

⁓◦⁓

"… he's got big dreams, that one," Shoe said as he turned onto Marshall Road.

"'Scuse me?" Peter said, giving himself a shake.

Shoe laughed. "I don't know where you were, but you sure had a big smile going. Anyways, I was saying about Kevin, he's already thinking of Florida State or Miami, but I'm not sure he's got the raw talent, even if he get serious. I suspect he'll end up here at Shenandoah U. There's nothing wrong with being a big fish in a little pond."

"Nothing wrong with that at all," Peter said. "As long as you love the pond."

27

Rachel rubbed her eyes again and stared at her monitor. Cutting two hundred thousand dollars from a two-million-dollar budget. Why, it'd be almost impossible without closing one of the libraries and laying off several people.

She ran the scenarios again. Reduce hours at Central and both branches. Close all the libraries on Mondays. Nothing provided enough savings. You still had the operational expenses. Closing the Round Knob branch was the only option.

It was a hard decision, but she didn't see any way around it. The next closest branch was twenty miles away, too far for kids who lived in Round Knob to drop in after school or for the elderly in the community to walk to. A lot of those folk didn't have the money for computers or internet access at home. But the other branches were even farther apart.

Rachel stood up and stretched. It'd be especially bad for Leitha Wells, the head librarian at Round Knob. Leitha had been with the county library system for twenty years. She was running the children's department at Central when Rachel was hired to work in circulation, and showed Rachel the ropes when she became Leitha's assistant in children's. But Leitha had moved to Round Knob five years earlier after her husband left her. She wanted to raise her three boys in a more rural setting. After Rachel was promoted from children's librarian at Central to head librarian of the system, she'd asked Leitha about coming back to her old job. Leitha had declined, not wanting to negotiate the mountain roads daily.

Rachel walked out of her office and into the main library. Being out in the stacks always made her feel better. Central's children's/young adult department was one of the biggest and best in the state for its size, thanks to her leadership. But somehow, she didn't think that reputation would convince the county board to rethink that ten percent cut at Monday's meeting.

Ten o'clock. Story hour. Sandy was seated cross-legged on the floor, reading *If You Give a Mouse a Cookie* to a group of preschoolers. They all leaned forward, not wanting to miss a word. One little girl with a long red braid and freckles, sitting apart from the rest, was mouthing the words as Sandy read. Rachel smiled. It could have been her, thirty-odd years ago.

She wandered over to the Friends of Gilroy County library shop. "Good morning, Mrs. Gregory," the volunteer said. Rachel nodded and headed for the YA area. *Pick a New Dream* by Lenora Mattingly Weber. Why in the world was that 1961 classic being discarded? Rachel picked it up. "I need to take this one to my office," she said.

Rachel checked the circulation records at her computer. *Pick a New Dream* hadn't been checked out since she bought the reprint edition years ago. Not once! Well, the children's librarian certainly had been within her rights to discard it. But while Rachel read and liked today's popular YA series, it broke her heart to think people were no longer reading about Beany Malone and Carlton Buell. *Pick a New Dream*'s language and situations were dated, but the message wasn't. When Beany's post-high school plan to work at the local newspaper didn't work out, she found happiness—and love—in a position at the community center.

Rachel was still reminiscing when Michael Manning, the beefy county board chairman, stepped into her office.

"Good morning, Rachel. Have a few minutes?"

Odd. While she and the retired truck driver had a cordial relationship, it had always been formal. In the months since she'd become head librarian, he'd never stopped by to chat unannounced.

"Of course," Rachel said, shuffling the three pieces of paper that were on her desktop into a single pile. "I've just been running some numbers. A ten percent budget cut is pretty difficult for us to handle. I'll keep working on it over the weekend, but it's tough."

Michael shut the door behind him and sat at Rachel's conference table. "Yes, it is a lot. But you know the county's revenue situation." He coughed. "Rachel, would you join me over here?"

Why hadn't he sat in one of the two overstuffed chairs that were opposite her desk? They were so much more comfortable, especially for someone Michael's size. "All right," she said, picking up a manila file folder as she rose. "I have some preliminary recommendations I can go over with you, if you'd like to hear them from me rather than the library board chairman."

At the table, Michael was tapping his thick fingertips together, forming and unforming a church with each move.

Rachel sat. "I don't see any way around closing Round Knob," she began.

Michael nodded. "I've come to the same decision. In fact, so has the county board. We had a meeting last night."

"You met last night? I didn't know."

"Yes. We called an emergency meeting. We found out yesterday afternoon that we won't be getting a five-million-dollar state grant we'd counted on for that sewage improvement project. You know the feds have been after us about getting that taken care of. We'll have to move funds from some other programs, like the library, to come up with the money."

Rachel nodded and began running the numbers in her head again. The library system likely would be asked to take a share of that hit. Besides closing Round Knob, that would mean reduced hours and programs everywhere—and more layoffs.

"Rachel," Michael said, "I'm here this morning because the board tussled with this situation for five hours last night. We got to cut managers across the board, and we decided to do it by seniority. I'm sorry."

Rachel felt her face go white and then red. "What are you saying?"

"We got to let you go. All the branch managers got more years in than you do, and you're right, we got to close Round Knob. I called Leitha last night. She's just sick about all this, but she's agreed to take over the head librarian position."

Rachel's head started spinning. "This isn't right," she said, standing up slowly. "You didn't even give me a chance to come up with a proposal to deal with these cuts. You had a secret meeting, which I daresay is illegal."

Michael opened his briefcase and took out a folder. "It was an emergency session dealing with personnel, and we were within our rights. Now, I got your severance package here."

She sat down and did her best to listen. Two weeks of salary for every year she'd been at the library full time, plus payment for the six weeks of vacation time she hadn't used. The option to buy health insurance.

"And Rachel, if you'd like, we'll pay for outplacement counseling and a job search workshop. We hate to see you go." Michael put his hands in his lap and looked down.

Outplacement counseling and a job search workshop! They were taking away the only professional position she wanted in the entire county. The neighboring counties all had head librarians who'd been there forever and, like Gilroy County, required employees to be residents.

"There's not much to say, is there?" Rachel didn't even try to keep the bite out of her voice. "When is my last day?"

"Well, we thought since today is Friday…"

"I see." Rachel stood up again and moved to her desk. "I'll just call a quick meeting so I can say goodbye."

"Um, Rachel?" Michael fidgeted with his briefcase. "I'll meet with them. I got to ask you to pack up your things, and then I'll walk you to your car."

"You have to stand here while I pack? What do you think I'm going to take?"

"It's what the lawyer said to do. Do you need some boxes?"

Rachel set her lips and let out a slow breath. She was being fired. Or downsized. Or laid off. Or whatever other name you wanted to give it. But it didn't mean she had to give them the satisfaction of seeing her fall apart.

It only took about ten minutes. Rachel had never been one of those people who brought a lot of her personal life into work. She took the library keys from her keyring. She printed out her computer passwords, and gave a silent prayer of thanks that she had no personal documents on the server. The certificate she'd received two years earlier as the state's outstanding children's librarian, Jill and Eric's wedding picture, a bag of cosmetics, a little box of pinecones collected a lifetime ago with Peter, and a half-dozen books filled the box Michael brought from somewhere.

"I'm sorry, Rachel," Michael said as they reached her car and he put the box in her trunk. "Hard times."

"Indeed," she choked out. It took every bit of strength she had to shake his hand, get in the hybrid, and drive home without crying.

All that strength vanished when she lugged the box into the house, put it on the kitchen table, and realized that *Pick a New Dream* was on the top.

28

The bug had finally won.

Peter prided himself on going to work no matter how he felt, and he'd felt pretty punk the past two days. But two hours into his shift, he knew he'd met his match. Wad of tissues in hand, he clocked out and got in the truck to go home. Maybe a three-day weekend in bed and Rachel's homemade chicken soup would turn the tide.

He rounded the bend on Marshall Road and saw the hybrid in the carport. What was she doing home at eleven on a Friday morning? He blew his nose again, parked, and entered the kitchen.

"Wife?" Peter shouted. "I'm home. Down for the count with this blamed cold."

He could never remember. Was it feed a cold and starve a fever, or the other way around? No matter. He didn't have the energy to rustle up food anyway. Peter headed to his bedroom, took off his shoes, blew his nose again, and got under the covers. No energy to change into his pajamas.

He didn't know how long he'd been asleep when the smell of chicken soup managed to get through even his clogged nostrils. Peter opened his eyes to see Rachel standing in the doorway with a tray. She was smiling kind of crookedlike, the way she did when she wanted to cry but didn't think she should. And she was wearing jeans and a sweater, not her usual workday jacket and skirt or pantsuit.

"Well, Miss Florence Nightingale, if you ain't a sight for sore eyes—and a sore throat and a sore nose, for that matter," he said as he sat up and accepted the tray. "I thank you. But what are you doing home at this time of day?"

Rachel rubbed her eyes and sat down in the chair at the opposite end of the room. She mumbled something.

"I couldn't hear you," he said, spoon in midair. "Are you sick now too?"

"I said I got fired."

Peter screwed up his face. Maybe the cold had stopped up his ears too.

"Did you say fired?"

"Yes."

"Are they crazy?" he shouted, upsetting the tray and spilling soup all over the bed and himself.

"You old fool," Rachel shouted back, shaking her head. "Get out of those clothes. I'll set you up a spot on the couch." She picked the tray and bowl and water glass and left.

Peter took a quick shower and dressed, then pulled the sheets off his bed and put them in the washer. His runny nose and scratchy throat didn't seem so important anymore.

He headed into the living room to find Rachel curled up on the couch, rocking herself back and forth.

Peter coughed and blew his nose again. Then he lowered himself to the floor and sat about three feet from Rachel. More than anything in this world, he wanted to stroke her hair and make everything all right. This is what happens when you don't feed a marriage; it starves to death, he thought. Your insides get tied up so bad you don't know what to do when your wife needs you. Anything I say could be wrong, and most likely would be.

"What happened?"

Her face stayed in her hands as she spoke. Peter couldn't make out all of what she said, but it sounded like it was about the budget. He still didn't like it, but he could understand that. At least it wasn't personal.

"Did you call Jill?"

Rachel rolled over on her stomach. The back of her head shook vigorously.

"How about Lizzie?"

The shaking was even more vigorous.

"So you came home to lick your wounds in private, and now here I am, sick as a dog and taking up your space."

Finally, Rachel sat up. Her face had red marks from where it'd rubbed against her hands, and the front part of her hair was standing straight up. They stared at each other for a few minutes, him wiping his nose occasionally and her wiping her eyes.

"What can I do?"

"You? Nothing. I'll act like I'm okay when people ask me what happened and then tell me everything's going to be all right. I've had plenty of practice pretending nothing's wrong."

Every time he thought they'd made some progress, it seemed she had to slap him in the face. "Now, wife," he said, ready to say exactly what he'd been thinking.

But something made him stop and consider her viewpoint the way Marsha the therapist had suggested. She'd lost her schoolgirl dream of going away to college and then working for the Library of Congress. She'd managed to build herself a nice little oasis with the county among people who respected her, even though he suspected some of them chafed under her bossy nature. For so long, work and church had been all Rachel had had to herself. He'd horned in on one, and now she'd lost the other.

"What about the Library of Congress?"

"The Library of Congress!" she said with a snort. "Do you have any idea how many applicants they get for positions at my level, and how long it takes to fill them when they're advertised?"

"Tell me."

"Well, I don't know exactly, but probably thousands and probably months. And what would we live on in the meantime? Your salary?"

Peter closed his eyes. *God, the woman I love is still in there somewhere. Let me be kind.*

"You said something about severance pay. And you know our books better than I do. This place is paid for, free and clear other than property taxes and repairs. We don't owe a cent on the truck or the hybrid. My salary may not be what yours is—I mean, was—but based on what you showed me a month ago, it'll cover our basic expenses, even without your severance. And if we need to tap our savings, well, so be it. Jill and Eric are set financially thanks to his folk and the Marines. They won't be looking to us for anything other than love."

Rachel looked at him.

"I suppose I could apply if they have something," she said, with the first smile he'd seen. "Or maybe do some volunteer work there."

"So you could. And they'd be lucky to have you."

The frown came back.

"Except there'd be the commute—nearly ninety miles each way."

"People do it every day. They drive or they carpool or they take them big buses from the commuter lot over to Winchester. Could you try it just a day or two a week?"

Rachel tapped her fingers together several times. "No," she said after a minute or two. "I don't think this is the time for us to be apart. I don't feel I'm taking to the counseling the way you are. But I want to see this through, and that won't work if I'm gallivanting off to the District."

Peter blew his nose again. "How much would an apartment there run, do you think?"

"Did you not hear me? I just said I don't think this is the time to be apart."

"I'm not talking about being apart. I'm a fair mechanic. That Metro system likely always is in the market for folk like me. I could go with you."

"You would do that? You've always sneered at people who live in those city high-rises, called them cliff-dwellers."

"The Library of Congress was your dream. We could still make it happen, I think."

"What's your dream, Peter? Isn't it living here, in a small town in the mountains, and being able to leave your doors and windows unlocked?"

"I got my dream a long time ago." He sneezed. "Drat this cold."

"And what is that dream?"

"You."

Silence.

At least she didn't laugh.

"You're serious," Rachel said with what sounded like surprise. "You would really move to the city if that's what I wanted."

"I would."

He blew his nose again. Living among the cliff-dwellers and not being able to see the mountains wouldn't be his ideal, and who knew what they'd do with Callie or if they'd find renters for the house or a million other things. Peter just knew he wanted to see more of that shylike smile she had when she mentioned applying with the Library of Congress.

"That was a long time ago," Rachel said after a few moments. "We've got lives here now, real adult lives and responsibilities and obligations. First Corinthians says, 'When I became a man, I put away childish things.'"

"What brought us together was no childish thing, even though we were all but children. I can't explain what's kept us together, but I know that's not childish either." A coughing spell wracked Peter, and when it was done, he found himself leaning against Rachel, arms touching arms.

"That cold has gone to your head," she said with a giggle as she moved away. "Let's get you a nap, and see where you are in a couple days."

Peter clambered onto the couch. Rachel was right; he was worn out. He smiled as she pulled the sheets and blankets up around his shoulders. He was tired from the cold and the talk, so he couldn't be sure. But he thought he felt her lips graze the top of his head before she turned away, whispering, "Sleep tight."

The washer was still on rinse when Rachel got downstairs. She pulled a set of fresh sheets from the cabinet that housed Peter's linens and took them over to his bed. The mattress cover appeared to be chicken-soup-free. The pillows seemed dry too. Well, that was something.

She smoothed the blue plaid sheets over the double bed, then tucked his pillow under her chin to slip on the case. It smelled… not of chicken soup, but of Peter. She sat down hard on the bed, pillow still under her chin, and shivered.

He had always smelled the same, she thought, tightening her arms around the pillow. Warm. Strong. Masculine. A little sweaty, but still good. Secretly, she'd always been glad he thought cologne was for sissies.

Rachel put the pillow at the bed's head, then picked up the blue corded spread from the floor. Unlike the mattress cover and the pillow, the spread had not escaped the chicken soup accident. She bunched it together and put it on top of the washer. Still, he'd need a cover for the night.

She went back to the cabinet and opened the deep drawer that held the extra blankets. The top one was too heavy; the second one, too light. The third one was a fraying stained-glass coverlet she'd hand-pieced so long ago from one of the Grossmutter's patterns.

Rachel spread it upon the bed, then lay on top of it, her head resting on his pillow and her fingers tracing the pattern. She had finished it the night before their only date, not long after her high school graduation day. He'd been asking for a long time, and finally had told Lizzie to tell her he wasn't going to ask again.

They had hiked about a mile in the Shenandoah National Forest's late afternoon sun, picking up a few pinecones here and there as they walked and talked, then unpacked their backpacks. From hers, Rachel brought out the new coverlet and spread it for them to sit on. Then she removed peanut butter and jelly sandwiches, and oatmeal raisin cookies. From his backpack came a six-pack of beer.

Rachel felt a knot in her stomach. "I don't think that's allowed here. And besides, you won't be able to drive after six beers."

"I was figuring I'd have some help. And I know one of the rangers. We'll be fine."

Rachel stood up. "If you think you're going to get me drunk and naked, you've got another think coming. We can go home right now."

Peter remained seated. He gave her that lazy smile and winked. Then he put five of the cans back into backpack, and opened the sixth. He took a swig.

"As you wish. Let me finish this one, and we'll go home. You can drive."

Rachel sat down and listened as he talked about his day. Construction work was hard, he said, but he liked it. They were paving a dirt road out in the hinterlands, and an old couple whose house was in the work area had hobbled out with lemonade at lunchtime.

"If those folk get sick come winter, it's gonna be a lot easier for the ambulance to get to them," Peter said. "Today, I felt good, like I was doing something that'll mean something."

Rachel nodded. This was the guy who had been her chemistry

partner, not the boy with the bad reputation.

"I changed my mind," she said. "I'll try one beer. But don't get me drunk."

"Not a chance," Peter said, smiling as he reached into his backpack. "I like you sober."

The beer tasted better than she had expected and went down easily with the sandwiches and cookies. It went down so well that she joined him in a second. When Rachel asked for a third, Peter shook his head.

"Remember what I said about liking you sober," he said, moving closer to her on the coverlet and putting his arm around her. She could feel his warmth through the back of her blouse, and moved tighter against his chest. His fingers moved slowly down her arm. She felt happy but nervous at the same time.

"So, anyway, my roommate is from Gaithersburg and we talked on the phone last week and she seems really nice and she's pre-med," Rachel said.

"I still don't get why anyone would go all the way over to College Park for school when the finest university in the country is right here in the Commonwealth."

Rachel giggled. "College Park is twenty miles closer than Charlottesville. Plus, UVA doesn't have a library science program. Plus, UVA didn't offer me a full-ride scholarship. Maryland did."

"Still, it's not the Commonwealth," Peter said. "What with DC traffic, you'll be looking at a lot longer commute home."

"It's not like I'll be coming back often, and when I do, I'll find a ride. I'm not taking a car."

"Really? I had kind of hoped..."

Then he kissed her. It wasn't like the boys who had taken her to homecoming or Sweetheart dances or proms, who pecked her on the cheek and lips and touched her shoulders with nervous, clammy hands. This was a kiss like you saw in the movies, the way grownups kissed.

"Wow," she said with an embarrassed laugh as she broke away. "Wow."

Peter looked at her with an odd smile on his face.

"You, well, I mean, I, I mean, um, we probably need to start back."

"What do you call this color?" Peter asked, putting his arms on her shoulders and lifting the heavy braid that ran down her back.

"Red, I guess."

"No, it's not red. My truck, now that's red." He lightly stroked the wavy wisps of hair at her temples back off her face. Rachel shivered and closed her eyes.

"Auburn, then."

"No, not that either."

Would he ever stop talking about her ugly hair?

"I don't know. My dad says it's the color of a rusty nail."

"Rusty," Peter murmured in her ear as he removed the rubber band from the end of her braid. She felt his hands move through her hair, loosening it and scattering it over her shoulders. "Rusty. Rusty, you are one beautiful girl."

Then he kissed her again.

⁊⁊⁊

"Rachel?"

She rubbed her eyes and sat up. Peter was standing in the doorway to his bedroom.

"Are you all right?" he asked.

Rachel could feel herself turning red. She'd have given him a tongue lashing if she'd found him asleep in her bed.

"I am so sorry. I was remaking your bed and I…" And I what? I was remembering the first time we were together?

"Not a problem. You've had a tough day. The chicken soup and a nap seem to have helped whatever bug I had. I finished up the wash. It's nearly six. I thought maybe I'd go get us some burgers at the Cave for supper."

Rachel ran her fingers through her hair, as much to buy some time as to make herself presentable. The action reminded her of him running his fingers through her hair, and she blushed more. How long had he watched her sleep? What was he thinking? Had she called out his name?

"That'd be great. The usual for me."

"Turkey burger with lettuce and tomato, wheat bun, no fries. Be back in a half hour."

Rachel waited for him to go up the stairs. She waited to hear the door to the carport open and the truck engine come to life. She waited to hear the truck back out and start down the road. She waited until she couldn't hear it anymore.

Then she held the pillow tight to her face and kissed it.

29

The Cave didn't look like much from the outside, just a hole-in-the-wall, locally owned, mom-and-pop joint. But it was clean and well-lit and the food was fantastic, especially the burgers and the frozen custard. Jill had worked there in high school, and the owners had become family friends. Small wonder, then, that on the few occasions Peter had to get takeout, he thought of the Cave.

Most of the Shenandoah Valley shared Peter's love of the place. The parking lot was full, and the drive-through line was all the way back to the street. Peter parked next door at the bank, blew his nose and used his hand sanitizer yet again, and walked over.

Rachel would call this pandemonium, he thought, proud that he remembered the word. The twenty or so booths were filled with young families, giggling teenagers, and some older couples. He finally reached the front of the line and placed their order—Rachel's turkey burger, his usual third-pounder burger with cheese and bacon plus fries—and a couple of cups of banana pudding frozen custard, just because.

"I apologize, sir, but it'll be a bit," the boy behind the counter said as he counted back Peter's change and gave him a sign with his order number, seventy-five. "As you can see, we're crazy busy with folk in town for the high school basketball sectionals."

Ah, so that explained it. Peter felt a little bad. He'd never gotten back to Shoe about going to the sectionals. Kevin was on the basketball team too and would probably warm the bench the whole night, but it would have been a good outing with Shoe, David, and Dot nonetheless.

"Forty-three!" a girl called out, holding up a bag.

Peter sighed and moved toward the back of the restaurant. He asked an older woman at a table for two if he could sit at the other chair and turn it toward the television located right above the table. "It seems I'm gonna be here a spell," he said, showing her his number. She nodded.

Given the sectionals, he figured the TV would be tuned to the local news and a possible preview of the game. But instead, there were four women, two about his and Rachel's age and two about Jill's age, seated around a table. They were talking about, as best he could figure, whether women really did need different purses for each outfit. The ones Jill's age, Tamar and Sheba, were passionate yeses. One of the women Rachel's age, Ruth, was a passionate no, and the other, whose name he didn't catch, didn't seem to have an opinion. Peter rolled his eyes.

"And after a break, we'll be joined by an *On My Own* magazine contributing writer who's been creating quite a stir with her article, 'Five Rules for a Countercultural Breakup,'" Tamar said.

"Forty-nine!" the counter girl called out.

Peter took out his phone and called home. "I'm at the Cave, but it's packed," he told Rachel. "Be back as soon as I can." As he put the phone back in his pocket, he heard Tamar say, "And now, we welcome writer Kara Lane to talk about what she calls the countercultural breakup." The studio audience burst into applause.

Kara Lane.

Peter looked up at the TV, and there she was. While the four show hostesses or whatever you would call them were all dressed in showy sweaters and jewelry, Kara was walking out the way he'd almost always seen her—jeans and a fitted shirt, stark white this time, and black boots. She had a single, familiar silver strand around her neck. She gave that long red mane a toss as she joined the others at the table, a little bit of a smile on her face, but biting her lips.

His heart stopped. It was the chain he'd given her for her birthday. And he knew that smile. She put it on when she had to do something she really didn't want to do, like speak with a difficult editor on the phone, or like the day she dumped him.

Peter wondered if he could get someone to change the channel since he seemed to be the only one watching TV anyway. But the line at the counter was four deep.

"Kara, we're so happy to have you with us today," Sheba said, turning to the camera rather than to Kara. "Everybody's talking about your article. Can you explain what a countercultural breakup is?"

Kara looked for a second at each of the women, then seemed to settle on Ruth as the person she'd talk to.

"Well, I'd heard so many of my friends go into dramatics over leaving a relationship, whether or not they were the ones who initiated it," she said slowly in that throaty voice. Peter could feel his body growing warm, starting with his ears. His nose and his throat didn't seem clogged at all anymore.

"And I thought, why can't we treasure those times rather than diminish them? That doesn't mean we need to stay stuck in something that's gone, but we also don't need to despise ourselves or the other person."

Ruth nodded. "Those are pretty words, but having a marriage or other relationship end after decades because the person isn't who you thought they were, or they find some bright new shiny toy, well, who's not going to get bitter for a while? What's wrong with a little negativity?"

Kara ran her hands through her hair and leaned forward. "That's exactly the point. A little negativity has a way of growing into a lot of negativity. And that eats away at us."

Ruth leaned forward too. "Let me tell you, Kara, in all honesty, this sounds like a lot of pop psychology that is good in theory but doesn't work in practice. Our viewers know that I divorced my husband last year after I learned about his series of affairs. He deceived me for years. I went through hell. I'm still going through hell. I think hating him is the natural, healthy thing for me to do right now."

"Fifty-three!" the counter girl called out.

"After the break, we'll be back to talk about countercultural breakups," Tamar chirped, looking a bit uneasy. "And Kara, maybe you can share some of the rules from your article."

Peter thought about leaving the Cave and going to one of those chain fast-food drive-throughs. The last thing he wanted to do was hear any more of Kara's voice… especially since it seemed that Ruth person had it in for her and there wasn't anything he could do about it. But he wouldn't be able to get Rachel's turkey burger anywhere else, and how would he explain his change of plans?

"And now we're back with Kara Lane, who's got everyone talking about countercultural breakups," Tamar said. "Kara, your article in *On My Own* had five rules. Could you share them with us?"

Kara settled back in her chair. She looked more confident, Peter thought. She always felt that way when she was talking about the stories she'd written.

"Absolutely. Rule one is don't do anything radical to yourself. Don't cut or color your hair or get a tattoo or a piercing you wouldn't have gotten when you were together. Your brain's probably as big a mess as your heart is, and this is not the time to do something reactive."

The women around the table nodded at each other. Kara took a deep breath.

"Second, be gentle with yourself. Heal. If healing means an extra scoop of ice cream or a new lipstick or some other reasonable treat, do it. Don't think, regardless of what was said in the breakup, that you need to lose twenty pounds or double your workout routine or be more or less social. In a couple months, think about what was said, and whether you want to act on any of it. But not right away."

The woman who hadn't talked before—it said Rae underneath her on the screen—started laughing. "Amen, sister! I dated a guy for a while who I really liked, but who was always on me about my weight. Eventually, he said he was breaking up because I was too fat. I went on a crash diet and ended up in the hospital!"

Kara gave a real smile and nodded. "Exactly. Don't let someone else tell you who you are, ever."

And that was one of the best things about you, Peter thought. You were comfortable in your own skin, and you were comfortable with me in mine. No nagging about my wicked ways. You just took me as I was. He shifted a little.

"Rule three is end all contact," Kara went on. "No text, no email, no social media friends, no calls. Consider changing your routine—groceries, dry cleaning, coffee—so that you're not likely to run into each other."

"But what if you work with them?" Sheba asked, looking per-plexed. "I mean, I've dated a lot of guys who are coworkers. That gets really uncomfortable."

Kara sat back in the chair and gave Sheba what Peter knew was her oh-you-poor-thing look. "Sheba, I'd say maybe that's a sign you shouldn't be dating guys at work."

"Sixty-seven!" the girl behind the counter called out.

Kara sure had changed her routine, Peter thought. He wondered if moving ninety miles away didn't violate her rule about nothing radical. But he guessed that wasn't like Su-ZAHN and going blond or anything and, after all, Kara'd always had the place in the District. She was still writing. She was still dressing the same. And she was still giving off that attitude of not really caring what other people thought about her or her opinions.

He started thinking about her rules and him. Had stopping

drinking and smoking been radical? He supposed so, but he hardly missed either anymore. It probably had been radical to accept Jesus, but that couldn't be a bad thing, could it? And the only ungentle thing he'd done to himself was to humble himself and try to accept Rachel as she was… and hope that one day soon, she'd trust him again. But that sure was taking a long time.

"Rule four is find some joy. Laugh. Most times, breakups don't come as a total surprise, so you've probably been under some stress for a while whether you realized it or not. Play with some kids. Do a silly dance. Take a class in comedy. Volunteer."

All four of the women nodded.

"Seventy!"

"And Kara, what's the final rule?" Rae asked.

"Oh, it's the most important rule of all, I think," Kara said, tossing her hair yet again. "Never, ever, to yourself or to a friend say, 'What did I see in him or her?' Even if the person ends up having been a total con artist and even if your next relationship turns out to be with your true soulmate. It may be that you saw them at their true best, that what you saw was something he or she hasn't shown the rest of the world and maybe never will."

Peter closed his eyes. *Oh woman, you speak truth.*

"Well now, Kara, again, I have to say those are some pretty words," he heard the Ruth woman saying. "But really? If you saw someone at their true best, why would you ever leave them? What's wrong with calling a cheat a cheat and a liar a liar, and being grateful to be rid of him? You're talking like an enabler."

"Seventy-five!"

He opened his eyes to see a split screen, Kara on one side, Ruth on the other. Ruth looked self-satisfied, as if Kara were a bug and Ruth was preparing to squash her. Kara's jaw was working.

"I believe there is good in all of us," she said. "It can be hard to see. But we get glimpses of it, and we show glimpses of our own goodness. Sometimes, we need to move away from someone we love to be a better person… or to let them be a better person. There's no-bleness in that, I think. Why destroy that by focusing on whatever bad there might have been?"

Ruth pursed her lips. "And you know that firsthand, I suppose?"

"Seventy-five! Second call for seventy-five!"

Peter knew it was his number, but he didn't care. He needed to see her answer. He needed to hear her answer.

Kara looked at the hostesses, one by one, for a second or so.

"Yes," she said as the camera pulled in tight on her to show the start of tears. "I know that firsthand. Indeed I do."

The audience started clapping like crazy.

"Seventy-five! Final call!"

Peter shook himself the way Fifth did, and went to the counter and got the order. He called Rachel to say he'd be right home. But he took the long way, past the place where Kara used to live. Just for old times' sake, he told himself. He had wondered so many times if he'd been wrong about that year with her, if maybe she hadn't felt about him the way he felt about her. The tears showed the answer. She had loved him, maybe still did.

Peter slowed down just a bit as he approached Kara's place. Chris's husband was pulling into the driveway, and Chris, holding their baby, was standing in front of the big window, waving. Not for the first time, Peter wondered what life would have been like with Kara, permanentlike, in that house.

When he got home, he found he didn't have much of an appetite, not even for banana pudding frozen custard.

30

I wish we could hire you today," said Maureen May, the Museum of the Shenandoah Valley's human resources director, as she and Rachel walked to the main door of the museum's administrative offices. "But with the search for a new director, well, you know how it is."

Rachel nodded. "Of course, Maureen. I just wanted you to know I'm available. And it'd been too long since we'd seen each other. Thanks for lunch. Hope you and Harvey have a great weekend."

"You too," Maureen said, giving Rachel a warm smile as the women shook hands. "Hope to see you at church soon."

Rachel smiled a noncommittal smile and nod and walked through the door. She hadn't really expected the museum to have much need for someone with a master's in library science. But she was trying to get out and network at least a couple times a week, besides scan the internet for jobs in the Valley, and the museum was a great place to pass a few hours.

A passel of schoolkids were horsing around as they waited to enter the nearby Glen Burnie Historic House. But that wasn't Rachel's destination. She turned left at the circle drive and entered the

Chinese garden. She shivered a little, from both the beauty of the flowering dogwoods and the slight chill in the spring air, and took a seat on the bench outside the pagoda.

Jesus was here. Rachel was sure of that. She could hear Him in the robin's chirp, smell Him in the evergreens, feel Him in the breeze. "It's impossible for me to be angry with You in nature," she said out loud. "But we are still on the outs. If You love me as much as that squirrel over there or the lilies of the field, I need You to show it. I know my faith should sustain me. But it isn't, not right now anyway."

Rachel waited a minute or two to make sure she wasn't going to be struck down by lightning. "All right, I know You don't work that way. But Lord, I do need You to show me Your love in a way I can understand."

She rose from the bench and turned right on the road, visiting the Parterre Garden, the Statue Garden, and the Rose Garden. The roses were looking a little peaked. She wondered if the gardener had thought of using bonemeal on them. Then, on to the scent of chives in the herb garden and the smell of freshly turned earth in the formal vegetable garden. It was there that she noticed the sun's position and looked at her watch.

Quarter of four! Where had the past nearly three hours gone? The museum would be closing in fifteen minutes, and she hadn't given a thought to supper. As she picked up her pace, she heard a laugh and turned around. It was a tall, lanky thirtysomething man, pushing a wheelbarrow overloaded with nasturtiums. "Don't rush, miss," he said with a smile. "You got plenty of time. Enjoy yourself."

Rachel smiled, embarrassed. "No, really, I need to get going. But thank you."

∼♃∽

178

She had white turkey chili bubbling on the stove and was prepping green salads when she heard the truck turn into the carport. Rachel smiled and kept her face to the window over the sink.

"Smells great," Peter said as he closed the door behind him. "Anything I can do to help?"

"Nope. Just change and then come tell me about your day." She put the salads on the table and had just finished ladling the chili into two blue stoneware bowls when Peter returned and sat down.

"Would you like to pray, Rachel?" he asked as he had nearly every meal since Christmas, always with what sounded like a note of hope in his voice.

"You go ahead," she said, as she had since Christmas.

He nodded and bowed his head. "Lord, we thank You for the gift of this day and for the food we are about to eat. We ask that You hold Eric close wherever the Marines have him. In Jesus' name we pray, amen."

"About my day, they made me an offer that I don't think I should refuse," Peter said as he poured far too much blue cheese dressing onto his salad.

"What's that?"

"Day shift manager. Fifteen percent raise."

"I must say I'm surprised." Rachel leaned forward to better watch his face. "They've offered you permanent days before. You always said you liked having the occasional night or overnight differential."

He nodded. "The differential is nice, and so is the difference in the pace of work. It's the first time they've offered the shift manager part, and I think I want to say yes. I'm honored that they think I could handle it."

"You really don't know, do you?"

"Know what?"

"How good you are—good with people. People like you—look

at how the committees at church are fighting to snap you up. Plus, you're fair and a good listener. I'm surprised they haven't asked you before, frankly."

Peter squirmed in his chair. "Boss said he'd thought about it, but he was asking now because he'd heard and seen that my, whatcha call it, extracurricular activities were more in a family-friendly way these days. You know he goes to Redeemer."

Rachel could feel her heart pound faster. "That's just not right. What you were or weren't doing outside of work shouldn't have mattered to him. You could sue for that."

Peter waved his hand. "It's okay. But what would you think of me being on days only, Monday through Friday? Do you think you could stand having me around all weekend, every weekend?"

She laughed. "It's spring. There's a garden to cultivate, a yard to feed, trees to tend, hedges to trim. I can use all the help I can get in the evenings and weekends. And, well, one of these days, you're going to run out of excuses for not fixing my bathroom tile."

"It's decided then." He nodded. "I'll let him know tomorrow. How'd it go at the museum?"

"As expected. They're not doing any staff hiring until there's a new director. Maureen and I had a good lunch at that new vegetarian place. Then I kind of got lost in time in the gardens until right before they closed."

"You ought to apply for that director job."

Rachel laughed. "I've had enough of meeting with boards and preparing budgets. Besides, I've never had any experience as a fundraiser, and that's the biggest part of the position."

"But you could do it. And after all, we gave them five hundred dollars back when they opened."

Rachel had to smile. Peter was so smart about some things—how to nurse along an ancient piece of machinery, how to get folk to see his point of view on almost anything. But he was a babe in the woods about the ways of business.

"I know five hundred dollars was a lot of money to us back when they opened," she said. "But there were plenty of people who gave thousands, even tens or hundreds of thousands. Our donation didn't get us any special privileges."

"It did mean we always get in free to that Gardens at Night reception in the summer."

"I stand corrected," Rachel said, laughing. "It did get us something at that."

"Anyway, I'm kind of glad they don't have anything right now." Peter stood. "I wanted to talk with you about something else. First though, I'm going to get that peach ice cream out of the freezer. Want some?"

"No thanks. I'll just get some green tea while you do that."

She wondered what that "something else" was going to be. The previous Sunday after supper, he and Jill had been talking in whispers for a long time while Rachel was reading magazines.

Rachel went back to the table and let her tea steep. Truth to tell, having Peter around in the evenings concerned her more than the weekends. His presence would cost her a considerable amount of alone time for reading and the like, and she needed that. Of course, right now she had plenty of time for that during the day, but when she found another job…

Suddenly, Peter was seated next to her, no ice cream in sight, just a stack of paper about an inch high.

"I did some research," he said, pushing part of the stack toward her. "The Library of Congress only does training for guides—they call them docents—in the fall. Takes four months. But you can start as a researcher guidance volunteer anytime. Here's the application. You fill it out online."

What in the world?

"I called them and told them about your background and they said they'd love to have you as many hours of the week as you care to volunteer. You'd help new researchers figure out what they need to do to find stuff. Then, if you liked, you could take the docent course in the fall."

"But Peter, we talked about this before. We agreed that it would be a bad time for us not to be together, when we're in counseling and all."

He nodded. "I know. But I've been thinking a lot. Maybe being apart for a few days a week for a while would help us break some bad patterns, like Marsha recommended."

Rachel found another part of the stack being pushed toward her. "Now, I know you're not keen on driving into the District," he said. But I looked into the commuter bus, and it's pretty reasonable. Maybe take the bus in on Wednesday mornings and come home Friday evenings?"

"Washington hotels are expensive," she said. "That's a nice raise for you, but it won't cover all this."

Peter pushed another part of the stack toward her. "I found these listings on one of those internet roommate sites. And Jill says a lot of people who work on the Hill will be looking for house sitters because it's an election year. It's not so much as we can't handle it for a few months."

Yep, he had it all figured out, all right. Rachel started to say as much, then looked at her husband's face. He was twenty-one again, showing her the wooden floor he'd just finished laying in their bedroom. He was twenty-five again, anxiously watching Jill at Christmas as she opened the dollhouse he'd built for her. He was… he was thirty-eight, walking toward her into their bedroom with a dozen red roses after he'd come home from taking Jill to college, not long before they stopped sleeping together.

"You went to a lot of work," she said. "This was so thoughtful, I hardly know what to say."

"Say yes. Maybe you'll like it so much you'll get a full-time job and we'll move over there. Maybe you'll hate it and be happy to skedaddle back here after a few months. It's a no-lose situation."

"All right," she said, surprising herself. "All right."

It feels more like a divorce," Peter said, putting the pages down on the table. "Ain't we both said we don't want to split?"

Marsha looked at him, then at Rachel. "As I've said, I've found, and the literature supports this, that controlled separations are most valuable when the parties agree on written conditions. This is simply a template. What is it you object to, Peter?"

He picked up the document again. "Well, for starters, splitting up the finances. Why would we do all this, one account for Rachel, one for me, how much goes where? We're not even sure how long she'll be going to the District. Here's how it works now. All our money goes into a joint account. Rachel manages the money; she does it on the computer. Every week, we talk about where we are, and she gives me some cash on Sunday night. Whatever she gives me, I make it last for a week. I'm happy, she's happy. Where's the problem?"

Rachel nodded. "I'm with Peter. It may sound simplistic, but it's worked fine for us for years."

"You don't think you need to formalize the amount Rachel will have to spend while she's in DC?" Marsha asked, turning toward him.

"As long as I've got my Sunday-night cash and the debit card in case of emergency, that's all I need."

"Now, Marsha, I did wonder about this section on spending time together, since I'll still be in Lyman half the week," Rachel said, moving closer to the therapist.

"I left something in the truck." Peter stood and stretched. "You two lawyer-esses do what you need to do, and I'll sign it."

He supposed it wasn't exactly polite, but he couldn't stay in that room much longer and still be on good behavior. Out in the truck, he pawed through the glove compartment, between the seat cushions, under the seat. He found a lighter buried in the passenger seat. There had to be a cigarette somewhere.

Finally, he found one, behind the seat in the duffel bag where he usually kept a change of work clothes and a towel. It was in an outside pocket, a little crumpled but still smokable.

He held it, unlit, in his fingers, the way he'd held cigarettes for decades, lifted it to his nose, closed his eyes, and inhaled.

That agreement was just plain silly. Why did they need something in writing? Of course they wouldn't be physically intimate, with each other or anyone else, during this time. Of course Rachel was the one moving out, and she wasn't exactly moving out, just living in the District part of the week. Thousands, maybe millions, of people in the United States lived apart for job reasons. Did they all have written controlled separation agreements? He doubted it. What was going to be next, writing down who'd be responsible for feeding Callie the calico on the days they were both home?

Peter put the cigarette in his mouth and ran his tongue against the unfiltered end.

Everyone was so excited for her—Jill, who got all sparkly when she heard the news and started reaching out to her UVA friends to find house-sitting opportunities for Rachel near the Capitol. Lizzie, who was getting to the District more for estate sales thanks to her new beau, wanted to make theater plans for the three of them. No talk of Peter coming in. Of course, he didn't care for live theater, but it still stung not to be included. The old library crowd, who surprised her with a luncheon at a swanky place in Old Town Winchester. Even Shoe, who told Rachel once she was settled in to please come by and pick out a house plant on him for the new place.

For more than twenty years, Rachel had been the constant in his life. Jobs had changed. Friends, other than Shoe, had come and gone… or died, in some cases. Jill had grown and left. Cats and dogs had come and gone. Whether he'd been excited about getting home to Rachel or dreading it, she'd always been there.

But what if she was looking forward to being away from him? He stroked his chin. It'd be a whole new world for her, one he knew nothing about. She'd be meeting folk smart as she was, people who liked to dress sharp and talk about literature and politics. But they wouldn't know her the way he did, that she was way more beautiful up to her elbows in the garden, dirt on her nose, than in any suit. That behind those smarts and reserve was a scared little girl who put out her arms to keep you at a distance, but glory, once she put those arms around you instead…

He hadn't even heard a simple "I thank you" or "how wonderful of you" about all this, and it was his idea. Nobody seemed to think about that it wasn't going to be easy for him, coming home to an empty house two nights a week.

. He knew she'd cook him some meals ahead, that was just who she was, and he could make himself a hot dog in a pinch. The wash didn't worry him. He'd been doing at least some of his own for years anyway, and pretty successfully other than that time he put a red flannel shirt in with his briefs.

'Course, at least one person was suspicious of why this was happening. Lizzie had had a dozen of the church bunch over the day before after services to celebrate Rachel's news. Peter had gone into the kitchen to refill a water pitcher and ran into Lizzie, who was taking another round of mini-quiches out of the oven.

"So," she'd said, putting the tray on the cooling rack. "Who is it?"

"Who is who?"

"Who you're planning to take up with." Lizzie put the tray on the counter, stood up and moved inches from his face, hands on her hips.

He felt himself get red all the way to his hair roots. "You're wrong, Lizzie. Dead wrong."

"I've known the real you even longer than she has, remember? You want her out of the way for a reason. It's the way you are. You've got her back in a love and trust place, and it's going to kill her when you let her down again."

Peter thought about throwing some love and trust Scripture at her. But what was the point?

"Believe what you want. Rachel knows the truth, and that's all that matters to me." He went to the water cooler and started refilling the pitcher. He heard Lizzie give a disgusted sound, then walk away.

He knew it hadn't been all that long, but he'd really worked at changing. He knew it and God knew it.

Cigarette still in his mouth, Peter reached for the lighter.

He rolled the wheel with his thumb and set the spark. He'd always liked watching the flame flicker for a few seconds before lighting the cigarette. Somehow, waiting made the smoke that much better. Delayed gratification, he thought they called it.

The cigarette in his mouth. The lighter flame in his right hand.

He could resist. He knew he could. He'd played this little game with himself a few other times since January, and he'd never lit the thing. 'Course, it'd always been for fun, idle curiosity, not because he really wanted a cigarette.

Things were different right now.

Peter remembered that first inhale and exhale of every cigarette. Calm. Soothing.

He looked up to see Rachel leaving Marsha's building. Quickly, he put the lighter out and dropped the cigarette to the truck floor. When she realized he'd seen her, she started waving, big smile on her face. Peter stepped out of the truck.

"Ready for my John Hancock?" he asked.

Rachel looked down for a second, then laughed. "No need for your John Hancock. The more Marsha and I talked, the more I agreed with you. It was pure silliness, no matter what her experience and the literature show."

"You're sure?"

"I'm sure."

"Then let's go home."

Rachel talked the whole way back, mainly about her to-do lists, it seemed, but Peter didn't listen, truth be told. Rachel was still talking as they entered the house, and he figured he'd best pay attention now, just in case there was something she needed him to do.

"I do think a little space will help us put some of the past behind and work on today, like Marsha said, don't you?"

Peter nodded.

"But we're still wife and husband and that won't change. We've already got the only piece of paper we need. Anyway, I was thinking about reheating some black bean soup for supper, if that suits?"

"Yes," he said. "That'll suit just fine. I thank you."

32

Rachel pressed her forehead against the big bus's window and tried to nap. How could there be so much traffic on Interstate 66 at 6:15 in the morning? She knew people did this every day, but it still seemed crazy. She'd already been up for nearly three hours and on the bus since 4:40, and they wouldn't reach the Capitol South area for another forty-five minutes.

It had all happened so quickly. Her Library of Congress volunteer application was accepted within two weeks, even after she'd told them she wasn't ready to make the standard two-year commitment. A college friend of Jill's who worked on Capitol Hill knew someone who knew someone who was looking for a house sitter for her tiny condo at Constitution Avenue and Second Street in Northeast DC.

"It's perfect for you both," Jill had gushed. "She needs to be back in Wisconsin Wednesday through Sunday for the campaign, and you need a place Wednesday and Thursday nights. You couldn't ask for a better location—three blocks from the Jefferson Building."

Peter had taken a day off work and driven Rachel over to see the place. She wasn't sure "perfect" was the word for it, a five-hundred-square-foot studio on the top floor of a four-story brick building that didn't have an elevator. But then Peter had told her that someone else in the same building was advertising a condo for rent for more than he made in a week, so free sounded pretty good. The place turned out to be cute, mainly in a turret, with three long windows facing south, a comfy futon placed right in front of them. Rachel was looking forward to a couple-hour nap on that futon, since her orientation wouldn't begin until 10 a.m.

⁓⚬⁓

"This is what heaven will be like," Rachel whispered. She was on the second floor of the Jefferson Building, looking down into the main reading room. Rachel had been to the Library twice as a child on school trips and then several times for meetings after she joined the Gilroy County library staff, but the view never got old.

The figures of eight women, each atop a huge marble column, each represented a characteristic of civilized life and thought: religion, commerce, history, art, philosophy, poetry, law, and science. Sixteen bronze statues were interspersed among the column figures. Rachel recognized most of them, including Moses and Paul, without looking at the guide. The pink walls and almost arcadelike arches. Sun streaming in from the half-circle windows. On the first floor, study desks and people at work.

"Better than heaven," a male voice said from somewhere behind her. "First visit?"

Rachel turned around. The man who belonged to the voice was a little older than her, maybe fifty-five. He was slim and angular, about five-eight, with a salt-and-pepper goatee, neatly trimmed. Looking at him, Rachel suddenly felt like an overdressed country bumpkin. She was wearing a black pantsuit, one she used to wear to work, while he had on jeans and a white turtleneck sweater. His gray hair was pulled back in a ponytail. He had a gold stud earring in his left ear.

She blushed, though she wasn't sure why.

"No sir, but it always overwhelms me."

He peered at Rachel over the tops of his wire-rimmed glasses without saying anything. She could feel him taking in the pantsuit and her flat shoes. She ran a hand through her hair to make sure there wasn't something amiss there.

Then he nodded and took a step toward her. "You're not from here, are you? Talk some more."

"N-n-no, sir, I'm not, though I can't see as it should matter to you," Rachel said, stepping back. "I'm here to take training as a researcher guidance volunteer."

The man nodded again. "Western Virginia, but not West Virginia. Shenandoah Valley. Educated, but you didn't go away to college when you were young. Neither of your parents went to college."

Rachel was intrigued in spite of herself. "How might you know all that from what I've said?"

"You didn't grow up in town, but you went there for high school. You've worked hard to get rid of the accent, but sometimes you slip up when you're nervous, like now. You were born in Gilroy County. Farm near Bridgewater, maybe."

"Near Duffy," she blurted out. "I went to high school in Lyman. Who might you be?"

The man laughed and extended his hand. "Jonathan Richman. I didn't mean to frighten you. I'm a freelance researcher, and my specialty is Virginia genealogy. I spend a good deal of time here and at the Daughters of the American Revolution library on my clients' behalf, and the variety of accents in the Commonwealth fascinates me. Placing them is a little hobby of mine."

Rachel wasn't sure how to take the man but shook his hand. "I'm no linguist, but I know you're not from here either."

"No, I'm not. Minneapolis. Moved here to attend Georgetown thirty-five years ago and never left."

"I'd best go," Rachel said. "My training starts in a few minutes and I wouldn't want to be late."

"Yes, you'd best go." Was he making fun of her? "See you around, Duffy."

Duffy? Then Rachel realized she hadn't introduced herself.

Training was supposed to be a full week, but Rachel had been excused from the first two days due to her familiarity with some of the collections and the fact that her master's in library science had been earned in the past five years. In retrospect, she wished she'd come in on Monday. Most of the other ten trainees had backgrounds at least equivalent to hers, and she struggled to keep up. On Wednesday and Thursday, she stayed at the Library until it closed at 8:30 p.m., working on memorizing the layout of the three buildings and all the reading rooms. She thought she saw Jonathan Richman at a corner desk at one point, but she couldn't tell for sure.

Rachel was glad the walk to the apartment was only three blocks, because even at that, she was seeing a different side of the District than she'd ever observed on her work visits or trips with Jill's grade school and high school classes. People, mainly men, squirreled away in the nooks and crannies of building exteriors, settling in for the evening with only blankets and large plastic bags that must have held all their worldly belongings. Occasionally, she saw people passing small packets and cash back and forth. No one approached her, but it all made her feel uneasy.

She talked to Peter and Jill both nights, each for fifteen minutes or so, about as long as she could manage to stay awake. Peter said he, Callie the calico, and the garden all missed her, in that order. Jill bubbled over about her plans to meet Eric in Frankfurt for a long weekend as a birthday present to him. Rachel told them both she was loving life in the District.

At the Library, the others in her class and the trainers seemed nice enough. But all the small-talk questions were about what people had done or were doing and who they knew. It seemed to Rachel that she was the only one who wasn't related to or didn't know a member of Congress or cabinet secretary or Supreme Court justice or at least someone who worked for somebody like that.

Finally, 3 on Friday afternoon rolled around, and training ended. Rachel breathed a sigh of relief, and confirmed with the trainer that she'd be available on Wednesdays from 12:30 to 4:30 p.m.; Thursdays from 8:30 a.m. to 4:30 p.m.; and Fridays going forward from 8:30 a.m. to 12:30 p.m.

"Just come here next Wednesday, and we'll let you know your initial duty station," the woman said with a smile. "Have a great weekend."

"Thanks," Rachel said. The way she figured it, she had just enough time to get her bag from her locker, get to the commuter bus stop at 3:41 p.m., and sleep all the way back to Lyman. It'd be 6:30 p.m. by the time Peter picked her up at the other end. She hoped he didn't expect her to make supper. But on the other hand, she didn't exactly feel like going out either. *Good thing I have plenty of time to get over being cranky and tired before I get home,* she thought.

Rachel saw him before he saw her. He was sitting on the red brick retaining wall, wearing what appeared to be a new pair of blue jeans and a chambray shirt and reading one of those handouts people were always giving away on the street.

Peter didn't fit in, any more than she did. But she suspected he cared a lot less about that than she did. What she did care about, even more than she would have expected, was that he'd known how tired she'd be, and drove nearly ninety miles in the type of traffic he despised to pick her up. Rachel could not think of a time she had been happier to see him—ever.

"They'll let anyone in the District, I see," Rachel said with a smile as she gave a little bounce to join him on the wall.

"So they tell me," Peter said, putting the piece of paper down.

That was when she noticed he was wearing his wedding ring. Had he had it resized? Or had he lost weight? "But I'm more concerned about whether they'll let anyone out of the District, especially a certain new volunteer who's knocking their socks off at the Library of Congress. I know you District trendsetters don't usually ride in trucks, but I think even with rush hour traffic, I can get us back home faster than that bus. Unless you'd rather stay here?"

Rachel wanted to start crying and tell him how alone she'd felt and how all she wanted to do was get back to the mountains and the cat, garden, house, Jill, and, yes, him, in reverse order. But that wouldn't do. After all, it'd only been three days.

"Oh, I suspect I can do without it for a few days," she said with a laugh. "Where did you park?"

The man couldn't stop talking: What did she think of the condo? Was the training interesting? Where did they keep all the books at the Library? What would she be doing next week? Were they impressed by how smart she was? Had she gone to any museums or exhibits over lunch? He didn't seem to notice her answers were short and vague. He was still asking questions when she dozed off before they were even halfway home.

33

The little old gray-haired lady with the pillbox hat and white gloves coughed one more time and smiled at Rachel.

"But my grandmother always said we were directly descended from George Washington," she said again, in an oh-so-cultured tone.

Rachel sighed again. "Ma'am, I've told you several times now that George Washington had no direct descendants. Martha was a widow when they married, and George helped raise John and Martha Custis, her children from her previous marriage. But he was not a father himself." Any Virginia schoolchild could tell you that—the father of our country, not of sons and daughters.

"But my grandmother always said we were directly descended from George Washington," the woman said again, just as politely, just as pleasantly as the first five times.

Rachel was about to offer to hail a taxi and send the woman over to the DAR library when she heard a cough.

"Excuse me." Rachel turned to her as she turned to see Jonathan Richman. "Madam, I wonder if perhaps your grandmother was referring to descendancy from the Lewises, Washington's sister's children."

The old lady smiled. "That may be."

"Excellent," he purred. "If Ms.... er...Duffy doesn't mind, I'll be happy to show you where the Lewis papers are housed." He offered his elbow, and away they went.

Rachel watched until they were out of sight. The first lesson of training had been not to focus on an individual's research project, but rather to help the person feel less overwhelmed at the sheer volume of materials available. She had failed already.

"I should have just directed her to the Virginia genealogies or the presidential papers," she said, half out loud, as she walked back to her station. "What in the world made me think I could do this?"

The next four hours passed in a whirl: An undergraduate student from George Washington University working on a paper about folk music. A graduate student from somewhere in New England looking for the Walt Whitman Notebooks collection. A young artist who wanted to see some of the posters one of her relatives had created for the Work Projects Administration. After that, Rachel lost track. Finally, it was 4:30 and the next volunteer arrived.

"How'd it go?" the other volunteer asked.

"Great! Everything went great!" Rachel said with a big smile. Then she walked to the Main Reading Room and picked a vacant desk in a corner and put down her face. She thought about crying, except her head was spinning so fast, she didn't think she could. Maybe in the evening, after she got back to the studio.

"Patience is a virtue, Duffy," she heard that Minnesota voice say. "Patience with others—and yourself."

She raised her head, and was surprised to see a gentle smile on Jonathan Richman's face instead of the sneer she'd seen before.

"So is kindness, and I didn't do too well with that one either today," she said. "Thank you for helping her."

"She wasn't so bad, just confused and scared. Confused and scared people say silly things, I've observed. Other than her, how'd the day go?"

She started to put on her bright smile, then stopped.

"I'm not sure. There's so much to remember, so many collections. I did the best I could."

"That's all any of us can do. If you're done for the day, there's a coffee shop down the block. My treat."

"I drink tea," Rachel said before she could stop herself.

"It's all right," he said, swinging a backpack over his shoulder. "They have tea too."

For the next hour or so, Jonathan told her stories of his research adventures. She laughed especially hard when he shared that one client asked him never to tell anyone of his discovery that her American Revolution ancestor had spent time in jail for running a disorderly tavern in Connecticut. "I think she was afraid I was going to blackmail her with that information," he said as he finished his coffee. "I told her that her secret was safe with me."

"Until now," Rachel said.

"Still, I didn't tell you her name, or the ancestor's name. Discretion is the name of the game in my line of work. Enough about that. Are you feeling better?"

Rachel thought for a minute. Honestly, she was.

"Yes," she said. "I thank you for the tea. I think I can come back and face tomorrow, anyway. That's more than I thought a couple hours ago."

"'I thank you,'" he repeated. "That's a new one for me. Charmingly archaic, more formal than 'thanks.' Possibly specific to the Valley?"

"Specific to my husband, I think. That's what he always says. I don't know what prompted me to say it that way."

Jonathan nodded. "I'd be curious. When I meet him, I'll have to ask if he remembers the origin."

"I doubt he even notices he does it," Rachel said, standing up. "And besides, he lives ninety miles away, so you'll likely never meet him. Anyway, you two wouldn't have much in common."

"I see."

No, you don't see at all, Rachel knew she should say. I've just made this sound like we're estranged, when in fact he's giving me what he thinks is the greatest gift possible, to let me see what it'd be like to work at the Library of Congress. But the words wouldn't come out. Instead, she smiled a crooked smile.

"Goodnight, Jonathan."

"See you around, Duffy."

"My name isn't Duffy. It's—"

Jonathan put his hand up to stop her.

"See you around, Duffy." Rachel watched as he walked away. His rear looked good—not as good as Peter's, but good.

She had two voice mails from Peter by the time she got back to the apartment. "Just checking on the first real full day of school," said the first one, from his break at 3:15 p.m. "Just checking in— miss you, wife. Call when you can," said the second one, received at 5:08 p.m., right after he got off work.

But she waited. She waited until after she changed her clothes, after she had supper, and after she'd listened to a little dulcimer music. Finally, at 8 p.m., she called him.

"I was starting to worry," Peter said with a bit of a chuckle. "I was afraid maybe you'd run off with some senator. How'd it go?"

"Fine," she said, hoping he didn't hear the choke in her voice. "It was fine. What's new there?"

"Jill got the go-ahead for Frankfurt. She's leaving out of Dulles Friday night around eleven. I checked the schedule, and it looks like your commuter bus stops there about six. I was thinking she and I could meet you there, and we could all have supper together at that steakhouse outside security before she has to board. How's that sound?"

"Fine."

"Are you sure you're all right? You sound a little off."

"No, really, I'm fine. Just tired, that's all. What else is up?"

"I interviewed a couple of guys for that opening we have on the line. I don't know, I liked 'em both. Good work records, good references. Got a couple more coming in tomorrow. This hiring stuff is all new to me. I wish you were here to talk it out, but maybe we can do that Saturday. Oh, and Pastor Doug, he says he sure hopes to see you on Sunday. Some new project or other. And…"

He went on and on and on, all the little details of his life that she had missed for years at that silent supper table, but had been too proud to ask about.

"…and we've got an appointment with Marsha Monday evening. She's keen to hear how this controlled separation is working for us. I told her if the goal is to make me miss you, it's working." He laughed.

What to say to that?

"Rachel? Are you still there?"

"Yes. I'm just tired. I think Lizzie and I have something planned for Monday night. I'll have to check with her. I should go to bed."

"It's not even eight thirty. What happened to my night owl wife?"

"Maybe I just need a dose of mountain air. I'm fine, really. Good night, Peter."

Not even eight thirty or no, Rachel washed up in the tiny bathroom, put on her pajamas, and got onto the futon. She watched the traffic go by for a while, trying to collect her thoughts and emotions.

She wondered what was making her feel so topsy-turvy about Jonathan. After all, she'd just had tea with him, a man who didn't even want to know her name. He hadn't touched her. Peter could have been there; neither of them had done or said anything suggestive. But to Rachel, the devil was in what she hadn't said. She hadn't told Peter about it at all. And she hadn't told Jonathan that she was in the District because her husband had so wanted to give her this opportunity. Instead, she'd implied they were separated. And she knew she wasn't ready to talk about any of it with Marsha.

She thought of Micah 6:8, the King James version that was above the Religion statue at the Jefferson Building: "And what doth the Lord require of thee, but to do justly, and to love mercy, and to walk humbly with thy God?"

She hadn't done any of those things during the day. *Lord, please forgive me, and hold my hand to help me back on the narrow path, for on my own, I may become lost.*

"Our Father, who art in Heaven, hallowed by Thy name," Rachel prayed out loud, thinking about each word. "Thy kingdom come, Thy will be done on earth as it is in Heaven. Give us this day our daily bread, and forgive us our trespasses as we forgive those who trespass against us. And lead us not into temptation—"

She turned off the lamp.

34

"Well, that's that," Peter said as Jill turned back beyond the security checkpoint to wave one last time.

"I still don't much like the idea of them trying to get pregnant again so soon, regardless of what Dr. Kidder told them." Rachel shook her head.

"It scares me too. So does him being on the battlefield, and her being inside a metal tube going across the Atlantic Ocean."

No response from Rachel. But then, responses had been hard to come by from her, in person or on the phone, ever since she went to the District. She was working through something, he knew; you don't live with someone for more than twenty years without knowing when something's weighing on her. But he had pushed as far as he could without pushing her away. He knew that from hard experience too.

The trip back to Marshall Road was quiet, but quiet comfortable. Every time he glanced at Rachel, she was leaning against the back of the seat, eyes closed. She didn't stir when he pulled into the carport. Peter decided against waking her. Instead, he went inside the house to her room and turned down her perfectly made bed.

She still was sleeping when he got back to the hybrid and opened the passenger door and scooped her into his arms, then pushed the door shut with his elbow. She stirred briefly, then snuggled into his chest, like a million years ago.

As light as the day he first held her. He inhaled her scent—no perfume, just Rachel, but that was perfume enough—and carried her inside and up the six steps to her room. He placed her on her bed, took off her shoes, and pulled the sheet over her. "Sleep tight," he whispered and went downstairs.

Peter brought in the newspaper, put on the coffee, and dropped a slice of whole wheat bread in the toaster to tide him over until she woke up. The house felt so much better, just having her in it. Same old, same old in the headlines: Property taxes were going up. A printing company was going to build a big new plant over in Berryville, probably meaning 200 or 300 new jobs for the Valley long term. A couple who looked ready for the grave were celebrating their fiftieth wedding anniversary. He wondered what he and Rachel would look like on their fiftieth. One of the benefits of marrying young; they were already halfway there. He'd be sixty-nine and Rachel would be sixty-eight. Maybe they'd have a great-grandbaby or two at the party.

As he was buttering his toast, he heard Rachel come down the steps.

"Good morning. Sleep well?"

"I guess," she said with a little smile. "I must have fallen asleep as soon as we left Dulles. I don't even remember getting to bed. All I took off was my shoes."

He nodded. "I carried you up there and took them off."

Peter hadn't thought a thing about it at the time, other than that he didn't want to wake her. But the way she was fidgeting, standing on one foot, then the other, not looking back at him, made him wonder if he'd done something wrong. Was she upset that he'd touched her?

"Well, what's on the schedule today, chief?" Peter asked finally. "Feeling reckless and daring? Maybe this is the day we get started on the garden."

"Cultivation couldn't hurt, but you'll not get me to risk tomato plants outside this early." Rachel laughed. "Onion sets and lettuce would be good to get started. Maybe some mushroom compost for the sparse spot on the north side?"

"Sounds good. I'll start a list."

Compost. Onion sets. Lettuce seeds. Gas for the tiller. Stakes. Ties. Annual bulbs. Take in the hedge and tree trimmers for sharpening.

"I know you're busy, what with being away three days a week, but I wonder about the landscaping at church," Peter said, hoping he sounded very casual. "Shouldn't that be starting up soon too? Things are looking a little bleak there."

"I don't know," she said, frowning. "The back and forth seems to be taking a lot out of me. It's not complicated, just putting a few annuals in the same places as last year. Maybe Jill could do it when she's back."

"Jill's the best daughter in the world, but we both know she ain't got your green thumb or even mine."

"Maybe they could start a committee. I'm surprised we don't already have one, to be honest. There must be other people in the community who like to garden."

Peter snorted. "Redeemer needs another committee like I need another dress suit. Think about it, okay? We need to swing by there anyway to drop off the canned goods for the pantry. Then, the warehouse club and Shoe's."

⌒♋⌒

Pastor Doug was outside washing his car when the truck pulled into the parking lot. Peter chuckled. Another reason he was glad he wasn't a minister. Couldn't imagine having to keep a vehicle clean and shiny all the time like that. He turned off the engine and looked at Rachel.

"You coming with me, or staying here?"

She sighed. "I'll come."

Pastor Doug turned off the hose and was drying his hands as they approached.

"Hello, Peter, Rachel. How's the Library of Congress doing?"

"It's all right," Rachel said. "I truly do appreciate the opportunity. It does keep me busy, though. I'm pretty worn out on the weekends when I'm home. Sorry I haven't been here for a while."

Not since Jill's miscarriage back at Christmas, if you want to be real technical about it, Peter thought. And what was that about the Library of Congress being "all right"? Did that have anything to do with her being so tired? He shook himself the way Fifth shook himself after a bath. No need to think about all that right now.

"We thought we'd drop off some canned goods for the food pantry," he said. "We'll be running some errands after this, yard work type, and were wondering about the landscaping."

"Well, Rachel, you did a great job as always with the winter plants. Is it too early to think about spring annuals?" Pastor Doug asked.

"I'm not sure I'm in a place to help this spring."

Pastor Doug nodded. "I understand. What would you recommend, though, for those beds right in front of the church, the ones we all walk by?"

Rachel was quiet for a few seconds. "Pansies this year, I think. They're always pretty, and come in so many colors. They can take a light frost, so they could go in now. Maybe a few dwarf snapdragons. You wouldn't want them to overwhelm the pansies."

It was the most engaged Peter had seen his wife in a few weeks.

"Wife, what say while we're running about we get enough

plants for just those beds? Even if you don't have time to plant them yourself, it'll be a help that they're bought and here, right, Pastor?"

"Absolutely. That would be a big help. See you both tomorrow?"

"I'm not sure about that," Rachel said. "I'll have to see."

"It would mean a lot to have you here, Rachel. We miss you."

⁓ͽe⁓

"I wish he'd just leave me alone about the church business," Rachel said as she and Peter entered the hardware store's garden supplies area. "I'll go back when I'm ready. Just now, I'm still too cranky with God."

"You used to tell me cranky with God was the best time to go to services, to get it sorted at church," Peter said as he loaded another bag of compost onto a metal platform truck.

"And you didn't listen to me, did you?"

"No, that's a true fact." Peter moved on to the grass seed and bagged dirt. "But I never claimed to be as smart as you."

They picked out masses of pansies and snapdragons for the church beds, then the sets and seeds they needed at home. The platform truck filled to nearly overflowing, they checked out, loaded up their own truck, and headed back down the highway and into the carport.

It was a good afternoon, a quiet afternoon. Peter tilled the garden and worked in some of the compost, then spread compost, grass seed, and dirt over on the north side. They'd tried everything they could think of on that bare spot over the years—fall seed, spring seed, a profusion of hostas, a variety of ground cover—with no permanent success. But the rest of the lawn looked so good, it didn't make sense to stop trying. Rachel worked on the strawberry and asparagus beds and started some tomato plants in peat pots that would remain inside until after Mother's Day.

Supper was quiet too, Rachel picking for a few minutes at the vegetables she'd roasted and then excusing herself to her room to do some reading.

Peter went to his room and turned on the television to watch some baseball. The Washington Nationals were having their heads handed to them by one of the West Coast teams. He wondered why he bothered. At the end of the sixth inning, he turned off the television and got ready for bed.

I feel so helpless, Lord, he prayed. I'd rather have her yelling at me than quiet like this. Something's weighing on her soul. If she can't bring it to me, I pray that You give her the confidence to take it to You.

Sunday morning, 9:30. Peter finished his coffee and bagel. Fifth, who was staying with the Gregorys while Jill was in Germany, was curled up at his feet; Callie was purring by the sink. Strange. A second straight morning with Rachel at home, and no breakfast waiting when he arose. It was lonely, somehow lonelier knowing she was in the house than when she was in DC.

Ask if she was coming along to church, or just go? Her bedroom door was closed; he could tell that from where he sat at the table. An invitation can't hurt, he decided. But as he got up to knock at the door, it opened and Rachel came down the stairs, dressed for services.

"Good morning. Sorry you had to fend for yourself for breakfast," she said.

"No worries. I had a bagel and coffee, and maybe afterward we'll go to the diner with Shoe and his family and Lizzie?"

"Maybe."

Maybe was good enough for now. They got in the hybrid and were nearly to Redeemer before he realized they should have taken the truck since it still had the flower beds in the back. When they got there, folk were friendly and asked how things were going in the District without making too much of a fuss about how Rachel hadn't been to Redeemer for a while.

At the diner, he was happy to see Su-ZAHN wasn't working. Peter half-listened to Shoe's bragging about Kevin's grand slam in the big game the day before. The day's big surprise was that Lizzie had brought the fellow she was dating, an older, barrel-chested bald man she called Jed. He dove right into the conversations and seemed nice enough. Peter guessed he was glad for Lizzie, but it seemed odd to see her with a man other than John, even after two years. Maybe it was a good thing they weren't including Peter in their theater plans.

He kept watching Rachel. She seemed as disinterested in what was going on at the table as he was, not taking more than a couple bites of her vegetarian quiche and continually looking at her watch. That's some demon she's working, he thought.

Back at home, they changed clothes and read for an hour or so in silence. Then Peter got up and stretched.

"I'll just run over to Jill's and check on things, then maybe come home and change the oil in the truck," he said.

Rachel coughed and looked at her cuticles.

"I wonder if you could drop me and the plants at Redeemer. It'd be simpler than me moving them to the hybrid and then going over myself."

"Sure," he said, somewhat surprised. "Let's go."

Once there, he helped her unload the plants and tools and her kneeling pad. "I'll be back in a couple of hours. Call me on the cell if you're ready before then and I'll come for you in the hybrid if I'm not done with the oil. And wife, I thank you."

He wasn't sure what he had said that annoyed her so much, but it had been months since she had given him that look that could cut right through him.

"Why do you say that?"

"Because I appreciate that you came to church with me, and

that you're helping our community when you could be at home. Rachel, when will you talk about what's wrong?"

She shook her head. "Not that. I mean why do you always say, 'I thank you'?"

"What's wrong with saying thank you?"

"But you don't say thank you, or thanks. You always say, 'I thank you.' It's so archaic, so Valley, so uneducated."

He put his hands on his hips and stared at her. "You're gonna have to fill me in on what archaic means if you want me to answer that. But I am Valley, and yes, I guess uneducated compared to you. See you in a couple hours."

Peter got in the truck. It was only the power of prayer that kept him from driving the other way down Marshall Road and past Kara's place, just for the memory of someone who hadn't made fun of him for thanking people.

35

Rachel, I'm glad you could join us today," Marsha said, entering the hallway after Rachel closed the front door. "Peter wasn't sure you'd be able to make it."

Rachel nodded. "He isn't here yet?"

"No, but it's only five of six."

"Could I talk to you alone until he gets here?"

Marsha ran her fingers through her hair. Rachel thought she looked a little uncomfortable.

"I'll pay you for it. I'm not trying to get anything for free."

"No, that's not it. I'm finishing up something on the phone. Please go on in, and I'll join you as soon as I can."

Rachel took a seat at the small table. Their most recent sessions had happened there, and it seemed less threatening, them all sitting together, than when she and Peter had hugged ends of the couch and Marsha sat in the recliner.

"Hey, I thought you and Lizzie had something on." Rachel turned her head. Peter was standing in the doorway, arms folded across his chest. She swallowed hard, and looked toward the window. Storm clouds were coming in from the west.

"I was wrong," she said. "And anyway, this would have been more important. Missed you at breakfast."

He nodded and moved toward the table, sitting across from her rather than beside her. "I should have said something instead of just leaving for work early."

"I'm sorry to be late," Marsha said as she entered. "Let's pray. Heavenly Father, we thank You for Your presence in our lives and in our souls. We ask that You help each of us to listen, to share, and to love. In Christ's name, we pray. Amen."

After a bit of silence, Marsha spoke again.

"The two of you were talking about something as I walked in. Is it something you'd like to discuss further? I can leave you alone."

"No, stay," Peter said. "Rachel told me yesterday that I'm 'archaic' because I say 'I thank you' instead of 'thanks.' I didn't know what that meant, so I looked it up."

He pulled a piece of paper out of his pocket. "'Of, relating to, or characteristic of words and language that were once in regular use but are now relatively rare and suggestive of an earlier style or period.' Now, that don't sound like a horrible thing to me. But it sounded horrible when it came out of her mouth."

Rachel started to squirm. He was right; it had sounded horrible, and she hadn't intended it to sound otherwise.

"I don't know why I say it," he said, turning toward her. "But I do know this: I never pretended to be any great thinker. I ain't been in a classroom since I graduated high school. Still, I've worked hard. And even when we were at our worst, I thought that counted for something with you."

Rachel swallowed hard. "You're right. That has always counted for a lot with me. I'm sorry. Please forgive me."

She watched as the set of his face relaxed, his mouth becoming less rigid and then showing signs of a smile. The crinkles reappeared in the corners of his eyes as he tilted his head to the side. Rachel felt the way she felt when he'd look at her in the old days and then take her in his arms.

Peter let out a little chuckle that grew and grew.

"Aw, wife," he said, laughing so hard he almost couldn't get the words out, "not only do I forgive you, but *I thank you.*"

Rachel leaned back in her chair and shook her head. "Old man, it's a good thing you're a superior mechanic, because you'd surely never make it as a comedian."

"Well," Marsha said, "if that's resolved—"

They both nodded.

"I'm wondering about your thoughts regarding the controlled separation so far."

Wham! Just what Rachel didn't want to talk about with Peter there, but of course Marsha would ask.

Peter raised his eyebrows at her. She knew he was asking permission to go first, and she nodded, grateful. He turned in his chair a bit to better face both women, and stretched out his legs in Rachel's direction.

"I miss you."

A few seconds passed.

"Peter, perhaps you could expand on that a little," Marsha said.

He leaned forward, elbow on the table, palm holding his chin. As she watched him, Rachel tried to think about what she was going to say when it was her turn. Talk about Jonathan? Talk about how much she felt like a fish out of water in the District? Talk about how much she missed the mountains and their cozy little house?

Rachel was getting itchy. "I suspect you miss my cooking."

Peter gave her that look again.

"You're a great cook, that's a true fact. But that's not it so much; you leave plenty in the fridge and freezer. I miss praying with you at meals. I miss knowing that you're safe upstairs sleeping when I get up in the middle of the night and get some water. I miss your busyness. When you're at home, there's always something doing—cooking, cleaning, gardening. It's lonely without you."

His words were making Rachel tingle. And, the more he talked, the less she would have to. "Sometimes, it was lonely for you even when I was home. How is this different?"

"It was lonely sometimes when you were home, I'll not deny that." Peter shifted his focus to Marsha. "You asked me, back when I came here on my own, before Rachel started in, whether I thought I was addicted to sex because of the other women. I've thought a lot about that since that day, especially since yesterday."

"And have you come to any conclusion?" Marsha asked.

"I don't think I am. I read those books you gave me. I can only think of one time that the woman wasn't someone I knew at least a little from work or bowling or the bar or some such, and she…" His voice drifted off, and Rachel wondered about that woman.

"Anyway, it wasn't like I was carrying on randomlike with every gal in the county. Matter of fact, I said no a lot and took some pride in that. Stupid, I know now, but I did. Mainly, it happened when I was lonely or hurt or mad, and I thought that was the way to fix that."

"Did it?" Marsha asked.

Rachel wished she were home. If Peter wanted to spill this part of his life to Marsha, she supposed that was all right. But did he have to do it in front of her?

"For a while. Sometimes, longer than others."

"You were hurt yesterday," Marsha said.

Rachel stood up. "I wonder if it wouldn't be better if I waited in the car."

"Stay," Peter said. "I don't mind."

Well, I do, she thought. But before she could say anything, there was a flash of lightning and rumble of thunder. Rachel sat back down.

"I was hurt yesterday," he said. "And I thought about someone who used to give me comfort—not so much by listening to me whine, but by just being herself."

"Fantasized, you mean," Rachel snapped. Here we go, she

thought. All his catting around was really my fault. I knew we'd get to that eventually.

Peter shook his head. "It wasn't like that. But I prayed my way through it. Took about an hour, but I did it. God helped me resist that temptation."

"You'll forgive me for not hiring a marching band to celebrate," Rachel said. "You resisted once. Congratulations. Come talk to me when you've been on a right path for decades instead of days or weeks or months. Those temptations you talk about come to us all. The devil is lurking everywhere. You have to always, always be on your guard—"

The room flashed with lightning, then went dark.

More thunder and lightning. The rain started pounding hard against the office windows.

"Let's go ahead and end this for now, given the weather," Marsha said. "It's a conversation the two of you might want to have without me first anyway."

"Sounds good," Peter said. "I brought in an umbrella. Let me walk you ladies to your cars."

Rachel got home first. No electricity there either. She brought in the flashlight from the hybrid, and lit the cinnamon-scented candles she kept in the living room and kitchen. She went to her room and changed into sweats. If she remembered correctly, there was some lentil soup in the freezer. Wouldn't take too long to thaw it in the microwave. Then she remembered about the electricity.

She was reaching for her phone to call Peter when she heard the door from the carport open. "Hope you're in a mood for Chinese," he hollered.

When Rachel got to the kitchen table, she had to smile. He was laying out containers of what appeared in the candlelight to be her favorites: hot and sour soup and kung pao chicken. It would mean extra time on the elliptical, but it'd be worth it.

"Thanks. I forgot electricity would probably be out here too."

"No problem. Shall we pray?"

The kung pao tasted especially good, but Rachel managed to restrain herself and gave half to Peter. She politely declined any of his moo shu pork.

"Wonder what this means," Peter said, peering at the slip of paper that was inside his fortune cookie. "'Behind an able man, there are always.'"

Rachel giggled. "You know the Lord tells us the devil is in fortune telling and horoscopes and the like. But I would have thought the devil would finish his sentences."

Peter nodded and rolled the paper into a tiny ball. "That's a whopper of a storm," he said. "Brings to mind the one we had that day you and Jill came home from the hospital."

"It was the worst March storm I remember, or maybe it just seemed that way because I was so worried I'd drop her before we got inside the trailer. We neither of us knew much about babies."

"But we made out fine. And there was a beautiful double rainbow afterward. Remember how when she settled down, we went out on the stoop and admired it?"

The microwave beeped and flashed. The refrigerator hummed. Things were back to normal.

"I need to get some wash done," Rachel said, standing up and moving to put out the candles. "Thanks again for supper."

"Wait just a second, okay? I wanted to ask you something. With my navel gazing and the storm and all, you never got a chance to say how you feel about being in the District."

"Oh, well, you know," she said, turning away to clear the table and hoping he couldn't see her face. "It's still too early to tell."

"Do you miss me?" She turned around slowly.

"Yes, I believe I do. You and Jill. I'm glad I'm not gone for more than a couple nights at a time."

"Do you like the work?"

"How could I not like being at the Library of Congress?" She hoped he wouldn't notice she hadn't answered the question.

"That's good," he said with a nod. "We've got all the time in the world to decide if we should move over there permanent. Change seems to come no matter what. When Eric gets Stateside, Jill'll be moving away with him. There won't be much to tie us here."

Other than the mountains and our house and our friends and the garden and our church. Yeah, not much to tie us here at all.

"Making any friends over there?"

She started. "Friends?"

"Yes, friends. You never talk about anyone."

Rachel thought for a minute. She'd need to watch her words. "We're so busy helping the researchers there's not much time for conversation. And most of the people I do know live in Maryland or Virginia, so they're hot to get home to their families as soon as work is done. It's all right. I'm usually too tired to do anything but go back to the studio and read anyway."

Peter nodded. "Makes sense. I'll leave you to your wash; the Nats are playing Baltimore, and I'd like to watch. Good night."

Lord, I wish I could tell him being at the Library is different than either of us expected, Rachel thought later after she folded and put away the last of the warm-from-the-dryer towels. But he is so joyful about giving me my dream at last. I ask You to help me appreciate this gift.

The electricity went out again.

36

"And we're finally, finally done with tax season, at least until the October extension period ends," Jill said.

"That's good," Rachel said, shifting her phone to the other ear. "What do you hear from Eric?"

"That he misses and loves us all. He asked about how you're doing."

"That's nice."

"Mother, how are you? I mean, really, how are you?"

"This going back and forth is harder than I thought it'd be. But it's truly a great opportunity, and I appreciate what your father's done for me." Rachel wished she had a quarter for every time she'd said that to someone in the past month.

"Speaking of Dad—Pastor Doug asked me to remind you about the volunteer of the year dinner on Saturday. I think Dad's got to be a shoo-in, don't you? After all the work he's done?"

"Yes, he certainly has done a lot of work." And been an active member of the congregation for less than a year.

"Anyway, it starts at six and they're putting all of us past winners at one table. I'll come by around five thirty so we can go over together. Good night, Mother! Love you!"

"Love you too," Rachel said, then shut off the phone.

She didn't know which irked her more: the prospect of having to spend a meal at the same table as Connor Newman, who had been the volunteer of the year two years earlier for beginning a summer work camp program for teens, or having to smile and pretend she was excited when Peter was announced as this year's recipient.

God had to have inspired Peter's turnaround. There was no other way to explain it. He'd stopped smoking and drinking and, by all appearances, catting around. He'd given her what he thought was the best gift ever. And then there was his new relationship with the Lord, and all the handyman work he'd done at church, not to mention his heading up the usher ministry and teaching the work camp kids what they'd need to know to repair homes in Appalachia this summer.

But it still didn't seem fair.

Maarten and Mavis had been part of the church for twenty years before they convinced Pastor Miller to establish the Volunteer of the Year award. He'd argued that every volunteer was special, and it would be divisive to honor specific people. Finally, he relented, and the Grossmans were honored the first year. But it hadn't come quickly enough for them. They moved to Calvary the following year.

Rachel had volunteered every week in every way she could think of for going on twenty years before she was selected. And it was the talk of the congregation last year when Eric and Jill won; they were the first recipients ever under the age of thirty. Eventually, most folk agreed with the selection committee that the hours the Stantons had put in redoing the church library from scratch—painting, putting in new flooring, and rearranging and recataloging all the books—were impressive.

It's not exactly envy or jealousy, Lord, Well, okay, maybe it is. But I just don't understand how You let his walk back be so sudden...and so easy. I feel like the older brother in the prodigal son story. Where's my party? She shook her head and rolled over to sleep.

———— ✦ ————

"Hey, parents! Are you about ready for the big event?" Jill sang out as she walked into the kitchen. Rachel was taking lattice apple pies out of the oven.

"I will be shortly," she said. "Just need to put on a little lip gloss. Your dad's downstairs if you want to nudge him along."

Jill stood and stared.

"Sweetie, what's wrong?"

"Mother, are you wearing that?"

Rachel looked down. Khaki pants. Navy polo shirt. Blue deck shoes.

"Yes. Is there a problem?"

Jill sighed. "What did you wear last year when Eric and I got the award?"

"That was a year ago! How do you expect me to remember?"

"You wore a black pantsuit and low heels. You dressed like you were going to work, like you knew it was important to us. How do you think Dad's going to feel?"

Rachel rolled her eyes. "As I recall, your father didn't even go to the dinner last year. What's that say about how important it was to him?"

"Dad wasn't a Christian then. I don't think he understood. I'm not even sure we asked him to come. But you understand."

Rachel felt her heart beating faster. "I think you're making a big deal out of nothing. After all, we don't know for sure that he's going to win."

"As a matter of fact, I doubt I will." Both the women turned to see Peter at the top of the stairway that led to his room. He was wearing his only suit, dark blue, and a white shirt. A red tie was in his hands. Rachel looked down. He had on what clearly was a brand-new pair of black wingtips.

"I don't expect to win," he said. "I've been a member for less than a year. A lot of people work real hard at our church, and have for a long time. That's what makes it a great congregation. And Jill, I apologize for not going last year."

"Jill, please tie your dad's tie for him," Rachel said. "I'll be ready in about ten minutes."

She walked upstairs to her bedroom with what she hoped was a shred of dignity, then raced through her closet. She still had that black pantsuit Jill remembered—but it was at the studio in DC. So were most of her other clothes from the library days. Finally, she came across the dress she'd worn to somebody's wedding the previous summer. It was a sheath dress, sleeveless, light green, sweetheart neckline. Way too dressy for a church potluck. She rifled the closet again. Everything else that wasn't wool was too casual.

"Mother, we're going to be late."

"Two minutes," she shouted back, pulling on the dress, grabbing a navy shawl, and shoving her feet into a pair of mules. Rachel took a quick glance in the mirror; no time for makeup or jewelry, but she ran her fingers through her hair.

As she came down the stairs, Jill whistled and clapped. Peter tilted his head and gave her that lazy smile. "You clean up real fast—and real good," he said. Rachel tossed her head and gave a little bow like a beauty queen, and they were off.

"Rachel, is this your apple pie?" Connor Newman asked as those seated at the past honorees' table made their way through the food line.

"Why, yes, it is. How did you know?"

"You're the only one in the congregation who puts lattice on top of apple pie. I guess you didn't understand. People with last names starting with A to G were supposed to bring salads and appetizers. Dessert was for people with last names from R to Z."

"Oh, Connor, for heaven's sake," Rachel began. Then she felt Peter put his hands on her shoulder blades from behind and squeeze, tight enough that she jumped.

"Connor, it's my fault," Peter said with a chuckle. "I suspect I forgot to tell her. But isn't it great that we all get to enjoy that award-winning pie of Rachel's?"

"Well, it was in the bulletin. I can't see how you could have missed it," Connor said.

"Tell you what," Peter said. "You can have what would have been my share of the appetizers, and I'll have your share of the desserts. How's that sound?"

Rachel fumed as she watched Connor trying to figure out whether Peter's proposal would solve the problem. She glared as Connor took two pieces of her pie.

"Mother, there's a spot on the back of your dress," Jill said after they'd put their plates on the table. "Let's pop in the ladies' room."

It figured, Rachel thought. She'd never dressed so fast in her life, not even to go to the gym. She hoped Jill could arrange her shawl so that the spot wouldn't show.

"Where's the spot? What do you think it is?" Rachel asked, standing with her back to the mirror and craning her neck around.

"There is no spot!" Jill said. "You look fantastic. You could have spent an hour getting ready and you wouldn't look any better. I just wanted to remind you of two things. One, you made a New Year's resolution to get along better with Connor—"

"But he's an idiot!"

"—even though you think he's an idiot. He's still our brother in Christ. Just let it go. And two, this is Dad's night. It's not about you. Okay?"

"But—"

"Okay?"

Rachel sighed. "Okay."

They walked back into the church hall to find they'd missed

Pastor Doug's blessing. Connor was talking Peter's ear off, and Peter was nodding now and again. Finally, Connor stopped.

"Just let me know if you need help getting Craig to chemo again," Peter said, patting Connor's hand. The scowl that Rachel usually saw on the man's face was nowhere to be found.

"Connor, what's going on with your brother?" Rachel asked.

"Lung cancer."

"I'm so sorry! I didn't know he smoked!" How could she not have known? She remembered Connor saying something about Craig having a cough that wouldn't stop, but nothing as serious as cancer.

Connor closed his eyes and shook his head. "Craig never smoked a day in his life. Asbestos."

An awkward silence fell over the table. Connor kept his eyes closed. Jill looked up at the ceiling. The two other couples stared at Rachel, and not kindly. *Lord, please just make me disappear. If You can't do that, please help me keep my mouth shut so I don't make matters worse.*

"Craig's chemo is over to Woodstock," Connor said after a few more minutes. Then he smiled and looked at Peter. "My eyes aren't what they used to be, and Peter's been real good about driving us there every other Thursday. Don't know what we'd do without him."

"It's not a big deal, really. I don't have to take a lot of time off to do it. Happy to help," Peter said, looking a little embarrassed.

People went back to eating, which made Rachel happy. It gave her a chance to think about what was going on. Maybe Peter did deserve to be the volunteer of the year. She didn't have any idea he'd been helping Connor, any more than she'd known about him helping Felicity from the library on the night of her prom. What else had he done that she didn't know about?

Pastor Doug came over to their table. "Hello, everyone! Thanks so much for coming tonight. Connor, I think we're ready to get started."

The men moved to a microphone and small table opposite the hall door. Pastor Doug thanked Connor and the other five people on Council for their service in the past year, and said he hoped the coming twelve months would be just as fruitful for the whole community.

Then they started handing plaques and certificates and taking photos. The members of the Flower Guild. The members of the choir. It seemed like everyone in the place but Rachel got called up at least once. Peter was out of his chair more than he was in it.

"And, now, it's time for the Volunteer of the Year award," Connor said. "Pastor Doug, I'm going to turn this one over to you."

The pastor smiled and pulled a handkerchief out of one of his suit jacket pockets and wiped his shiny face. He put the hankie back, then took a folded piece of paper out of his pants pocket.

"The Volunteer of the Year award is special to all of us," he read. "Our church is full of love and volunteerism, and selecting the recipient becomes harder each year. Let's give everyone a round of applause, for all our community does to feed the hungry, clothe the poor, aid the elderly, and guide the children."

A hearty round of clapping ensued.

"I'd like to recognize the past honorees who were able to join us tonight. Please stand as I read your name, and remain standing until I'm finished." Rachel was called first, followed by Patricia Kobbemann, who had established Redeemer's food pantry; Frank Webb, who had set up a network to help the homeless find shelter in the winter; Connor; and Jill.

"Let's give them all a big round of applause!" Pastor Doug said, dropping his script as he led the clapping. Rachel had to laugh. She loved this place and these people. It was all very aggravating and disorganized sometimes, but it was home. She could see the Lord's light in every face, even Connor's.

"As you all know, Jill shared this award last year with her husband for the work they did on the library," Pastor Doug said. "It was the first time we honored two people in the same year. Eric isn't with us tonight because he's halfway around the world protecting our freedom. Please remember him in your prayers tonight and always until he's home for good."

More applause. Then the past honorees took their seats.

The pastor picked up his script from the floor and started to read from it again.

"This year's Volunteer of the Year award is very special to me and I believe to our entire congregation. It's the first time since I've been here that the selection committee's decision was unanimous." Pastor Doug stopped, took out his hankie again, wiped his face, and then threw the script on the floor.

"I wrote it all out because I was afraid I would cry, and darned if I'm not going to anyway," he said with a little sniffle. "I'm just going to speak from the heart. Tonight, we honor Peter Gregory for the hours and materials he donated to repair the church, for the time he's spent with the work camp crew, and for the things he's done for so many of us quietly. Peter, we are all blessed that, when you found your way back to the Lord, this was the place He led you."

Pastor Doug wiped his eyes. *Lord, we are all blessed, me in particular,* Rachel thought. The room was silent as the pastor struggled to compose himself. Rachel stood up and began clapping. Everyone at her table and the other dozen tables did the same. Peter put his face in his hands. His shoulders shook.

"Okay," the pastor managed to push out. "Peter, please come up here."

Slowly, Peter got out of his chair, walked to the pastor, and extended his hand.

"Wait, Peter," Pastor Doug said with a crooked smile. "I'm not done yet. You're going to be sharing this award—with the same woman with whom you share your life. Rachel Gregory, come on up."

What? But I haven't even been coming to services since December! Everyone was clapping again. Jill was laughing and crying at the same time. Rachel bit her lips together hard and looked down at the floor.

"Rachel, you've held just about every position except pastor at Redeemer, and I think you would have succeeded at that too. We're honoring you for all that—and for knowing, in the past year, that it was time to help some other members of the congregation step up. You made room on Council for Karen Jones. You successfully transitioned Seniors on Call to Connor Newman. We all know your prayers helped Peter find his way back to the Lord. The past six months have been tough for you for reasons we all know, yet you found time to do our spring landscaping. You exemplify volunteer-ism, and we thank you."

Pastor Doug led the room in one final round of applause. Then Rachel felt a rough hand on her bare upper arm.

Peter.

She didn't dare look up as she stood and walked over to Pastor Doug with Peter's arm around her shoulder. Ever so slightly, as they stood for the photo, she leaned into Peter's chest.

❧

"I told Mother that Dad was going to win, and I told Dad that Mother was going to win. Can you believe it? I kept a secret!" Jill bubbled on the way home, not seeming to notice that neither of her parents had had much to say to her or to anyone else since the announcement.

"Well, it certainly was a surprise," Rachel said. "I can't speak for your father, but I'm pretty beat. Are you coming over for breakfast before church?"

"Sure thing!" Jill said as Peter pulled into the carport. "See you guys around eight thirty. Sleep tight. Love you!"

They watched as Jill got into her car, locked the doors, turned on the lights, and then drove away.

"Quite a night," Peter said, turning toward Rachel and putting his arm around her as they stood in the carport.

"It was."

"May I kiss you, Rachel?"

Everything in her wanted to wrap her bare arms around him and bury her face in that clean white shirt. But then she thought about the trouble in her brain about being in the District in general and about Jonathan specifically. *Lord, when I come back to him, I need to come back whole and honest.*

"Not just yet," she said, swallowing hard and looking down. "Please be patient. Not just yet."

"All right," he said, putting his hand under her chin and tilting her face upward. "Good night, and congratulations." Then he put his hands in his pockets, started whistling, and opened the door from the carport to the house.

37

Peter dreaded Wednesday nights.

It wasn't just that he was tired from being up by five thirty to get Rachel to the commuter bus lot and then going home and showering before leaving for work himself. Wednesday nights lacked hope, unlike Thursday nights, when he knew he'd be seeing that brisk walk and shy smile in less than twenty-four hours. No matter when he went to bed on Wednesdays, he slept lousy and knew he was a regular bear to deal with at work on Thursdays.

He hadn't said anything to Jill about how long the time got, but she'd figured it out. A few weeks after Rachel started volunteering, Jill had scheduled father-daughter date night for Wednesdays. She'd come over and share one of Rachel's pre-cooked suppers. Then they'd play Yahtzee or Monopoly or maybe Go Fish or some other game until it was time for him to get ready for bed. It was a lot better than watching baseball or a movie on TV and feeling sorry for himself, that was for sure. He appreciated his daughter's thoughtfulness; to him, it had always seemed like she and Rachel had a special connection, and at times he'd felt a little of an outsider, truth be told.

But that Wednesday after work when he was setting the table, he got a breathless call from Jill. "Dad? Any chance we can have supper over here tonight?"

He considered the vegetarian quiche that was thawing in the fridge. He could take it to work for lunch the next day, he supposed, and maybe share it with one of the guys.

"I guess. What's going on? Something there need fixin'?"

She laughed. "Oh, no. Eric wants to talk with you about something, and he probably won't be able to do it again for a while."

Peter frowned. Jill and Eric had standing date nights too, Sundays, Tuesdays, and Fridays, when they used those web cameras and internet phones to talk with each other. He didn't know how it worked, exactly.

"Can't he just email me?"

"Nope! We want to do it together, like around nine o'clock, but you could come over now and we could eat and talk. Please?"

Peter smiled to himself. She was pregnant again. Must be just barely.

"See you in twenty minutes or so."

The tuna casserole was tasty but a little salty; Jill still had a few things to learn from her mother about cooking, Peter thought as Jill added her third house on Boardwalk. She had a few things to learn about decorating too; Rachel would have never used plastic placemats, even when they were just getting started, and the bathroom's green guest towel didn't go with the light blue wallpaper. It had taken Rachel going away for a while for him to see how some of her little touches made their place so cozy, he realized.

"Bankrupt again," he scowled good-naturedly as the game ended and they put away the pieces.

"You know, Dad, when I was a kid, I thought you let me win all the time. But now I realize you're just not good at games."

"It's a true fact. I can think twenty or thirty steps ahead when it comes to laying a floor or putting up drywall. Checkers or Monopoly or Crazy Eights, not so much. I don't know why that is, but I hope it'll make me popular with my grandkids."

Jill blushed. "It's about time to talk with Eric. Come in our room."

She fiddled around with the computer and that little thing on the top that Peter supposed was the camera, and then put two chairs in front of the monitor.

"Here's what you need to know. It's nine o'clock here, but it's five in the morning tomorrow where Eric is. It's a long way away, and the sound and video won't always match. Sometimes it'll take his words a few seconds to catch up with the picture. And, you have to talk toward the camera up here. You're going to be able to see Eric on the screen and you're going to want to talk to his face, but if you do that, all he'll see is the top of your head. Got it?"

"Not really," Peter said, shaking his head. "But I'll just do what you do."

"Love you, Dad," she said, putting her left arm around his shoulder and kissing his cheek. Then she typed in some web address, fast as lightning, clicked on Eric's name, and then "video call."

Suddenly, there Eric was! Wearing fatigues, in front of a computer in what looked to be a makeshift office, he appeared a little sunburned and, if anything, thinner than he was at Christmas. He waved and they waved back.

"Hi Eric!" Peter shouted.

Eric's mouth moved, but nothing happened.

Peter turned to Jill. "Is it broke?"

"Hi Dad!" Eric's big voice boomed.

Jill laughed. "Remember what I said about the delayed sound?" Then she pointed to the little picture in the corner of the screen. "And see, all Eric can see of you is the top of your head. See how you can see my whole face? That's because I'm looking up here at the camera."

Peter felt like an old fogey. He knew Jill had told him those things before they started, but he hadn't understood. He was starting to regret his refusal to take that technology class at the community college she had suggested. If he had, maybe he'd figure out how to use a phone like Jill's and Rachel's instead of his trusty flip phone.

"I told him we wanted to talk about something all together," Jill said. Eric's mouth moved and his hands gestured. He seemed very excited. After what seemed like a long time, his voice came through the computer.

"Dad, Jill and I have been talking about something ever since Christmas. We've decided I'm not going to re-up with the Marines when the time comes."

Peter's mouth fell open. "But all the time we've known you, you've planned for a military career. What changed?"

"Just listen," Jill whispered in her father's ear.

Eric talked for a long time, but what it came down to was that, when Jill had the miscarriage, he thought a lot about what would have happened if he hadn't happened to be on leave. He talked with his parents when he was in Florida about how hard it had been for them to raise a family when they were separated from each other and the rest of their friends and relatives.

"The short of it, Dad, is that I love my country, and if she's attacked, I'll be there in a heartbeat. But my priority has to be my family. Do you understand?"

Peter felt so proud of Eric he thought he was going to burst. He nodded and squeezed Jill's hand tight. "You picked a good one, Jilly-Bean."

After a few seconds, Eric was talking again. "Now, Jill, show Dad the property, would you please?"

Jill opened the file folder that was in her lap. "This is the outside," she said, pointing to a page of photos of a snug little cabin surrounded by spruce trees. The front door was red, and a little deck sat to its right. The next page showed a wooded backlot and ancient swing set. You could see a river on one side, and mountains loomed on the other side.

"And this is the inside," she said, flipping to the next piece of paper. A kitchen with those old avocado-colored appliances from Peter's childhood. A dark blue dining area with full-length windows overlooking the woods. The next page showed a large bedroom with windows facing the river, and a smaller bedroom that looked out onto the woods.

"There's a finished sleeping loft too, but I was so busy thinking about how many kids we could fit up there that I forgot to take a picture," Jill said.

Peter had all kinds of questions, but he could see Eric was talking. Then Eric's mouth stopped moving again. Peter waited.

"A friend of a friend of a friend's grandpa, George Burdett Smith, built this cabin," Eric's voice said. "It's over by Lyndhurst, across from the entrance to George Washington National Forest. Mr. Smith is eighty-nine. He had a bad bout with pneumonia last winter, and his kids and grandkids have finally talked him into moving to Charlottesville with one of the granddaughters."

"Isn't it just perfect?" Jill clapped her hands so enthusiastically that the folder flew off her lap, the paper scattering around the room. She laughed, then started picking them up.

"Mr. Smith built this place when he came back from World War II," Eric said. "He did all the work himself. He and his wife had six kids, then she died in childbirth with the seventh one. He never remarried, just raised all the children on his own, here in this cabin that didn't even have running water or electricity until the 1960s."

Peter groaned. Jill was right; it looked adorable—on the surface. But he could imagine the condition of the plumbing and wiring. A lot of these old coots who insisted on doing everything on their own had no idea about codes and safety.

Peter looked at the screen again. Eric wasn't talking, and no sound was coming out. He waited a few more seconds, then waved to let Eric know he was going to say something.

"I take it the two of you are thinking about buying this place?"

Jill nodded. "Just think, Dad. It's only two hours away! You and Mother could come down and visit us for the day, or we could come up here. You could come here for he-man hunting, not to mention fishing and canoeing."

Peter cocked an eyebrow at the camera. "What's he want for it?"

Eric came back with a figure so low that Peter had to ask him to repeat it. Jill then pulled out an email confirming the price. It was half what Peter would have expected. He read the rest of the note. Mr. Smith had told his family he was looking for a "sweet young couple, like me and Ruthie in the day."

"Six kids, and not a one of them nor their kids wants this cabin?"

Jill smiled. "Eric wondered about that too. But they've mostly scattered and no one is interested in the property. Mr. Smith is a bit…strong willed, I guess you'd say…and the family is used to just letting him have his way."

"Sounds like you know a lot about him, Jill," Peter said.

"I went to see him last Sunday. He's a real sweetie. Told me to call him Georgie. Showed me all over the property. I fell in love, with it and him." She giggled. "Sorry, Eric. You know what I mean."

After a few seconds, Eric's mouth moved in a laugh, and then he talked some more.

"Dad, everything sounds good about this cabin—in fact, a little too good. That's why we're hoping you'd go take a look and see what it would need. Mr. Smith said it'd be all right with him. But it'd have to be in the next few weeks. He'll need to put the place on the market or rent it for the summer if we're not going to buy it."

Peter nodded. "It'd be good for your mother to go along and look at the appliances and get an idea about paint and wallpaper. Maybe next Monday?"

Jill looked a little uneasy and waited for Eric to hear Peter's words.

"The thing is, we don't exactly want Mom to know just yet," Eric said. "Jill, you explain to him, please."

Jill turned to her father and took his hands. "We've got the money for the down payment, and if the place is in good shape, we'll rent it out this summer to cover the mortgage. Then when Eric's back home, he and the baby and I—" She blushed.

"I knew it!" Peter hollered. "Congratulations!" He gave Eric a thumbs-up, then turned to Jill and enveloped her in a big bear hug.

"Thank you!" Eric's voice said.

"We want to wait to tell Mother until we're past three months," Jill said. "The miscarriage brought back all kinds of bad memories for her, and we'd rather not give her something to fret about right now. She's got a lot on her mind anyway, what with going back and forth to the District."

Peter frowned and looked first at the camera, then at Jill.

"I can respect that. But why shouldn't she go to check out the cabin with me? I should think you'd value her advice too. She don't need to know you're pregnant."

"Dad, I couldn't help it. Mr. Smith and I got to talking and he told me about how his wife and the seventh baby both died. I don't know why, but I told him about our miscarriage and we both started crying, and it didn't seem like he was going to stop. So, I said not to worry, that I was pregnant again now. I'm concerned that he'd forget and start talking about it with Mother if he met her right now."

Peter shut his eyes and sighed. "I thought this family was done having secrets."

Jill and Peter both looked at the screen. Eric appeared to be listening, then his mouth moved.

"Dad, it looks like the perfect opportunity for us. Whenever I think of owning property, I think of the Valley. I've had enough desert between here and Twentynine Palms to last a lifetime. But I understand what you're saying about no more secrets. We're just asking that you keep this one for us just for a bit, just for six more weeks. After that, you can be the one to tell Mom if you like. Please?"

Peter shook his head. "I have to tell you both I don't like this idea of keeping things from Rachel one bit. But if you promise me it's no longer than that, I'll do my best. Now, how do I get in touch with this Mr. Smith?"

38

When she took her lunch break, Rachel found a text from Lizzie. Jed had surprised her with tickets to a big Kennedy Center event for that evening, and they wondered if Rachel would like to join them for supper first—their treat—at a fancy restaurant on the Potomac.

The idea tickled Rachel. This Jed was working his way into her best friend's heart, and the only time she'd seen the two of them together was that day at the diner after services. And in her time in the District, Rachel had gone out to supper exactly zero times. She texted back a big "yes" right away.

Rachel hurried back to the studio when she was done at the Library to shower and change and, feeling reckless, hailed a cab to the restaurant. She was early and took the opportunity to drink in the Washington Harbour shops. The clothes, home goods, and furniture were all too pricey for her tastes, but it was still fun to look. Not far from the restaurant, she stopped at an empty circular area. "What do they do here?" she asked out loud, confident none of the milling tourists were paying any attention to her.

"They ice skate," a familiar voice said. "You didn't miss it by much; it just closed in March. It's quite fun."

Rachel turned and smiled in spite of herself. It was Jonathan, dressed in running clothes and just a bit out of breath.

"That's right, you're from Minnesota," she said. "Do you skate here?"

"Indeed I do, Duffy. A rink's not a lake, but it'll do. I try to skate for an hour three nights a week from when they open in November until they close. This time of year and again in the fall, I run. June through August, I hibernate."

"So, the opposite of bears," Rachel said with a laugh.

"Yes, you'll find much of the District shuts down in the late summer, especially August. Too blasted hot and humid for words."

"If I'm still here then."

"Why wouldn't you be?"

"It's hard, going back and forth for a volunteer job. I don't really feel like I have time to explore here the way I'd always dreamed, and I haven't met anyone to explore with me, anyway." Rachel was just about to add, "and I miss home and the people there, silly as it sounds since I'm there most of the week," but Jonathan spoke before she could.

"Duffy, I'll explore with you anytime." He looked her up and down and smiled. Rachel wasn't exactly sure what he meant but she thought this Duffy person he kept calling her probably would smile back. So she did.

"Rachel! How wonderful you brought a friend!" She turned in the direction of the voice she knew so well. Lizzie was dressed to the nines, all in aqua and mauve, perfect with her blond hair and fair coloring. Her hair was mostly swept off her face in what Jill and her friends called a messy bun. Her skin had the kind of glow it had had when John was alive. Jed had the same glow.

"Jonathan Richman," Jonathan said with a smile. "I'm a friend, but Duffy's, er, she's not bringing me. We visit with each other at work, and I just happened to see her while she was waiting for you. I live nearby. I'm mid-run, and not fit to join anyone for anything, I'm afraid."

Rachel could feel her skin blushing furiously. Why, she wasn't sure. They hadn't been saying anything other than that remark of Jonathan's about exploring that she wouldn't have been comfortable with Peter and Jill hearing. She noticed everyone was looking at her. So, she made the introductions, and Lizzie and Jed decided nothing would do but for Jonathan to go home for a quick shower and join them.

The food was wonderful and the conversation even better. The four of them talked about Jed and Lizzie's latest finds for their shops, and Jonathan regaled them with stories about some of his research clients. And, he made it sound like Rachel was practically running the Library of Congress, she was so efficient in the way she guided visitors to the right collections.

"I say, Jonathan, Lizzie and I are coming in next month for a play at the Warner Theatre," Jed said as they all stood to leave. "We already have a ticket for Rachel. Should I see about getting one for you as well, so we can continue this?"

Jonathan gave Rachel that same smile he had about exploring. "What a lovely offer. Certainly. I'll clear my calendar for that. Duffy—er, Rachel, I'll get the date from you."

"Yes," Lizzie said. "Rachel's husband, Peter, isn't much for live theater. I'm sure he'd be relieved to hear Rachel had a companion." Rachel wondered if either of the men heard the bite in Lizzie's voice.

Jonathan made his exit, and while Jed went to say hello to some friends he'd espied across the restaurant, Lizzie grabbed Rachel by the shoulders.

"Now, what is this all about?"

Rachel shrugged out of her grasp. "I don't know what you're talking about."

"Oh, yes you do. That man is after you, and you're not doing a thing to discourage him."

"Hey, the two of you are the ones who invited him to supper. This is the first time I've seen him outside the Library, well, other than when he took me to coffee, oops, I guess it was tea."

"Are you that innocent? The innuendo? The looks? The smiles? The fact that he has a special name for you?"

Just then, Jed returned. "Rachel, thank you again for joining us. Lizzie talks about you all the time, and I can understand why the two of you are so close. May I get you a cab?"

"We'll talk about this back in Lyman," Lizzie said as Jed got the cab.

"Or not," Rachel said with a butter-wouldn't-melt-in-her-mouth smile.

What was Lizzie so concerned about? So Jonathan paid a little attention to Rachel. After all, Peter had paid a whole lot more attention to a whole lot more women before his conversion. And neither Lizzie nor Jill nor Peter had any idea just how lonely she felt in the District. Ending the volunteer experiment so soon would disappoint all of them. She had an obligation to stick it out a while longer, and Jonathan was making that a little easier—for her and for everyone, really.

Rachel paid the cabbie and, after climbing all those stairs, fell asleep almost as soon as her head hit the pillow.

Wednesday morning of the following week brought requests for guidance with projects on colonial music, Middle Eastern birthing traditions, and Russian iconography, one after the next. Finally, lunchtime.

Rachel collected her bag from the employee lounge's refrigerator. Sometimes, she liked to walk the National Mall during her lunch break, but this day, she needed to sit and ponder. Bartholdi Park in the national botanic gardens, just over on the U.S. Capitol Grounds, would be perfect. She perched at the base of the fountain, facing the perfectly manicured landscaping to the west, and closed her eyes.

Rachel had spent nearly a week ignoring Lizzie's texts, phone calls, and emails. She had begged off services the previous weekend to avoid her. But what Lizzie had said about Jonathan—was she right? Was Rachel truly blind to Jonathan's signals? She'd never flirted with anyone, not even Peter, really. She'd thought men in the District were just different. Whether she was here or at home, nothing seemed simple.

"I just don't fit in anywhere right now, Lord," she whispered. "Where do You want me? Please show me the way. Bless this food. Amen."

Rachel turned to open her lunch bag—except it was no longer there. She scanned the fountain in case the bag had fallen into the water or someone sitting nearby was eating her tomato, basil, and mozzarella salad, but there was no hint of what had happened. A group of schoolkids in uniforms were having their picture made. A few federal government workers with lanyards around their neck were seated on benches or the fountain edge.

"Something wrong, Duffy?"

It was bad enough that someone had stolen her lunch. Did Jonathan Richman really need to see her frazzled and confused yet again?

"Someone stole my lunch while I was praying. It's not the end of the world; I have money back at the library and can buy something. The person must have needed my lunch more than I did. And stop calling me Duffy. My name is Rachel Gregory."

"All right, Rachel," he said, sitting down next to her and opening his own lunch sack. "Care for half a soggy tuna sandwich?"

She couldn't help but laugh. "Please."

He said he'd been working at the DAR library, coming to the end of a big project for a deep-pocketed client who was a lineage junkie.

"What's a lineage junkie?" Rachel asked.

"You know how some people are addicted to tobacco or drugs or their phones or chocolate? She's addicted to genealogy societies. I've already gotten her into the DAR, Colonial Dames, First Families of Virginia, First Families of Boston, the Associated Daughters of Early American Witches, the Jamestowne Society, Magna Charta Dames and Barons, the General Society of Mayflower Descendants, the Society of Colonial Wars, even Descendants of the Knights of Bath."

"My goodness!" Rachel said, laughing. "That's a curious obsession. What else is left?"

"The General Society of the War of 1812, and I fear I've reached a dead end there."

"But I don't understand. If she had folk in the Revolution, it would seem logical they had children or grandchildren in the next war."

"So you would think. But you see, Rachel, there's a problem. They either evaded service or became—" His voice took on a dramatic tone. "—pacifists!"

Rachel laughed harder than she'd laughed for a long time, so hard that tears rolled down her cheeks.

"I'm glad you're not upset anymore, but it's not all that funny," Jonathan said in an injured tone. "This project is becoming hopeless, and the woman is a major client. It will be difficult for me to replace the income."

"Oh, Jonathan, I'm sorry, but don't you see the lunacy here?" Rachel said between gasps, trying to dry her eyes. "People in this city so desperate or mean that someone just stole my lunch in broad daylight, and you're in a knot about whether a client can get membership in some nutty society?"

"Maybe it's crazy to you, but genealogy matters to people. So does history. Woman, you're volunteering at the Library of Congress, I presume because you have nothing else to do with your time. I imagine you have some sort of advanced degree and research background from some backwater college. But surely, even you understand the importance of documents and records and history."

"I do understand." Rachel put the uneaten sandwich half on top of Jonathan's brown bag and stood. "I spent nine years as a full-time librarian, including a few months as head librarian, in Lyman. You know, where we speak in an archaic yet charming manner. We won all kinds of awards for children's reading programs, and to me, it's a lot more important to build young minds than to obsess about getting into some stuffy old society. And, by the way—my master's? It came from Drexel's online program. It's a highly accredited university in Philadelphia. Maybe you've heard of it."

Jonathan stared at her, then stood up.

"You may be the most self-absorbed, defensive woman I have ever met," he said.

And then he drew her to him and kissed her.

Long.

Deep.

Hungry.

39

Rachel pulled back, shaking, and slapped Jonathan. Hard. "What in the world made you think you had the right to do that?" she shouted.

"Do you really want to do this here in public, Duffy?" He rubbed his cheek.

"You seemed to think it was a good idea to kiss me here in public. And for the umpteenth time, my name is Rachel. R-A-C-H-E-L."

She marched to a bench at the head of the triangular park. It was out in the open, as far from the Shade Garden or the Romantic Garden as she could get. Lizzie had been right. She had been blind. Jonathan followed and sat on the opposite end of the bench.

"You are incredibly attractive, you know," he said, looking straight ahead.

Rachel snorted. "Then why did you just say I was the most self-absorbed, defensive woman you'd ever met?"

"Because you are. That's part of the attraction. You're so focused on whatever's going on inside that Drexel-educated—see, I do listen sometimes—brain of yours that you have no idea of the way those eyes flash when you're challenged, whether it's me or the pillbox hat doyenne. You don't know the way your face lights up when you figure out the first step for a newbie researcher. You also don't know about that confused scowl that appears on your face anytime you see me. It's why I kissed you. I wanted to—and I thought you wanted me to."

Rachel shook her head. "Pretty words. But whether any of them are true doesn't matter. The fact is that I'm married, and you know that."

"You said he's away in the hinterlands and that I'd never meet him. I took that as code."

"Code for what? What are you talking about?"

"That something wasn't working for you in your marriage—and you'd be open."

"Open to what?"

Jonathan sighed and rested his face in his hands for a few seconds, then looked toward the fountain.

"Rachel, are you truly that naïve? Because if you are, it's charming in its own way. But do not try to play the innocent if you aren't. You're not sophisticated enough to pull it off."

What language is he speaking? Rachel thought. Why am I even still sitting here?

"It seems you know a great deal about me," she said. "I'm self-absorbed. I'm defensive. I'm married. I hail from Duffy, Virginia, and I worked for the library in Lyman. I have a master's degree from Drexel. As far as you're concerned, I can pass for beautiful at least some of the time, when I don't have a scowl on my face. All I know about you is your name, you appear to make a good living doing research for rich people, you went to Georgetown, you're a good conversationalist, and you grew up in Minneapolis."

"And you know that I kiss well."

Rachel let the remark sit.

"I'm fifty-six," he said finally, continuing to look at the fountain, tapping his fingertips together. "Widowed five years ago. She had MS. I quit my job at the National Archives to care for her full time. That ate up all our savings, and I don't regret it. No children. I'm lonely, Rachel. You seemed to be lonely too. That's all. No offense intended."

Lonely? Is that all this man thinks there is to kissing a woman, loneliness?

"My husband and I have a grown daughter," she said. "I've been married for twenty-six years. I was eighteen and pregnant. I convinced myself that God was punishing me for having given into temptation. I buried myself in righteous church work, even though my motivation wasn't very godly. As long as God was punishing me, I thought I'd punish my husband. He got lonely, as you put it, frequently."

Jonathan coughed and started to say something, but Rachel motioned for him to be quiet.

"Something happened last fall, and he found the Lord. Sometimes, I think he knows the Lord better than I ever have. He also knows it always was my dream to work at the Library of Congress. He's making a lot of sacrifices for me to volunteer here a few days a week."

"Rachel, this isn't a conversion opportunity. Nor do I want another wife. I'm simply looking for someone reasonably attractive and intelligent with whom to spend time, to explore as you put it. If you're not interested, you're not interested. I'll live."

"You did interest me; I can't say that you didn't. For a few weeks, I've let that work up something in me. But I never encouraged you or flirted with you, Jonathan. My conscience is clear on that part. If I were truly interested in finding another man, I would have left my husband years ago. I love him."

Rachel stopped, short of breath, and put her hand to her chest.

Had she just said it? "I love him"? Not "I loved him," but love him, present tense.

"Maybe this isn't a conversion opportunity for you, Jonathan, but it is for me. I don't belong here in the District, where people steal my lunch bag and talk in code. I'm afraid to walk three blocks after dark here and to drive anytime. I miss the mountains. I miss my garden. I miss my husband. And now, if you'll excuse me, I need to do something about all that."

Rachel patted Jonathan's hand, and spun around, walking quickly back toward the Jefferson Building. She looked at her watch: 2 p.m. People at the reference desk wouldn't be happy with her. Well, another ten minutes wouldn't matter. She pulled her cell phone out of her jacket pocket.

"You've reached Peter Gregory. Pease leave a message at the tone."

When had he added his name back to his voice mail greeting? How many other little signs had she missed?

"Hi, it's me. I'm coming home for good. I miss the garden, Callie, and you, not in that order. The bus gets to the commuter lot at 6:25 p.m. If you could pick me up, I'd be much obliged. I—"

Goodness, she thought, I can't say for the first time in years that I love him in a voice mail!

"I thank you, Peter."

She explained to the research volunteer supervisor that she'd be leaving, and fifteen minutes later was back at the studio, packing up. Then she stopped. Why not stay till Friday and take a little time to see the museums? Who knew when she'd have this opportunity again? It'd be a shame not to take advantage of it, and Lyman would keep.

Her phone chimed at 5:03 p.m. It was Peter. She waited a few chimes. What was he going to say? What was *she* going to say? Finally, she picked up.

"Hi there," she said as cheerily as she could with a knot in her throat. "Did you get my message?"

"I did. You're sure?"

"Positive. Except I'm going to stay until Friday."

"It's only Wednesday. If you're positive, why wait? It's only Wednesday. I can drive over yet tonight."

Rachel giggled. "Hold your horses. I'm going to hit some museums and galleries tomorrow and Friday morning, stuff I love that drives you crazy and that I never had the energy to do after work."

"All right, I guess," he said with a mock growl in his voice that made her laugh all the more. "I'll be waiting at that lot with rings on my fingers and bells on my toes on Friday. But tell me more about why you're quitting?"

"Somebody stole my lunch today, right out in broad daylight at a fountain. I closed my eyes to pray and when I opened them, it was gone."

"Whoa! Are you all right?"

"I'm fine. A friend came along who was all self-absorbed about something that wouldn't matter a hill of beans to you or me, and that was the final thump on the head I needed. I'll tell you more at home. But enough about me. What's going on with you?"

Peter laughed. "Talking to Callie too much. Forgetting to recycle. Playing the radio too loud. Eating too much fast-food garbage since my wife isn't here to make me eat right."

"Yes, I've heard about your wife," she said. "She's a strict one. Makes you walk the line."

"The good Lord knows someone's got to. See you soon, Rachel. Love you."

"Bye-bye," she said and ended the call. And then, when she was sure he was no longer there: "Love you too, Peter."

40

"Yee-haw!" Peter shouted, picking up Callie and twirling around. "Hallelujah, Callie, she's coming home for good!"

Callie gave a bit of a yowl and scampered away as soon as Peter put her down.

"Callie! I say, Callie! Aren't you excited? She's coming home!" Peter went running after the cat for another dance, and found her hiding behind the toilet in Rachel's bathroom.

"Now there's a thought, cat." Peter rubbed his chin. "If I can get the time off work, I'd have time to get the old tile out and the new tile in, even if it turns out the subfloor's a mess. Wouldn't that be a surprise for her?"

Nothing crazy was going on at the factory, and the two new guys seemed to be working out fine. Peter made a quick call to his boss. He apologized for the late notice, and asked if someone could cover for him till Monday. No problem, the boss said.

The next call was to Shoe. "Any chance of borrowing your electric chipper first thing tomorrow?"

Shoe laughed. "Finally gonna take on that bathroom tile, eh? What's the occasion? Mother's Day? And isn't Rachel's birthday coming up?"

"I'm gonna level with you," Peter said. "Till you said that, I forgot Mother's Day is Sunday. So's Rachel's birthday. But Friday is a way more special day on Marshall Road. She's coming home for good, Shoe. Says the District ain't for her after all, and she sounds real excited about being back here full time. I've been jawing about that bathroom tile for months. It's time for me to stop talking and start doing."

"Praise the Lord. I'll bring over the chipper around eight, and help you pull up the old stuff. Dot can manage at the store by herself for the morning."

"Appreciate it. See you then."

That evening was game 5 of the hockey playoffs, and Peter had canceled father-daughter date night in favor of ordering pizza and holing up and rooting the Washington Capitals on to victory. But instead, he found himself prowling about the house like, well, Callie. He put contractor bags for the tile outside the bathroom door, and gathered up the sponges and rags he and Shoe would need. With any luck, they could pull up the old tile in the morning and even out the subfloor if needed. In the afternoon, he could cut and mortar in the new tile he'd had for months, then let it cure overnight and grout it all before Rachel got home.

From there, it was onto the living room, where he did his best to dust the bookshelves and photos. He was taken aback at how much came up on the rag. It wasn't like Rachel hadn't been doing any housework during the part of the week that she was home, but it gave him a new appreciation for just how much there was to do around the place.

He decided to wait until Friday afternoon to vacuum, then headed for the kitchen. Just for good measure, he set the oven to self-clean overnight, wiped the refrigerator shelves—they were sadly bare, maybe he'd pick up a few groceries on Friday as well—and put some baking soda down the garbage disposal. He was surprised when he looked at the kitchen clock and saw it was ten. Where had the time gone?

Peter wasn't sure why, but he found himself heading up the stairs to Rachel's bedroom. He turned on the light and took a step inside.

The pine tree pattern quilt was on the bed like always. The nightstand looked bare without her Bible, but he figured she'd taken it to the District with her. That was when he noticed it. On her dresser, right beside the acrylic stand that held her earrings, was the small box he'd given her on their wedding day. He'd been proud of that box, which he'd made from a fallen limb along the old trail.

Peter picked it up. As he recalled, he'd done a right fine job mitering the corners before he stained it. He opened it to examine his craftsmanship and smiled. Inside were a half-dozen or so crumbling pinecones. From that day. Carefully, he closed the box and turned off the light.

After he'd cleaned up, Peter got into bed and opened his Bible to Mark 4. He read again about the seed that the birds ate; the seed that withered for lack of roots; the seed that was choked by thorns.

"Folk scattered a lot of seed on Your behalf over the years, Lord," he prayed. "Shoe. Rachel. Jill. Eric. John. Funny that You were able to use a wrong relationship to set this soil right for hearing Your Word and bearing Your fruit. I guess all that good seed was just lying dormant all that time, waiting. Lord, I thank You for giving me second chances, with You and with Rachel. I humbly ask that You continue to light the way for us. Amen."

As Peter reached to turn out the light, Callie jumped onto his chest and licked his nose. It tickled.

⁓୨ୡ⁓

Peter lifted his dust mask and smiled. "We do good work, Shoe." It was barely 11 Thursday morning, and all the old cornflower blue tile was pulled up and disposed of.

"'Course it helps that the subfloor was in such good shape,"

Shoe said as he stood up and stretched. "Kind of surprising in a house this age. Also helps that this bathroom's barely big enough to turn around in."

Peter laughed. "We decided nine-by-nine was plenty big enough, especially once we put the shower stall and tank in the basement when Jill got to be a teenager."

"Well, let's get the thinset down. Then I need to get back to the store."

Several hours later, Peter backed out of the bathroom on his knees and surveyed his work. Everything was squared and level. The faded green tile Rachel had picked out was just right with the beige shower stall, vanity, and patterned wallpaper.

He went into the kitchen and poured himself a cup of coffee as he made his Friday list: Get a haircut. Grout the tile. Pick up groceries. Buy a birthday card and flowers, some for Rachel and Jill, some to take to his mama's spot in the cemetery on Sunday. Meet Rachel at the commuter lot. Check in with Jill—

As if on cue, his cell phone rang with "Jillian's Song."

"Say, I was just gonna call you about Sunday brunch. Your place, or here?"

"Hey, Dad. I need to ask you a big favor."

"Anything," he said with a smile. This pregnancy thing seemed to be affecting her hearing a little.

"I just heard from Mr. Smith. He's been in the hospital. Pneumonia again."

"Oh my. Sorry to hear that."

"He says he's faring pretty well but gets tired easily. Dad, one of his daughters is visiting from Charlottesville for Mother's Day, and she can take him to the cabin tomorrow. Is there any way you could take some time off and go over and meet them? I know it's short notice, but…"

Peter frowned. "I'm already taking the day off to finish up the bathroom tile. I got a bunch of other errands to do before I pick your mother up from the bus around six thirty. She tell you she's coming home for good?"

"Yes, she texted me, and I want to know more about why. But Dad, if we can't give the Smiths a decision tomorrow, they'll put the cabin on the market. And you know how much Eric values your opinion. Painting and appliances we can handle, but we can't tell anything about the foundation from the photos. Neither of us wants to do this unless it's got the Peter Gregory thumbs-up."

"Having this house ready for your mother is important too."

"I should think—" Jill stopped. "All right. I'm not going to tease or beg. I'll abide by your decision."

"Give me a second, okay?" He put the phone on the table and mentally walked through the day. It'd take him two hours to get there, two hours to get back, assuming he beat those thunderstorms they said were coming in the afternoon. An hour to look the place over. The floor wouldn't be ready for grouting till four or so anyway. It'd be close, but he could get his haircut and the flowers between 5 p.m. and picking up Rachel.

"Tell your boyfriend I'll be at the cabin at noon," he said. "And Jill? I sure hope we can tell your mother about all this soon." As he closed the phone, it fell from his hand and skittered across the floor, the back coming off and the battery dislodging. He put it back together and went downstairs to catch the hockey game's recap.

41

Rachel was at the Renwick Gallery when it opened at 10 a.m. on Thursday. People were already taking photos by the White House a block up Pennsylvania Avenue and holding protest signs in Lafayette Square. But Rachel didn't care about any of that. She was on a mission.

Her schedule permitted precisely one hour at the Renwick, the home of the Smithsonian American Art Museum's craft and decorative arts program. She could have spent the entire morning looking at the quilts alone, but time was tight. So, she buzzed by the paintings and other decorative arts, and was at the Corcoran Gallery of Art three blocks away at 11 as she had planned.

Then her day began to fall apart.

From the online description, she'd figured a half hour would be plenty of time at the Corcoran. She'd decided to bypass the contemporary, European, and American art collections and race through the decorative arts and photography areas. Except it turned out she couldn't very well skip the Stuart portrait of Washington, and then there was the Peale portrait of Washington on his horse…

The next thing Rachel knew, it was noon and she had missed her reservation at the Old Ebbitt Grill across the street, and the wait without a reservation was more than an hour. To get back on schedule, she decided to buy an overpriced hot dog from a street vendor. But she hadn't counted on a bus full of indecisive Baltimore fifth graders unloading in front of the vendor while she was still half a block away.

If there was one thing Rachel knew for sure, it was that she wasn't going back to the Valley without seeing the America's Presidents collection at the National Portrait Gallery. Except that she ended up by mistake at the American Art Museum first, and she'd always been a fool for Mary Cassatt and John Singer Sargent. By the time she was done with those two stops and was back near the National Mall, she only had an hour to spend at the Freer Gallery of Art and the Arthur M. Sackler Gallery, and no time for the Hirshhorn Museum.

"The best-laid plans of mice and men," Rachel muttered as she lowered herself to a bench near the giant old-fashioned eraser in the Hirshhorn's outside Sculpture Garden. She pulled her phone out of her fanny pack to check in with Peter and found she had three voice messages, all from Maureen May at the Museum of the Shenandoah Valley.

In the first one, received at 10 a.m., Maureen said that the new director, Priscilla Poplin, was looking at résumés and wanted to talk with Rachel about a part-time job curating a new exhibition about education in the Valley. Rachel listened and nodded; the timing couldn't have been much better. Then she erased the message.

In the second message, received at 1 p.m., Maureen asked whether Rachel had received the first message and could she please call to schedule an interview. Don't quite get the urgency here, Rachel thought as she erased the message.

In the final message, received about fifteen minutes earlier, Maureen sounded a bit frazzled. Could Rachel come in for an interview on Friday afternoon? Maureen left her home phone number and asked Rachel to call her there, no matter how late it was.

A lot of fuss and bother for a part-time, temporary position,

Rachel thought as she entered the numbers. Maureen answered on the second ring.

"Rachel, I am so glad to hear from you! I know you've been in DC a lot lately, but is there any chance you could meet with Priscilla at 2 tomorrow afternoon?"

Rachel frowned. "I'm in the District right now, and hadn't figured on being home before suppertime Friday. Will Monday work?"

"Unfortunately, it won't. Priscilla has spent the past two weeks lining up the new leadership team, and we're having a news conference on Monday to introduce everyone."

"But surely, a one-time exhibit curator wouldn't be part of a leadership news conference."

"Excuse me?"

"You said the new director wanted to talk with me about curating part of the Valley exhibit."

Maureen laughed. "Is that what I said? It's been a crazy day. That's what Priscilla asked me to call you about originally. But didn't I tell you in the second voice mail? We found out late in the morning that a grant application came through, and so we're adding an assistant director position. The person will run the day-to-day operations at the museum while Priscilla focuses on corporate and large-donor giving."

Assistant director of the Museum of the Shenandoah Valley!

"I probably shouldn't say this, Rachel, but I think the job is yours if you want it. Priscilla was so impressed with your résumé—your roots in the Valley, your experience managing the children's department and then the whole library system, your service in the community. I wouldn't be surprised if she offers it to you on the spot."

"Well, thank you, Maureen. I'm sure I can figure out a way to be there at 2. I'll call to confirm in the morning, all right?"

Rachel walked on air the few blocks back to the studio. *God is so good,* she thought. *This sounds like the ideal fit, and I'll bet the money is at least as good as my salary at the library was.*

She called Peter's cell, which went to voice mail immediately. "Maureen from the museum called me. They're creating a position that's perfect for me and I need to go in for an interview Friday afternoon. Don't worry about picking me up at the commuter lot. I'll go on the rideshare sites and find something and see you at home afterward. Please pray for me, and call me when you can."

She powered up her laptop and checked a rideshare site, then called a young woman who was leaving around 10 the next morning for Lyman. Rachel arranged to meet her at the Ballston Metro stop in Arlington. She'd get Peter to bring her back on Sunday for the rest of her stuff.

Rachel tried calling Peter's cell again, but once again, he didn't answer. "Me again," she said. "I'm all set, got a ride. Please call me when you can. Thinking of you."

42

The photos hadn't done the place justice. Peter could tell that as soon as he took the final turn off the gravel road and up the little slope to the cabin on Friday morning. The green paint on the shutters couldn't have been more than two years old. The sheen on the wood exterior told the world it'd been resealed recently. He put the truck into park, took his tool kit from the passenger side floor, stepped outside, and inhaled.

"Nothing like the smell of mountain springtime, eh?"

Peter whirled around. Standing behind him was a bald, elfin man, stooped over but tilting his smiling face upward. He was wearing a pair of khaki pants held up by a rope belt, and a white shirt with the sleeves rolled up neatly to the elbows.

"There certainly isn't," Peter said, extending his hand. "I'm Peter Gregory, Jill's dad. You must be Mr. Smith. Pleased to make your acquaintance. You've got some place here."

"Call me Georgie." Peter had to chuckle at how vigorously the old man shook his hand. "And the pleasure's mine. That's some daughter you've got in Jill. A beauty, inside and out. You and your wife did good work."

"I thank you," Peter said with a nod. "Looks like you did some good work yourself with this cabin."

"I'll let you be the judge of that. Let's go inside."

The red front door opened without a squeak into the living room, dominated by a massive rock fireplace. Georgie sat on a blue sofa next to the fireplace and picked up a large, well-worn book. "The place be yours. I'll just be here with the Lord."

Peter nodded and started down his list, moving around the cabin. After a while, he forgot about the old man. The electric panel, his main concern other than the foundation, had a tag saying it had passed inspection when the place was rewired ten years ago. Plumbing had been redone at the same time. Same for the heat pump, which pleased Peter to no end. He hated those big ugly propane tanks so many of these places had in the yard. The appliances were as old as they looked in the photos, but that was all right. The refrigerator and the stove were functional, if outdated, and when Peter started up the washer and dryer, they seemed fine as well.

He poked and prodded around all the windows and doors on both floors. Nothing rattled, and you couldn't see daylight through a one of them. He wondered how long ago they'd been replaced; the big window in the master bedroom that faced the river seemed almost brand new.

Well, the foundation would tell the tale. Peter went out the back door and down the deck stairs to get under the place. It hadn't seemed that high from the road, but the back was on four-foot posts; the front posts were more like a foot in length. He opened his tool kit, took out his awl, and scooted under the cabin. Over and over, he jabbed the joists and the main beams, then the posts themselves. No sign of give. He was a little surprised; eastern subterranean termites were the bane of cabin owners' existence in these parts. There'd been some damage at the tri-level a few years back, and after dealing with that, he and Rachel had agreed that a professional's checkup twice annually was well worth the money.

Peter moved back from underneath the cabin and straightened

up. Then he turned around and looked at the place again. He had to hand it to Eric and Jill, asking him to check it out. It had taken him a long time and problems with his own house to see that it was the foundation that was important, not the pretty shutters and the beautiful mountain view.

The old man was moving his right index finger over lines in his Bible when Peter reentered the living room.

"Beg pardon, Mr. Smith, but—"

"Georgie."

Peter swallowed hard. The man was practically old enough to be his grandfather.

"All right. Beg pardon…Georgie…but I'm wondering if I might ask you a few questions."

Georgie leaped up, clapping his hands. "I knew you'd like it! You wouldn't be asking me questions if you didn't. I have what you want in the kitchen."

The men sat at the little wooden table for four, and Georgie opened a green pocket folder.

"A few years back, a heart attack knocked me out of commission for six months. The kids knew better than to try to talk me out of coming back, so they hired the wiring and plumbing redone from when I first put it in. They made sure I was up to code and such. Here be the receipts and certifications."

Peter nodded and started to read the documents, but then another sheaf of paper was thrust in his hands.

"We had us a hailstorm a while back, and it hit the windows pretty good. They be new too."

Georgie must have been a salesman, Peter decided. He had to smile at the old man's intensity as he thumbed through the papers in his folder.

"Here be the bills for the electricity. Includes the internet and the satellite TV. The grandkids like to have 'em when they visit."

Georgie was going on and on about how the refrigerator might be old, but it was better than anything they made today when Peter coughed.

"Beg pardon, but I have a couple of other questions."

Georgie gave that laugh again. It reminded Peter of the church bell in a way.

"'Course, son. Guess you can see how much I love the place. It's as much a part of me as my kids are. I do know how to carry on about it."

"I'm wondering about the water. I read on the internet about how the reservoir's got a problem with sediment."

"It do," Georgie said with a vigorous nod as he left the room. "Be right back." Within seconds he returned, a newspaper in his hands. "But maybe you didn't read on that internet thing about how we passed us a bond issue last Tuesday to take care of that." He took a pen from his folder and circled the headline on the front page. "What else?"

"I wondered about termite inspection."

"Well, I had 'em. Had 'em bad," Georgie said, leaning forward and almost whispering. Peter had to laugh. Georgie looked at him, mouth and forehead crinkled.

"Son, tain't nothin' funny about termites. You'd know if you'd a-had them."

"Sir, I apologize for laughing. You're right, nothing funny about them. And I did have a bit of trouble with them up in Lyman, but treatment worked. What did you do?"

"Replaced the beams. Redwood, treated with pressurized coal-tar creosote. Ain't had a problem since."

Peter gave a low whistle. "You're talking some money."

Georgie nodded. "Tweren't cheap. But it took."

"If you don't mind me asking, why didn't you try other options first?"

Georgie stood, more slowly this time, Peter noticed. He disappeared, then returned lugging a photo album. He opened it to the first page. A slim young man, baseball cap bill tilted back, standing in front of the cabin, his arm around a woman about his height. She had a blond ponytail and a toothy grin.

The next page showed the same blonde, this time in slacks and a flannel shirt, at the stove, stirring something in a pot, a toddler on the floor. Next to it was a photo of a picnic on the cabin deck, maybe ten years later. Five kids at the table, a baby cradled in the woman's left arm as she waved to the right with the camera.

"That's my Ruthie," Georgie said as he turned toward Peter. "She were the girl next door. Loved her from the time we could walk. Prayed every night I was off at the war that I'd make it back safe to her. We got hitched when I was home on leave after she graduated high school. We spent our honeymoon clearing this land. After I got back from the Navy, we didn't spend a night apart until she went to the Lord twelve years later."

Peter coughed. "Jill told me about her, sir. That's tough. My mama died that way when I was four, and me and the wife lost a couple of angels too. But I still have her."

Georgie nodded. "You be a lucky man. Anyways, I found out about the termites a few years after Ruthie passed. Some folk thought I ought sell the place as-is and take the kids and move into town. That were crazy talk. It's a real strong, good cabin today, and it were then. Didn't make any sense to quit it. I sold off a few acres yonder—" He pointed toward the west. "—and used what I got to fix up the foundation, top of the line."

"It's gotta be hard for you now to leave it," Peter said. "Charlottesville life must be a lot different."

"It'll keep the kids and grandkids from badgering me," Georgie said as he closed the photo album. "There's some peace in that. And I won't be doing it too long, I don't reckon."

Peter looked at him and nodded. He supposed he could tell Georgie he looked great and still had a lot of life left in him. But the man was eighty-nine years old and had had health problems. Peter suspected Georgie knew a lot more about the Lord's plan for him than Peter did.

"What will you tell Jill and her man?"

"That they'd best snap up this property before you come to your senses and ask the true price for it."

Peter thought that remark would draw a laugh, but instead Georgie shook his head.

"I got me a doctor, a lawyer, an engineer, a professor-doctor, a bank president, and some government muckety-muck for kids. They all be set for money, and so be the grandkids. I know the price is low. I did that a-purpose. I want a young couple like me and Ruthie in this place, want 'em to be able to buy it without a mountain of debt. Want 'em to be 'stay heres,' not 'come heres' who never put down roots. Jill and her man swear to me they want to do that, and I believe 'em. What say we call Jill right now?"

"Good enough." Peter pulled his cell phone out of his front jeans pocket. It was off; that was odd, he didn't remember doing that. He hit the power button. Nothing.

Peter removed the back of the phone and reseated the battery. That was when he noticed the small dent on the bottom. Then he remembered. The phone had come apart when it skittered across the tile the night before. He couldn't believe he hadn't checked to make sure it was working after he put it back together. He kicked himself for not thinking about why he hadn't heard from Rachel or Jill since then.

"Well, I won't be calling Jill right now," he said, shaking his head. "Seems my phone's broke."

Georgie smiled and took a phone like Jill and Rachel's out of his pocket. "We can use mine. She be in my recent calls." He pushed a few buttons and held the phone to his ear. "Jill? This be your friend Georgie." He nodded. "Yes, he be here." He listened for a while longer. Laughter. "Let me give him to you."

Jill was still talking when Peter took the phone. "But did he like the cabin, Georgie? Did he give it the Peter Gregory thumbs-up?"

"Yes, he gave it the Peter Gregory thumbs-up," Peter said, laughing and winking at Georgie. "He gave it a big thumbs-up, and he's looking forward to visiting his first grandchild here before too long."

"Dad! Thank you! Don't you just love it?" Jill was off to the races, chattering on and on about the cabin and the mountains. Peter gave up on trying to get a word in edgewise and closed his eyes and smiled.

"…and now, what with Mother's job interview—"

Peter snapped back to reality. "Jill? What's this about your mother having a job interview?" Had Rachel decided to reconsider coming back to the Valley? Had the Library of Congress offered her something full time?

The connection went dead as the beautiful view outside went white with lightning.

43

"And what would you say your greatest weakness is?"

Rachel smiled. The interview with Priscilla Poplin was going just as she had hoped it would. The position sounded wonderful, supervising a staff of ten, including curators, researchers, and the two dozen volunteers associated with the museum's eleven gallery rooms. Priscilla seemed personable and professional, and it appeared they had a real connection.

"My greatest weakness is my impatience. I like to get things done. At the library, I counterbalanced that tendency by making good hiring decisions and seeing that key staffers had appropriate training. It's much easier to delegate when you're confident of people's abilities."

The gray-haired sixtysomething woman nodded and made some notes. "I can have the same problem," Priscilla said in one of those cultured First Families of Virginia accents. Rachel thought of Jonathan and smiled. "Now, I see from your résumé you're very involved in community activities."

"I think it's important to give back. While I was at the library, the children's department consistently was rated one of the best of its size in the Commonwealth, in part because of the outreach program I began for the children of the apple orchard migrant workers.

The library received a governor's award for that program, and it's been replicated in five other counties."

"That's an impressive accomplishment. Early learning is so important." Rachel watched as Priscilla scanned her résumé again. "And it seems you're quite the gardener."

"Oh yes! Gardening's my passion. My grandmother helped me plant a strawberry patch back when I was five or so, and I haven't been without a garden since. I do a lot of the landscaping at Church of the Redeemer too. In fact, I have a master gardener's certificate. There's something so centering and peaceful about planting and then seeing the fruits of your labor." Had she talked too long about this? Rachel wondered. After all, she wasn't interviewing for a gardener's position.

"You know the history of our gardens, I'm sure. Mr. Glass and Mr. Taylor brought them back to life when they moved here in 1956, and then they began a major renovation in the late 1980s."

Rachel nodded. "My husband and I were here that day in 1997 when Glen Burnie House and the gardens opened. He had to drag me out at closing time. We come several times a year, mainly for me to ooh and aah and steal some of Mr. Taylor's ideas."

"That kind of theft, Mr. Taylor would have approved of. They say he was never happier than when he was talking with visitors about the gardens. And of course, Tom DeCristofaro and his staff have done a marvelous job of carrying on since Mr. Taylor passed."

Now that would be a job, Rachel thought. I wonder how he stays on top of it all, the Chinese Garden, the Rose Garden, the formal vegetable garden.…He must have a lot of hourly help and volunteers. The inside of that greenhouse must be something. How much do they grow versus buying?

"Rachel?"

She blinked twice, hard. "I'm sorry. My mind was off in your gardens."

"I'd like to offer you the new assistant directorship," Priscilla said with a warm smile, handing Rachel a portfolio. "You'll find information about the salary and benefits inside."

Rachel scanned the cover sheet. The salary was twenty percent more than she'd made at the library. Fifteen vacation days and eight paid holidays. She nodded.

"Would you like to see your office? At least, what I hope will be your office?" Priscilla asked. The women left the director's suite and walked to the other end of the long hallway. "It's been a conference room, but it seemed we have an excess of those."

It was beautiful; Rachel couldn't deny that. The windows facing the gardens were huge. Her feet practically disappeared into the sand-colored carpeting. The walls were muted green below the chair rail, a honey yellow above.

"You could pick out your own furniture, of course. As you can see, there's plenty of room for a desk, a couple credenzas, small table and chairs."

I should be dancing on the ceiling with joy, Lord, Rachel thought. It's a great job, great salary, fifteen-minute commute. This is the second time in a few months You've given me a professional opportunity that seemed perfect. Why am I lukewarm on this?

She looked out the window. A young man was going by with a wheelbarrow full of plants.

"Rachel? Rachel, is something wrong?"

Rachel shook herself. "Priscilla, I have to apologize. It sounds wonderful. I think I'm just still a little worn out from commuting to the District the past few months. I got home a couple of hours ago, and I haven't even had a chance to talk with my husband about this opportunity. Would it be all right if I gave you a final answer on Monday?"

For the first time since Rachel arrived, Priscilla frowned. An elegant, ladylike frown, Rachel thought, but a frown nonetheless.

"I had hoped to introduce the entire team at Monday's news conference."

Rachel nodded. "I understand. If you'll excuse me for a moment, I'll try calling my husband again. I do need to speak with him before giving you an answer."

"Certainly. I'll be in my office." As Priscilla reached the door, the room flashed with lightning.

It figured, and Rachel without an umbrella. She sighed, then speed-dialed 3.

"You've reached Peter Gregory—"

Where was he? She hit the star key to bypass the recording.

"Listen, I don't know where you are or why you aren't returning calls, but I need to talk to you. Now. It's important. Call me."

Thunder crackled. She speed-dialed 2, the landline at home. No answer.

Rachel put the phone in her purse and entered the hall to return to Priscilla's office. As she reached the front entrance, the young gardener she'd seen through the window came in, shaking his shoulder-length mop of brown hair and laughing. She'd never seen anyone who was drenched look quite so happy.

"Typical Valley storm," he said to her as he stomped his feet, apparently thinking that would help dry off his work boots. "Skies are clear and then, bang, we got us a soaker."

Rachel nodded and kept walking toward Priscilla's office. So did the gardener. When they reached the secretary, he stepped back to let Rachel go first. But the secretary turned to him.

"Tom! You look like a drowned rat!"

He grinned, showing white, even teeth.

"I suspect I do, Bess. Just wanted to let you and Miss Priscilla know I sent the crew home. Too dangerous to work outside with the lightning. I've got a few things to do in the greenhouse, then I'll be leaving too."

"I'll let her know. I'll have those applications ready for you to review Monday morning."

"How many'd we get?"

"So far, fifteen. Not bad for two hourly positions."

The man nodded. "Lot of folk in the Valley need work." He turned to leave, and then stopped and turned toward Rachel. "Where're my manners?" He stuck out a big, still damp, suntanned hand. "Tom DeCristofaro. You probably guessed I'm a gardener. Sorry I didn't introduce myself sooner."

Rachel laughed. "You had a few other things on your mind. I'm Rachel Gregory."

Tom stepped back and then ran his hands through his hair and shook off more water. "Don't remember seeing you before. Are you new?"

"Not exactly. I don't work here. I mean, I don't work here yet. I mean—"

He laughed. "In any case, Miss Rachel, pleased to meet you and welcome. Bess, you and Miss Priscilla have a good weekend. Happy Mother's Day."

Rachel watched as the young man sloshed out of the room, leaving a light trail of wet in his wake. Then she turned back toward the secretary. "I'd like to speak to Priscilla for a few minutes if she's available."

"I know she'll be available for you. Let me just check." Bess pushed a few buttons on the phone, spoke quietly into the receiver, then nodded. "You can go on in."

Priscilla rose as Rachel entered the room. "Rachel, thank you for returning. Were you able to reach your husband?"

"No, I wasn't. Would it be possible for me to call you at home tonight or in the morning?"

"It would be helpful if you could call tonight, Rachel. I hope your answer will be yes, but if I need to go in another direction, I'd like to get things resolved by midday tomorrow. My children and grandchildren are coming into town for Mother's Day, and it's important to me to spend time with them."

Mother's Day. It didn't hit Rachel until she reached the museum's front door. Sunday is Mother's Day. She did a quick calculation. It was also her birthday. The Gregorys didn't go in for big birthday celebrations, but Mother's Day and Father's Day were downright sacred, with trips to Peter's parents' graves and a family brunch. She'd even thought about seeing if Mavis and Maarten wanted to drive up this year. Rachel put on her best spreads of the year for Mother's Day and Father's Day, if she did say so herself. And here they were, less than two days away and she'd done no prep work whatsoever.

She checked her cell phone, though she knew it was pointless. She would have felt it vibrate if he'd called her back. She looked at her watch. No time to stop at the store. She'd have to go directly to the commuter lot, assuming he remembered to pick her up. Then Rachel stopped. What if the reason she hadn't heard from Peter was that he was hurt somewhere? It was a good thing she hadn't told Priscilla her true biggest weakness was self-absorption.

Rachel waited a few more minutes for a break in the weather and raced to the hybrid. Once inside, she called Jill, who picked up on the first ring.

"Mother! How'd it go? Did they offer you the job?"

"Yes, they did. But I need to talk with your father, and he's not returning my calls. Do you know where he is? Is he all right?"

"I'm, I'm, I'm sure he's all right. He's probably slowed down with the weather."

"Slowed down doing what? Isn't he at work? And I tried calling home too, and he's not there either."

Seconds ticked by.

"I'm sure he'll call you as soon as he can."

More seconds ticked by. They must be planning a surprise for me for Mother's Day, Rachel thought.

"Well, all right," she said with a laugh. "If you talk to your father, tell him I'll be at the commuter lot in a half hour just like if I'd been coming on the bus. It'd be too confusing for me to go home in case one of us can't reach him."

"Will do. Love you, Mother. Call me later and we'll talk about Sunday, okay? And congratulations on the new job!"

Still don't understand why I'm not more excited, Rachel thought as she turned on the windshield wipers, shifted into gear, and started to drive toward the exit. What could be better than coming here every day and sitting in that beautiful office?

She heard a horn honk and looked around. That Tom gardener was in a truck, stopped at the garden entrance to her right and waiting to enter the main road. He waved and gave her a big smile.

44

Slap, slap, slap. Even at top speed, the truck's windshield wipers couldn't keep up with the driving rain. Peter eased back on the gas even more. He was getting old, that was for sure. In the day, he'd have taken the mountain curves at forty or fifty miles an hour, rain or no rain. He'd still make it back in time to pick up Rachel at the commuter lot, but it would be close. And he could forget about grouting or groceries or flowers or that haircut.

God is indeed great, he thought, slowing down even more as he approached a curve he took with respect on the driest of days. That cabin is a true gift for Eric and Jill, and I've got the gift of Rachel coming back home for good. Wonder what that job interview business is about. Guess I'll find out as soon as I'm down the mountain.

Then, not one hundred yards ahead, Peter saw a pitiful sight. A green Mustang was parked just off the road without its emergency flashers on. A woman, soaked to the skin, was frantically waving a flashlight.

He would have known that car and that body anywhere, even without the KLN 699 license plate.

Peter knew the second that Kara recognized the truck. The stress went out of her and she tossed back that mane of red hair, drenched as it was. He pulled next to the car and waved her to get into the truck.

"Well, if you aren't the answer to a prayer," she said as she clambered in. "Got a towel?"

"Actually, yes." He reached behind the seat for his duffel bag. "It's been used, but it's dry."

"Dry is good. Thanks." She wiped off her face, then squeezed some of the rain out of her hair. "You're my knight in shining armor."

"What's wrong?"

"I came up early this morning to do some interviews for a piece on weekend getaways," she said, wiping her face one final time. "When I was done, I started down, but the view here was so beautiful that I pulled over and hiked for a while. Wouldn't start again when I got back. Then the storm blew up."

"Same old short, I suspect. You didn't call for help?"

"No cell service."

"I'd have just holed up in the car and waited for the storm to pass rather than do the drenched rat thing."

"You always were better at waiting than I was. You're the first person to drive by in a half hour. Any more questions?" She handed him the towel.

Peter laughed. She was right. What did any of that matter?

"There's an umbrella in the truck bed box," he said. "Go get it."

Peter hurried to the Mustang, popped the hood, and then stood in front of it. The next thing he knew, Kara was standing behind him. He knew because the rain no longer was beating down on his head—and because he smelled that clothes-on-the-line perfume.

Neither of them said anything for the next several minutes as Peter tinkered with the wiring. Then he lowered the hood carefully.

"Give it a try now."

He felt the umbrella leave and heard the driver's door open, but not close. He looked down at his dirty fingers.

Kara turned the key once. Twice. Three times.

No luck.

He looked at the windshield and motioned her out of the car. After she came out with the umbrella, he reopened the hood. He hoped the umbrella had protected the critical wiring, but who knew. It couldn't cover the whole engine. If the Mustang didn't start this time, he'd have to give Kara a ride down the mountain to wherever she needed to be. He'd do that for a stranger. But he sure wished he'd been able to reach Rachel.

"Try 'er again," he shouted.

Kara turned the key once.

The engine roared.

"Thank you!" Kara shouted.

"No problem," he shouted back. "I'll follow you down just to be safe."

Back in the truck, Peter looked at the dashboard. He was going to be late to pick up Rachel, there was no doubt. He tried his cell phone, knowing that was futile.

The rain lightened, but Kara continued to crawl along. What would have taken even a cautious Peter twenty minutes stretched into a thirty, then a forty-minute journey.

Peter considered his possible excuses. "My phone got busted" wasn't going to work all by itself.

"The guys were having a beer, and I went along for the conversation." Except that he hadn't done that since they began counseling, and he didn't smell like he'd been in a bar.

"I stopped at the mall." Except that he never did that without Rachel or Jill.

"I stopped by church." Except that he couldn't lie about that.

Finally, Lyman was in sight. The rain slowed to a light drizzle. Kara pulled into the Gas 4 Less and waved him over. They both got out of their vehicles.

"Thanks, Peter. I'm good to go. I'm headed back to the District. I moved—"

"I know."

"I figured." Kara scuffed the toes of her hiking boots against the asphalt. "The tenants said someone stopped by last fall. Thought it was probably you."

"Yes. It was a mistake."

"You're sure?" She stepped closer, close enough that he could see those green eyes that had captivated him for a year. She was as beautiful as ever, even wet.

"Yes. It was a mistake that I came by." Peter took a couple steps backward. "Rachel and me—well, you were right. I do love her; maybe always have, just like you said. We're in counseling. I thank you for turning on that light bulb in my heart."

He couldn't read the look on her face. Satisfaction? Sadness?

"I'm glad," she said after a few seconds. "And now, my friend, you'd best get home to her. Supper's waiting, I'm sure. Just like it always was. Godspeed, Peter Jackson Gregory."

Kara hugged him tight, but the way his mama had hugged him when he was a kid, not the way she used to. Then, without another word, they got into their vehicles, and Peter drove off as fast as he could for the commuter lot. He hoped he wasn't too late.

45

He was late. He'd probably be even later. And Rachel was done waiting. She ground fresh pepper onto her omelet and took a bite.

She was done being a fool too. "You can't teach an old dog new tricks after all," she told Callie the calico.

She had made it to the commuter lot just as the bus pulled up, just in time to see sixty or so more-or-less happy men and women get into their vehicles or hug and kiss the people who'd come to pick them up. No sign of him or the truck. She'd waited fifteen minutes. Still no Peter. Finally, she left Jill voice mails at the apartment and on her cell: "I don't know what little game you and your father are playing, but I'm tired of it. If you can reach him, tell him I'm headed home."

The Gas 4 Less was deserted, so she figured there'd be no harm in taking ten minutes to fill up the hybrid. She was just about done when the truck pulled into the station.

Rachel had started to wave him over. Then she saw him join the redhead. Then she saw the hug. Then Rachel knew she was done.

As soon as she got home, she called Priscilla Poplin and accepted the assistant directorship. She felt like a fraud when Priscilla went on and on about how excited she was and all the great things the two of them would accomplish for the museum and the Valley.

She calmed down a little when she went to put her toiletries away. He'd made an effort, retiling the bathroom floor. But it wasn't finished. The grout bag was unopened. A bucket, filled with a trowel, sponge, and gloves, was nearby. Maybe that's where he is, getting something for this project, she thought as she turned to put her things on her dresser. Maybe something's wrong with his cell phone. Then she remembered the hug.

She'd do her best to make it through Mother's Day, and then tell him it wasn't going to work after all, she decided as she finished her omelet and put the plate in the dishwasher. There wouldn't be much to fight over. They could split the savings down the middle. Rachel supposed any attorney would contend that since she had had the lion's share of the income, she should get the lion's share of the savings. But she didn't care.

He could have the house. All she wanted was her clothes and a few pieces of furniture. She'd rent herself a condo, maybe one of those renovated places in Old Town or in that new development out by the museum. She wasn't sure where. She was sure, however, that she had been wrong to begin opening even a tiny piece of her heart again to Peter Gregory.

Rachel heard the truck pull into the carport. Peter burst through the door.

"Well, this has been a comedy of errors," he grumbled. "Sorry I missed you, but I'm glad to see you made it home. Busted my cell phone last night and didn't realize it till I'd left to run an errand. Sorry about the bathroom not being done."

She nodded.

"How did you get here, anyway?"

"Oh, I got home this morning. I left you a bunch of messages. I had an interview at 2 for assistant director at the museum, so I looked on the internet and found a ride."

"So that must have been the job Jill mentioned," Peter said, that big lazy smile spreading over his face. "Her and me was talking on someone else's phone this afternoon and got cut off in the storm. How'd the interview go?"

"Fine. I accepted the position."

He raised an eyebrow at her. "Really? Without us discussing it?"

"Yes."

"I wonder if we might talk about that. But first, I apologize but I'm starved. Ain't had anything to eat since breakfast. Did you have a thought as to supper?"

"I ate without you."

"But you never..." His voice trailed off as she examined her cuticles. "What's going on here? I dropped my cell phone while I was working on your bathroom floor, and busted the battery. I apologized for you not being able to reach me, but it wasn't intentional. You needn't freeze me out for that."

What to say?

Peter disappeared downstairs, and after a few minutes came back to the kitchen, wearing a dry pair of jeans and a navy polo shirt. He went to the refrigerator and took out the bread, mayonnaise, mustard, salami, and lettuce. Rachel wanted to jump up and make the sandwich—he was using way too much mayonnaise—but instead she opened the morning's newspaper, which was still on the table. A big deal at the senior citizens center for a woman who was turning one hundred. Pictures of the high school seniors' trip to Luray Caverns. She heard him walk out of the room. The front door opened and closed. The sandwich was still on the counter.

Rachel put her face in her hands. *Jesus, I thought we were done tiptoeing around each other. We were so close to having a marriage the way You and I wanted. Is this how it ends?*

After a few minutes, the front door opened just a bit.

"Would you come out for a minute? The rainbow is something to see."

"I've seen rainbows," she snapped, hearing the words come out even more harshly than she intended.

"It's a double, like the day we brought Jill home from the hospital. Please?"

Against her better judgment, she went. Peter was sitting smack in the middle of the swing. A rag he had used to dry the seat had been carefully folded and put on one armrest. The rocker seat looked to still be wet. It'd be meaner than even he deserved to take the rag and wipe it off.

Peter was right, she decided as she sat down as close to one edge of the swing as she could. You couldn't have asked for anything lovelier. The pinks in particular were breathtaking, the same shade as the hedge of Queen Elizabeth roses that were beginning to bloom in front of the porch.

"It's a true fact you couldn't reach me because my phone was busted and I didn't realize it," Peter said, looking straight ahead. "But that's not what kept me from getting to the commuter lot on time."

She took one more look at the rainbows and shut her eyes.

"All right. Why were you late?" she asked in a tone as even as she could muster.

"I had to do something up the mountain today for someone. I can't tell you more than that, as I was asked to keep it a secret."

So much for truth.

"Go on."

"The storm blew in, and coming down was slow going. I was about halfway and then there was a woman whose car was out of commission. I was the first one to go by in a half hour. I jiggled the wiring enough to get it started, then followed her down. She went real slow. She's not built for mountain living."

No kidding, Rachel thought. Lord, You show me the evidence of a relationship with this woman, and then he expects me to believe this cockamamie story?

"Is that all?"

Peter stood up and moved to her side of the swing. He knelt in front of her.

"No, that's not all," he said, placing his hands on her knees. "She was the last woman I was with."

Rachel tried to stand up but Peter's hands held her thighs down.

"She dumped me last August. Jill found out about the woman, and went to her and asked her to end it. Remember that night you overhead me and Jill talking in the basement? Kar—I mean, the woman—told me she'd seen me and you together with Jill outside the hardware store. She said she thought we were still in love, 'cause of the way we looked at each other."

August. Rachel thought back. It fit, sort of. It was zucchini season when Jill went to see Eric. That was about when Peter started doing the work at the church. That night he and Jill talked…that was when she decided to join him in counseling.

She put her small hands on top of his large ones.

"Is that all?"

"No."

Peter clutched her knees so tightly they hurt, but she held back a yelp.

"She lived on my way to work. That place where Chris from church and her family live. I was prideful after she called it quits, and never called her. But one day when it was still bad between me and you, I went over there. She had moved out. Today was the first time I'd seen her."

"And?"

"And when we were down the mountain, we got out and talked for a minute at Gas 4 Less. She's living in the District now. I told her—"

Peter's arms shook as he looked Rachel in the face.

"Yes?"

"I told her I love you. She hugged me and then we both left. It truly was a harmless hug. I tell you this not to hurt you, but because this is a small town. Someone probably saw the hug. I want you to know the truth. I understand now how whispers hurt."

Rachel swallowed hard. "I saw the hug myself." She watched as his dark unruly eyebrows rose almost to his hairline.

"When I couldn't reach you on the cell, I went to the commuter lot. I waited fifteen minutes or so, then decided to stop at Gas 4 Less on the way home. I saw you."

"Do you believe me?"

"I want to," she said with a little catch in her voice. "I'm trying to understand everything that happened to you today, and there's still a piece that's missing. What you were doing up the mountain—was it for her?" This one question, Lord, please let him answer this one question truthfully.

"No." Peter shook his head. "It was not. It was for someone else, people you know and love and trust. I'm bound by my word not to tell. I can say that you will know soon, and it's nothing that will bring either of us shame. Will you trust me?"

"I need to think about that for a bit," she said slowly. "I want to. Let me clear my own mind before I chew on it any further."

"Yes?"

Rachel took a big breath. "I hated living in the District, even just part of the week. I appreciate the opportunity you gave me and your sacrifices more than I can tell you, but that dream needs to die. Maybe it would have worked when I was in my twenties, but not today. They're different over there, not so genuine as Valley people. A researcher who came to the Library all the time made fun of my accent. I didn't even know I had an accent. He's the one who told me saying 'I thank you' was archaic. I didn't like who I was around him or the way I felt."

"He sounds full of himself."

"A little. He's not all bad, but he's not built for mountain living either. I must say I felt confused over him. He ended up at supper over in the District one night with Lizzie and Jed and me, and Lizzie read me the riot act about how he was trying to get beside me. I didn't believe her. Then this week he kissed me, right out in public after my lunch was stolen."

Peter stood up and took a couple of steps back, arms crossed across his chest and an impassive look on his face.

"What did you do when that happened?"

"I slapped him across the face. Really hard."

Peter's laugh was so loud that Rachel was quite sure everyone in the county heard him. He sat down on the swing close to her, and draped his right arm over the back. It felt good to have him close.

"And I told him I love you." She held her breath and squeezed her eyes shut. There, it was out.

His arm moved tighter against her shoulder, and she could feel his nose against the top of her head.

"I love you too."

Who knew it would be this easy? Rachel thought. No big ah-ha moment in Marsha's office, no epiphany at some public event. Just simple, here where we belong, here where we said it to each other so many times in the early years.

"Now," Peter said as he stretched out his legs and flexed his feet, "tell me about this new hot-shot job, Mrs. Assistant Director."

"I wanted to talk with you about it first, honest." Rachel snuggled her back up against his chest. "It's a new position. Inside all the time, supervising staff and overseeing the gallery rooms. It sounds a lot like what I did at the library, only more money."

"And? You don't seem too excited about it."

Rachel stroked his hands. How long had it been since she had touched him like this? He felt so strong.

"I think I want to call them back and say no. I think what I really want to do is get an hourly job working in those beautiful gardens at Glen Burnie House. They have a couple openings."

She waited for him to laugh, but he didn't.

"I want you to do what's right for you," he said slowly. "I do believe you could do that assistant director job or anything else you put your mind to. But like I said when I pushed you to try the

Library of Congress, it ain't about the money anymore. We ain't rich, but we got what we need. I can't think of anything you'd enjoy more than working in a garden."

"And you don't think I'm crazy, not to put my education to use?"

"Who says you're not using your education? Master gardener classes. Years of landscaping our place and the church. How many blue ribbons and prizes? Different kinds of education, wife."

"As long as we're being so honest, Peter, I must say, I have always detested you calling me 'wife.' How would you feel if I called you 'husband'?"

He gave another one of those huge laughs. Rachel wasn't quite sure what was so funny, but she giggled a little to keep him company.

"Twouldn't bother me, as long as you were the one calling it. But I hear you. What would you have me call you? Rusty, like in the old days?"

Rachel pulled away and turned to face him. "You haven't called me that for years."

"I been calling you Rusty all the time in my head the past few months. I'm asking again, so we can put the mess of the past behind us and start living today. Kind of like you said about your Library of Congress dream being done. I've told you the truth. Can you believe me, Rusty?"

Rachel swallowed hard.

"Can you believe me, Rusty?"

Finally, she found her voice.

"Yes," she said, beginning to sob. "Yes, though I'm not sure why or how. Yes, I believe you."

Suddenly, Peter was kissing her forehead, his arms around her, his tears mingling with hers.

"Please forgive me. With God's help, I'll be the husband you deserve. Would you do me the honor of being my wife again?"

"If you'll forgive me, old man," she said, laughing and crying at the same time. "I've not been much of a wife either. There's plenty of blame to go around here. Like you said, there's no point in hashing and rehashing the past. But Peter—" Her voice cracked. "—I'm so scared."

"Don't cry, Rusty," he said, standing up and pulling her close to him. "I'll take care of you."

And then, Rachel Gregory stood up on her tiptoes and kissed Peter the way a wife in love kisses her husband.

Epilogue

It must have been a great place to grow up," the young woman said. She put the car in park in front of the George Washington National Forest entrance and reached for her grandfather's hand.

He looked across the road at the cabin. "It was. We worked hard, and played harder. I don't remember ever having trouble sleeping at night. The mountain air, I suppose, and all the physical activity. It sure built up our constitutions—all of us in our sixties and healthy as horses."

"And Great-Granddad. Ninety-one. I wonder if he had stayed here…"

Her grandfather shook his head. "It was the right thing for him to move to Charlottesville. He had access to world-class health care at UVA. Anyway, he was ready to go. He kept talking at the end about Mother coming for him."

"He'll be happy he's buried up here with her near the little church."

"Yes, I think so. And he would have been surprised and humbled by how many people came up for the service. He left his mark on this area, that's for sure."

"I love the stories you all tell about growing up here. Do you or the others ever wonder if selling the property was the right thing?"

"Not at all. You knew him. When George Burdett Smith made up his mind on something, it was best to just go along. And besides, no one had the time or the inclination to give the cabin the love he gave it. He was right to sell it to a young couple. I just wanted to see it again before we go back to California tomorrow."

The people at the cabin were having a picnic in the front yard. A young woman with dark hair, about the granddaughter's age, and obviously pregnant, was seated on the grass next to a thin man. He was rolling a ball back and forth to a carrot-headed toddler, who was pretty good at standing up but not so great at walking. Every time he took a couple steps successfully, the little boy would laugh and clap his hands and fall…then get back up. "That's the way, Michael," the thin man said. "That's the way."

An older man who was the image of the woman—or was she the image of him?—sat on a quilt nearby taking it all in. His grin said he thought Michael hung the moon.

The granddaughter coughed. "Should we ask if we can go inside and take a look around?"

"No. Let's just stay in the car and watch them for a while."

The cabin door opened, and a small woman with graying red hair came out, bearing a birthday cake with candles ablaze. They sang, "Happy birthday, dear Eric," and everyone laughed as Michael attempted to blow out the candles for the thin man.

The cake cut and served, the younger woman sat cross-legged, Michael in her lap, hair blowing across her face as Eric put his arm around her shoulder. But it was the older couple who drew the grandfather's attention. The woman was on her knees, starting to gather up items, when the man, getting to his knees, whispered something in her ear, then placed his lips on her forehead. Even from across the road, the joy and love on the woman's face in profile was evident.

About the Author

Melanie Rigney is the author of several Bible studies and books on Catholic saints. She is a South Dakota native who has called Arlington, Virginia, home for more than twenty years. This is her first novel.

Learn more about Melanie at www.rejoicebeglad.com.

www.ingramcontent.com/pod-product-compliance
Lightning Source LLC
Chambersburg PA
CBHW021241060726
47590CB00005B/1854